"I'm sorry about last night."

"You've nae need to be sorry about anything," he replied. Then, reaching up, he brushed a stray tendril of hair from her cheek, his fingers caressing her skin.

She shivered from the tenderness in his touch, which transformed to waves of sensation that rolled through her body. Why? Because of one gentle brush of fingers on her skin? Was she that starved for human affection?

What would it feel like to let go of her tightly held control, just a bit more, with this man she had loved so long ago? And then, because she could not stop herself if she tried, she wound her arms about his neck, and raised her head to brush his lips with hers.

It was the barest of touches, as light and delicate as a flower's petal. Yet his reaction was deep and real, his entire body jolting as he drew in a sharp breath. When she raised her lids to look at him, his eyes seemed to have claimed all the brilliance of the rising sun.

"You dinnae have to show your gratitude that way, Seraphina," he said, his voice hoarse.

"It was not gratitude that had me kissing you, Iain," she replied softly.

He swallowed hard. "What was it, then?"

In answer she pulled his head down and claimed his lips with her own.

Praise for Christina Britton and Her Novels

"For readers who like to feel all the emotions of a story."
—*Library Journal* on *Some Dukes Have All the Luck*

"Endearing, complex characters."
—*Publishers Weekly* on *Some Dukes Have All the Luck*

"Sigh-worthy fare."
—*BookPage* on *Some Dukes Have All the Luck*

"This is a knockout."
—*Publishers Weekly* on *A Duke Worth Fighting For*, starred review

"First-rate Regency fun!"
—Grace Burrowes, *New York Times* bestselling author

"Moving and heartfelt."
—*Kirkus Reviews* on *Someday My Duke Will Come*

The Duke's
All That

The Duke's All That

CHRISTINA BRITTON

FOREVER

NEW YORK   BOSTON

Forever
Hachette Book Group
1290 Avenue of the Americas, New York, NY 10104
read-forever.com
twitter.com/readforeverpub

First Edition: February 2024

Forever is an imprint of Grand Central Publishing. The Forever name and logo are trademarks of Hachette Book Group, Inc.

The publisher is not responsible for websites (or their content) that are not owned by the publisher.

Forever books may be purchased in bulk for business, educational, or promotional use. For information, please contact your local bookseller or the Hachette Book Group Special Markets Department at special.markets@hbgusa.com.

ISBNs: 978-1-5387-1044-9 (mass market), 978-1-5387-1045-6 (ebook)

Printed in the United States of America

OPM

10 9 8 7 6 5 4 3 2 1

In loving memory of Pauline Secor, my wonderful Aunt Pauline. Thank you for being such an incredible, strong, supportive presence in my life. I just know you and Papa are laughing together in heaven.

I love and miss you, so much.

Acknowledgments

There are so many people I wish to thank for being with me on my Synneful journeys. First and foremost, a huge thank-you to my agent, Kim Lionetti, whose belief in me and these stories I create mean the world to me. Thank you also to my fabulous editor, Madeleine Colavita, and every single person at Forever who has loved my stories and characters, including Grace, Dana, Stacey, and so many more. I am so honored to be part of the Forever family.

Thank you also to my family and friends who have supported me and my writing, especially Jayci Lee, Hannah, and Julie. I'd be lost without you and adore you all so much.

Thank you to my wonderful husband and my two incredible children (and my writing companion, little Miss Emma), who always stand by my side and support every one of my endeavors—even though I *still* haven't put a sword with a secret compartment in the hilt in my books. I cannot begin to tell you how much I love you all.

Last, but certainly not least, to my readers: Words cannot express the gratitude I feel to every single one of you who has read, reviewed, and loved my Isle of Synne books. Because of you, I was able to create a place that will forever be a part of me, with characters who have become as dear to me as real people. Thank you, from the very depths of my heart.

Author's Note

The Duke's All That contains content that may distress some readers. For content warnings, please visit my website:

http://christinabritton.com/bookshelf/content-warnings/

Affectionately yours,
Christina Britton

The Duke's
All That

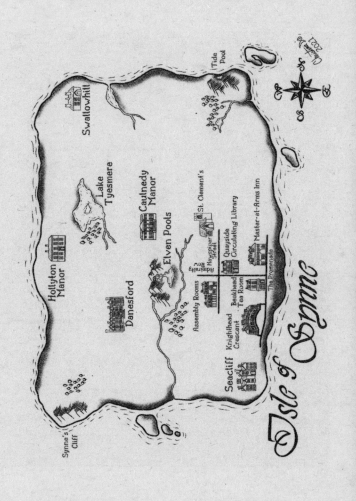

Isle of Synne

2021

Tide Pool

Swallowhill

Lake Tyesmere

Cautnedy Manor

St. Clement's

Hollyton Manor

Elven Pools

Quayside Circulating Library

Danesford

Mayfisher Street

Admiralty Row

Master-at-Arms Inn

The Promenade

Assembly Rooms

Beakhead Tea Room

Knighthead Crescent

Seacliff

Synne's Cliff

Prologue

Scotland 1808

I cannae believe you're my wife."

Seraphina smiled into Iain's bare chest, wrapping her arms more tightly about his waist. She could hardly believe it herself. How many summers had she spent at her family's Scottish holiday home slowly falling in love with this man, how many autumns and winters and springs at her family's English estate pining for him, how many secret letters written to him, how many furtive assignations gone on? And all because her father saw him as beneath the notice of his eldest daughter.

She perhaps might not have found the strength to accept Iain's proposal had her father not informed her that they were cutting their holiday short and would be leaving the following day, that next spring she was to go to London for the season and find a husband. But he had, and she had, and here she finally was, in the one place she wished to be. She had always felt like the selkies of legend, those mystical seals that could shed their skins to walk among humans, only to have their skins stolen and them unable to return to their rightful places. Now she had found her skin, had finally escaped the hateful home of her father, and was where she belonged: in the arms of the man she loved.

Her smile widened, one of such happiness that she felt it in every inch of her body. A body that was, if not singing with the aftereffects of pleasure, at least humming pleasantly. She rubbed her bare leg against his own. Had their first attempt at lovemaking been the stuff of her fantasies, something that the poets would write about? No. But they had the whole of their lives to perfect their bed sport. And she intended on practicing often.

A sudden commotion went up in the hall outside their borrowed room, two men arguing drunkenly, the sound of a woman screeching, some bit of pottery shattering. She tensed, her gaze darting to the rough wooden door. Iain's arms tightened about her and he let loose a low curse.

"But our first time shouldnae have been in such a place," he said gruffly into the crown of her mussed hair. "You're used to so much better, and I should have given you so much better. You deserve to be loved on a mattress of the softest down, under silk sheets, your body dripping with jewels—"

Heart twisting at the self-condemnation in his voice, Seraphina gripped his arm and pressed her face into his chest. It was an old argument, and one made all the worse for what they had just shared together, for what *she* had shared with him. "Stop," she rasped.

But he seemed not to hear her. "Even worse, I will never be able to give you what you deserve. You will never have a large house, or an army of servants. You will never set off on those travels you always dreamed of going on—"

She rose up and pressed her fingers against his lips, blinking back tears. "I won't have you speaking like that," she managed through a throat thick with emotion.

"Why nae?" he demanded. "'Tis true. You are used to wealth and beauty and privilege. You were brought up to wed a man of title and means. And instead you marry one who cannae give you better than a quick tumble in a borrowed room in the very worst part of Falkirk."

Frustration reared. She had foolishly hoped that, once she promised herself to him, their difference in status would no longer come between them. She saw now, however, that it was not something that could be put behind them so easily.

But she would tell him every minute of every day that he was enough for her, if that was what it took.

"Listen to me, and listen well, Iain MacInnes," she said through a throat tight with tears, cupping his rough cheek in her palm. "I don't want some gilded life, nor some stuffy, uptight Englishman for a husband. As for those travels I always wished to go on, I know for a fact that any far-off vista I may see would pale in comparison to the ones I can view at your side. I chose you. You are my future. I made a promise to you, for good or bad, that I would be by your side, and I do not take those vows lightly. You are stuck with me, husband, whether you like it or not."

His gray eyes suspiciously moist, he placed his large hand over her own, holding it to his cheek. "Aye, I like it, verra much," he said, his voice gruff, before pulling her down for a kiss.

But the kiss did not—could not—last long. A sudden pounding at the door had both of them tensing again. And then a voice out in the hall, in a loud, aggravated whisper.

"MacInnes, are ye done wi' yer lass? The innkeeper'll have my head if he finds I leant ye the room at nae charge."

A low growl rumbled up from Iain's deep chest as he turned to glare daggers at the door. "Aye, Ross, keep yer kilt on," he spat before turning regretful eyes back to Seraphina. "Nae the most romantic beginning to our life together."

"Nonsense," Seraphina said with a determined smile, smoothing a soft brown curl from his forehead. "I would rather be here with you than anywhere else."

His smile, a strained thing, said he did not believe her one bit. But he gave her one more quick kiss, silencing whatever platitudes she had hoped to utter to soothe him, before rolling from her arms and the bed. "We'd best make haste," he said as he reached for his loose linen shirt. "We've much ground to cover if we're to make Glasgow by nightfall."

Seraphina took a moment allowing herself to watch the play of his muscles under his bare skin, the taut curve of his buttocks, his strong limbs, before he covered them with his shirt. Then, with a small smile of anticipation for what would come later, she hurried from the bed. But there was no striding across the rough floorboards in her full naked glory. No, though she had lain with Iain just minutes before, her bare body joined with his, this was still all too new to her. And so, face flaming, she gripped the threadbare sheets to her bosom as she fumbled for her own clothing.

"From Glasgow we shall make our way up the River Clyde to Greenock, and then board a ship for Montreal," he continued as he secured his kilt about his lean hips. His deep voice had gone soft, almost caressing the words. "We'll find a good piece of land to settle on, Seraphina, a fine place to start our life together and bring up our children. Mayhap we'll have a strapping lad or two, or twin sisters with hair as bright a red as their mother's." He grinned at her, the future sparkling in his gray eyes.

But Seraphina hardly saw it. Her attention snagged and stuck on one word: *sisters*. Her heart twisted, her fingers stalling on securing the tapes of her gown. Elspeth and Millicent were the most important people in this world to her apart from Iain. They had been the only things making life bearable, the only good her father had ever put into the world. And she would never see them again.

She must have sniffled, for suddenly Iain was there beside her, pulling her into his arms. "Seraphina, what's wrong?"

She was not one to indulge in emotional displays. And she abhorred tears. Yet she could not begin to stem her grief at the thought of never seeing her sisters again. She buried her face in Iain's chest lest he see this proof of her weakness.

"Seraphina?" His voice sounded almost frantic as his large hands rubbed up and down her back.

She blew out a sharp breath. "I worry about Elspeth and Millicent," she admitted into his shirt. "They might understand if I could explain things to them. But my father will fill their heads with lies about you, about us. They'll hate me for it. And I cannot stand the idea of them hating me."

He was quiet for a time, his hands massaging her tense muscles, soothing her. And then he spoke.

"I know how important your sisters are to you," he said gruffly. "And I cannae stand the thought of you being in pain. While I secure our places on the coach and gather our things, why dinnae you return to them, to say a proper farewell."

Hope surging in her chest, she pulled back to gaze up at him. "Truly?" she breathed. "I can see them once more?"

"Aye." He smiled, cupping her cheek. "I shall have you by my side for the rest of my life anyway; what is one hour in the grand scheme of things?"

She grinned, her heart glowing. "I do love you."

"As I love you," he murmured.

Within minutes they were dressed and sneaking down the back stairs of the ramshackle inn, their hands clasped tight. The sun was high in the sky when they made it to the rear yard, their laughs free as they hurried down the dirt road. And when they reached the crossroad that led to her father's summer home, the swift kiss they shared was full of a bright hope for the future.

"One hour," she vowed.

"One hour." He kissed her again, smiling down at her. "And then forever, mo bhean."

Mo bhean. *My wife.* Happier than she had ever thought possible, she gave him one last long look before hurrying away from him, her heart counting the minutes until they reunited. And this time, no one could tear them apart.

Chapter 1

Scotland, early 1821

*H*is wife was alive.

Iain MacInnes, Duke of Balgair—a title that still felt about as comfortable and welcome to him as a starched collar after the loose-necked Jacobite shirts he'd been used to wearing all his life—stared down at the letter in his hands, feeling as if a ghost had just jumped out at him from the shaky handwriting and punched him in the throat. He read over the missive again, and then once more, his eyes scanning with increasing agitation, certain he must have read it wrong. But no, there it was, plain as day, information he had never expected to receive, had not thought it possible to get.

I did not know who else to turn to, who else might care. Her father lied. Lady Seraphina Trew did not die in a carriage accident with her sisters as her father reported. Rather, they are thought to be alive and well and possibly living under an assumed name.

Dear God. Seraphina was alive?

An image of her rose up, like a specter in a long-abandoned graveyard, from that last time he'd seen her: brilliant hair loose down her back, lips still bruised from his kisses, her smile bright as she bid him farewell, promising to see him within the hour. He had not thought of that painful scene in years—at least not willingly. Later that same day he'd been cruelly informed of her betrayal, all his fears that she could not love someone like him proving true. And when he'd learned of her death several years later, he had not mourned her. It was difficult to mourn someone who had broken your heart so brutally and completely.

But she was alive, and had been all this time?

He was out of his chair before he knew what he was about, racing from the study and through the massive house to the front hall. Donal, the ancient butler with his powdered wig constantly askew, was trudging across the tiled floor as Iain rounded the corner.

"Who brought the letter?" he demanded as he made for the front door.

"Wha's that, Yer Grace?" the man rasped, frowning at Iain. An expression Iain was all too familiar with, as unwelcome as he was in his new position as duke.

Gritting his teeth at that title he so despised, he nevertheless replied, "The letter that just arrived. It dinnae come with the rest of the correspondence. Who brought it?"

"Oh. Hmm. 'Twas a young woman, Yer Grace. Some wee blond thing, came on foot. She might still be in the front drive—"

The words were not yet out of Donal's mouth before Iain was out the door. And there she was, trudging down the long drive of Balgair Castle through fresh drifts of snow, shoulders slumped, as if the weight of the world were on them. He did not pause but leapt down the steps, sprinting down the snow-laden gravel drive. Blessedly the lass was so caught up in whatever was on her mind, she did not hear him until he was right atop her. Then she only had time to gape as he lurched into her path.

"You knew Seraphina?"

But even as he berated himself for the desperation in his voice, he realized the lass could not possibly have known his recently resurrected wife. This girl was just that: a girl, not more than fifteen or sixteen at the most. Certainly not old enough to have known Seraphina or her sisters in any proper capacity. Which meant she could not have been the one to pen the missive.

A fact that the girl verified a moment later, all while backing away and staring at him, as if he were a great big beasty about to swallow her whole. "N-nae, I know nae one by that name."

So saying, she made to skirt around him. But Iain could not let her leave, not until he learned who had sent him that letter.

He stepped in front of her again. The girl's eyes widened, a distressed squeak escaping her lips.

Damnation, this was no way to get information out of her. "Forgive me, lass," he said, thickening his burr, making his voice as gentle as he could. "I dinnae mean to frighten you. I only meant to find out who it was that sent the letter. 'Tis verra important, ye ken?"

But the girl did not look even remotely easy at his

assurances. Instead, her eyes narrowed in suspicion as she attempted to skirt around him once more. "If yer master wishes to know who sent the letter, he can do the asking himself. Good day, sir."

Iain very nearly laughed at that. His master, eh? Not that he was surprised the lass did not realize he was the bloody duke. Most dukes were not nearly so rough and unkempt as he, with three days' growth of beard and wearing his oldest, most comfortable kilt. No, dukes were by and large soft, selfish bastards, who cared more for their possessions and appearance than they did for the lives of those they were responsible for. As were all of the nobility, a group he had come to actively loathe in the past decade and a half.

And, he thought with no little bitterness, he was now one of them.

But the girl had made her way around him and was quickly making her escape. "I *am* the duke," he bit out, perhaps more sternly than he should have, considering the anger that his ruminations dredged up.

Another squeak from the girl as she turned back to face him and dropped into a curtsy so low he thought she might lose her balance entirely and topple face-first into the fresh snow. "Yer Grace," she gasped, "I'm sorry, I am. I dinnae ken 'twas you."

"Dinnae fash yerself," he grumbled, waving her to standing. Would he ever get used to the fawning obsequiousness that such a title brought with it? Surely not. It was no wonder those who possessed titles and wealth thought so highly of themselves.

For a moment he remembered one particular lord, and how cruelly he'd dealt with Iain when Iain had dared to look at his daughter, had dared to *love* his daughter. *Seraphina*.

But no matter it seemed the lass had risen from the dead—a fact that he could not seem to wrap his head around—he would not lower himself to think of her father and all the heartache that man had caused, all at the altar of his own self-importance.

"But perhaps you might now tell me who sent the letter," he said.

Whatever reaction he might have expected from her, it certainly wasn't the sudden sadness in her wide brown eyes.

"My gran," she said, her voice going quiet. "Mrs. Mary Campbell."

He sucked in a sharp breath, the cold air like needles in his lungs. Yet another ghost rising from the graveyard of his past. He tried to swallow back the memories that surfaced, but they were barbed and rough with age, and tore at his throat, refusing to budge.

Mrs. Mary Campbell. He had known her well. Housekeeper to Seraphina's father, Lord Farrow, the woman had been kind to Iain when others had not, taking him under her wing, securing him a position in Lord Farrow's stables so he might support himself, protecting him from those who would make him suffer for his father's mistakes and scandalous death. She had been a kind of mother figure at a time when he'd needed it most, and he had trusted her implicitly. So much so that, when he had been presented with tangible proof that Seraphina had left him to go off on those travels she had always dreamed of, only Mrs. Campbell's mournful testimony that she had indeed seen Seraphina leave with her own eyes had made him finally accept the truth.

And now here she was, writing to him, telling him that Seraphina had not died. That she was alive. He crushed the missive in his grip.

The girl standing before him stared solemnly up at him. "You recall my gran then?"

"Aye," he managed, his voice gone hoarse. He cleared his throat, fighting for composure. "And where is Mrs. Campbell now?"

Again that sadness in her eyes. "Gone to her Maker," she whispered.

He sucked in a sharp breath at the unexpected news. Mrs. Campbell was gone? "I am sorry for your loss," he managed. "The world is a dimmer place for it." And he meant it, down to his bones. Though he had not seen Mrs. Campbell since the day Seraphina had left him, that did not mean he did not mourn this news of her passing.

But apparently the world had been dimmer for a wee bit longer than he had assumed.

"Thank you, Your Grace," the girl said, dipping her head in acknowledgment. "But 'tis nae a new grief. Gran has been gone these ten years now."

He gaped at her. "Ten years," he breathed. "Did she write this from the grave then?"

Her cheeks, already rosy from the cold, darkened. "Nae. That is, she passed nae long after she wrote that note to you and she did nae have the time to post it before she died. And then 'twas bundled in a box with her other things when her rooms were cleared. My family did not discover it until some months ago."

She was growing more agitated by the moment under his incredulous stare. With enormous will he schooled his features to a calm he did not feel.

"Dinnae worry, lass. What is done is done."

But she seemed not to hear him. She took the edges of her shawl in her hands and twisted them as if she would strangle the life out of the frayed ends. "We knew she must nae be resting easy with unfinished business. We set out to find you." She let loose a bark of nervous laughter, made all the sharper for the hush of the snow-draped landscape. "Imagine our surprise to learn our gran was acquainted with a duke of all people. It was why I came in person, to make certain we were not mistaken."

The reminder of his title was potent enough to banish his shock. "Yes, well," he muttered. "I wasnae a duke when she knew me."

But the return of reality had other realizations becoming clearer as well. He looked down at the crumpled missive in his fist with new eyes, taking in the yellowed edges and stains that he had missed when first reading it, all indicators of age and wear. To think Mrs. Campbell had been in possession of this information all along, had meant to give it to him some decade past. He ground his back teeth together. All but for fate, that fickle, wanton creature.

The granddaughter dipped into a quick curtsy. "Your pardon, Your Grace, but I must go; 'tis a fair way to travel before nightfall."

He looked about at the snow-laden landscape, then back to the thin shawl held tightly about the lass's narrow shoulders, and nearly cursed. Damnation, he had kept the girl here quizzing her, and she had been freezing in her no-doubt worn shoes.

"You will come back to Balgair with me," he said gruffly. "I'll ready a carriage to bring you wherever you need to go."

He thought for a moment she would refuse. There was nothing like the pride of a Scottish Highland woman, after all. But in the end she must have been colder than even he realized. Cheeks flaming—all the more violent for the blue beginning to paint her lips and nose—she nodded and followed him back to the castle.

In no time he had the girl settled in a carriage, a hot brick at her feet and her purse heavier by a good quantity of coins. As the conveyance rumbled down the drive, creating deep gouges in the fresh snow, he turned away, heading back inside the house. All the while his mind was spinning and whirling like a child's toy with all he had learned, not the least of which was the inconceivable fact that Seraphina was not dead, but alive and well.

He felt as if she had betrayed him all over again. A string of Gaelic curses poured from his lips, echoing about the massive hall. It would have been an impressive thing to hear...if it had not been the dowager duchess and his cousin, Cora, just arriving in the cavernous space and heard the tail end of it.

"Oh," the dowager said weakly, thin hands going to her nonexistent bosom. She stared at Iain as if he had grown a tail. And horns. And perhaps cloven hooves to go along with it all.

Cora, blessedly, was made of sterner stuff—though not by much. While she initially appeared just as horrified as the duchess, she quickly managed to adopt her typical cool expression. Even so, her knuckles were white from her fingers gripping so tightly to one another, and he could quite literally see her throat working as she swallowed hard.

"Is something amiss, Cousin?" she queried, her voice without emotion.

Iain pressed his back molars tightly together. Cora always talked thus to him, as if he were a pebble in her path, something to be dealt with but given no more energy than what was strictly required.

"Nothing of import," he replied evasively, even as his hand closed tighter around Mrs. Campbell's letter.

But Cora, suspicious of him from the moment he'd stepped foot inside Balgair six months ago, narrowed her eyes and looked to the massive front door. "I thought I heard a carriage."

"Aye," he responded, his tone clipped. "A girl came with a letter. I called a carriage for her so she might nae be forced to walk back in the snow. If that is all right with you?"

"It is your home, your carriage," Cora replied tightly. "It matters not what I think."

The dowager, who was watching the back-and-forth with wide, anxious eyes, spoke up then in an obvious effort to ease the tension that never failed to crop up between Iain and Cora.

"That was very kind of you, Iain," she said with a too-bright smile. "But where are you off to now?"

"To my study. Unless you have need of me, madam?"

Her expression gentled. "I thought I told you to call me 'Gran.'"

Gran. Yes, she was his late father's mother. Yes, she was kin, his family, his clan.

But after more than three decades of believing himself to be alone, being looked down on, having no one—all but for that brief time with Seraphina—it was much too late for him to ever accept these women as family. How many years had Iain spent hating himself for his origins, clawing his way out of the literal gutter, using every ounce of cunning and luck and pure spite to turn his life around and lay claim to everything he had been lacking in life. And the whole time he'd had family, family who had never once looked for him in more than thirty years, never made an effort to contact him. Only when the old duke was dead and they needed to locate someone to take his place did they even bother to search out him or his father. No, they had been living a life of luxury and ease while he had been alone and struggling in near poverty, wondering where his next meal might come from.

"Yes," he replied evenly, though his anger burned hot as ever, "you have told me that."

Her features paled, and she seemed to shrink into herself. But he would not feel pity for her.

The dowager turned to Cora, still at her side. "Dearest, have I told you that the latest issue of the *Gaia Review and Repository* has arrived? Mayhap we might go fetch it and have a read."

"That sounds lovely, Gran," Cora replied quietly, even as her eyes blazed into Iain's. "But I need to grab my reading glasses. Why don't I meet you in your sitting room?"

The dowager nodded and, without a glance Iain's way, shuffled off. She was barely out of earshot before Cora turned on him.

"You don't have to be so cruel to her," she hissed.

But he would not rise to her bait. "I have work to get to. Is there anything else you needed?"

She blew out a frustrated breath, and for a moment he thought she would not let it go.

But in the end she merely said, "It is getting increasingly close to the season. I am fully aware that you have no plans to search for a bride, but I do hope you reconsider. For the sake of the dukedom."

With that, she turned and stalked from the great hall.

Another string of curses escaped his lips, this time much quieter so he might not have to deal with her judgmental stare again. As if he gave a damn about the dukedom, a title he had never wanted. He had no emotional connection to it, and he certainly didn't give a damn that he was last of the line. He'd had every intention of finding a wife...eventually. Though it was not to save the dukedom. With all he had amassed over the past decade, all the properties he had taken back from the sniveling English, all the bastard Sassenach he had bankrupted, he wanted an heir, someone to pass it on to. Someone who would not have to suffer and struggle as he had.

But he had not counted on the fact that his dead wife was not, in fact, dead.

Pressing his lips tight, he opened his fist and glared at the crumpled letter. "Well, I cannae verra well go off and marry another when I'm already wed, can I?" he muttered. He would find Seraphina, he decided. And when he did, he would divorce his devious wife and finally get her out of his life for good.

Chapter 2

Isle of Synne
Six months later
Late summer, 1821

"Miss Athwart. I say, Miss Athwart."

But Miss Seraphina Athwart, head proprietress of the Quayside Circulating Library on the idyllic seaside resort the Isle of Synne, hardly heard the increasingly annoyed voice at her elbow, far too caught up in the story she was hastily scribbling. It was highly unusual that she allowed herself to get caught up in her writing in such a public place. No, she had a strict—albeit silent—rule that any work she put into her secret alter ego, that of the mysterious authoress S. L. Keys, was to be kept starkly separate from her public persona. It was a secret even her beloved sisters did not know; that even her dear friends had never guessed at.

However, last night's dream, which had her once again reliving the worst moments of her life, had demanded she put it on paper immediately. Perhaps she should simply try to forget, as anyone else would have done. But writing it down, seeing it in simple black and white, was almost like lancing an infection, purging her of the poisonous memories.

But the telling of that story would have to wait. Phineas, her red-crowned parrot, nipped ever so gently at her ear, making her aware that she was needed.

"What is it, darling? Oh! Mrs. Juniper." Seraphina started upon seeing the woman peering so intently at her. Hastily turning over the papers she had been scribbling on, praying the nosy woman had not snuck a peek at her writing, she straightened and pasted a stiff smile to her lips.

"Forgive me," she continued, adjusting her spectacles. "I'm afraid I was quite immersed in my work. How can I help you today?"

But the woman was not to be soothed so easily. She pursed her lips, glaring at Seraphina. "I pay good money for my subscription to your establishment, Miss Athwart," she said, looking Seraphina up and down as if she were a cockroach—well, more up than down, as Seraphina quite towered over most of the women on Synne, and a fair number of the men as well. "I even make certain to encourage any of our customers who come through the Master-at-Arms Inn to patronize your premises. And so I expect to not be so rudely ignored."

Hot anger sizzled along Seraphina's skin. But she had not spent years controlling her more unwelcome emotions for nothing. She would certainly not let some insulting, self-important woman draw out her ire.

She smiled tightly and inclined her head. "Again, my apologies, Mrs. Juniper. It was horribly disrespectful of me and shan't happen again. Now, then, what can I assist you with?"

The woman, having no recourse but to back off in the wake of Seraphina's politeness—no matter how couched her words had been in disdain—narrowed her eyes. "I am hoping to borrow the latest Walter Scott. I trust you have a copy available?"

Seraphina nodded. "*Kenilworth*? Yes, we should have a copy for you, Mrs. Juniper. Please have a seat in the reading room and I shall check on that right away."

"I haven't the time to wait." The woman sniffed, adjusting her bonnet, a hideously loud confection of straw and ribbons and feathers that rivaled Phineas for gaudiness. "You shall bring it round to the Master-at-Arms when you've located it. At no extra charge," she added pointedly, giving Seraphina a stern look. "And don't think to foist this particular chore off on one of your sisters. You were the one to insult me, and you shall be the one to make it right."

So saying, she sniffed again and flounced toward the door.

"I'll locate the book for you, Seraphina," her youngest sister, Elspeth, said, rounding the counter as Mrs. Juniper stalked out to Admiralty Row and out of sight. "I don't know why the woman couldn't wait for me to be done with Miss Swan. She could see you were busy. By the way, what were you working so diligently on? I've never seen you so distracted."

"Nothing," Seraphina hastened to say, gathering up the loose pages lest her curious sister take a closer look at them. Of course, her sisters would be ecstatic were they to learn she was the one penning the popular gothic romances that had everyone clamoring for the monthly *Gaia Review and Repository*.

But she could not have them wondering at the contents

of her stories, realizing that there was more than fiction to them. Her sisters already knew that the year she had been away from them had not been spent traveling, as their father had claimed. If they read her work they would begin to understand where she had truly been, someplace so horrible that she had never been able to give voice to it except in her secretive writings.

She cleared her throat, putting those particular thoughts from her mind. "The reason Mrs. Juniper insisted on me helping her is because she despises me," she continued, folding her papers several times over and stuffing them in the pocket at her waist. "She does not think well of a self-made woman who has no need for a man or children."

Elspeth laughed as she thumbed through the list of their stock of titles. "Then she must not think well of Millicent and myself either, for we are right there with you."

Seraphina smiled down at the bent bright auburn head of her youngest sister, ever industrious and good-natured. "Ah, but you both have the good fortune of being quite sweet and cheerful. No one could despise either one of you, dearest. I, on the other hand, am very much set in my grouchy, grumbly ways."

Elspeth looked up with a gentle smile. "That is because she does not know you as we do."

At once Seraphina's light mood vanished. "Perhaps," she murmured quietly as, having found what she had been looking for, Elspeth hurried away. But then, even Elspeth and Millicent did not know Seraphina completely. They did not know the dark secrets in her heart, the cloud of fear and grief that hung over her head, ready to rain down on her at a moment's notice, the horrible memories that were like manacles.

Subconsciously she rubbed her wrist under the long sleeve of her gown, even as she told herself that there was nothing there. She pressed her lips tight. And there never would be, ever again.

Phineas, however, must have sensed her distress. He gave a low whistle, pressing his head to Seraphina's cheek.

"It's all right, darling," she murmured, reaching up to scratch the back of his neck. His feathers had regrown for the most part, but even after all these years she could still feel the bald spots beneath the bright green-and-red plumage. Proof of a stress that was not completely eradicated, no matter the years that had passed and the love she had given to him.

Much like herself, she supposed. No matter how far behind her she left that most horrible time, there truly was no escaping from it, not completely. "Which is why we are such a perfect pair," she murmured to the parrot. "Isn't that right, you handsome thing?"

"Keep the heid," Phineas squawked, tilting his head to eye her closely, not fazed in the least by her flattery.

"You are very right, darling," she soothed. "I shall calm myself right away. But we'd best hide these away in my room lest we are found out. And then we shall have a lovely walk down to the Master-at-Arms and concentrate on getting some much-needed sun and fresh air and not on the fact that we are forced to do the bidding of that horrid Mrs. Juniper."

A short time later Seraphina was in possession of the requested book and stepping forth from the Quayside into the late-summer sun. Despite the early hour the pavement was packed with all manner of holiday-goers, the looming end to the busy summer season prompting a barrage of last-minute shopping on Synne's main thoroughfare before the visitors headed back to their respective lives.

It was a time of year that always sat heavy on Seraphina's shoulders. She had moved her sisters here knowing it was far enough removed from their old lives that they could stay hidden, and yet with the hope that the busyness of such a place could keep her mind occupied. And in the summer months she was quite thoroughly occupied, the circulating library flourishing, demanding every bit of attention and focus from her that she could muster up.

The off-season, however, was another matter entirely. While the Quayside was never without patronage, there was nevertheless a lull that dragged on Seraphina. Perhaps that was the reason for her sudden increase in nightmares. She was all too aware that in a week or so she would be without that crutch of constant work she counted on. Mayhap she should begin to look at branching out. They already offered an assortment of stationery and perfumes and fans for purchase, and they provided tea to their patrons in the reading room. But perhaps she could pair up with her dear friend Adelaide, owner of the Beakhead Tea Room, to provide an assortment of baked goods as well. Or maybe she might convince Bronwyn, another of her good friends and now the Duchess of Buckley, to host several intellectual salons at the Quayside.

Mind humming, finally pleasantly occupied by something other than her troubling nightmares, she turned onto the Promenade and entered the Master-at-Arms. Mrs. Juniper was behind the front desk, laughing uproariously with her husband. When she spied Seraphina, her laughter died, to be replaced with a self-satisfied smirk.

"Is that my book then, Miss Athwart?" she asked, motioning to the volume in Seraphina's hands.

"Indeed it is," Seraphina replied in a carefully neutral tone, placing it on the front desk. "Please let us know if you need anything else."

"Oh, I will," the woman drawled, pointedly turning away without a word of thanks.

Breathing slowly through her nose to control her temper, Seraphina turned about and stormed for the door. But her path was quickly barred when a very tall, very wide, very male presence stepped into it. Strange, that; she was uncommonly tall, after all, and did not often meet men who made her feel small. In truth, only one man had ever made her feel thus, a man who had worn the same green-and-blue plaid kilt as this man was, who'd had identical overlong light brown hair, the same piercing gray eyes, strong jaw, chiseled lips...

Good God.

She stared at him, certain she must be imagining things. She had dreamed of him just last night after all, and so this must simply be a figment of her overactive imagination. Or perhaps a ghost, a spirit, come back to haunt her.

As if he had not done enough damage to her.

But then that figment of her imagination smiled, a slow, cruel thing, proof that she would not be so lucky to have him vanish in a puff of mist. And then he spoke, in that rumbling, deep brogue that had once made her insides melt but that now only caused them to freeze into painful ice.

"Hello, mo bhean. Fancy seeing you here."

Chapter 3

Seraphina's mouth dropped open, gaping like a trout's. And though she knew she must look a fool—especially as it was all too obvious from the satisfied look in his eyes that he had been expecting to see her, giving him a clear advantage in this encounter—there seemed to be nothing she could do to snap herself out of her shock. She had not seen Iain MacInnes since that day nearly thirteen years ago when she had parted from him at that crossroads, fully expecting to be reunited with him within the hour, her heart full of the promise of their future together.

How wrong she had been.

His lips, those firm, chiseled lips that had kissed her senseless on more than one occasion, kicked up at one corner. But where they used to be deliciously full and smile easily, there was no softness to them now. No, now they carried a certain cruelty.

"What, no kiss for your husband?"

That one question, said so quietly yet with a bite, broke her from her shocked stupor. She hastily stepped back, fighting the urge to wrap her arms about her middle. But Phineas chose that moment to dig his claws in tighter on her shoulder, making a low, agitated trilling sound, and she knew she could not let this man cow her. She was not the same innocent, naïve girl she had been. She was strong now, in both body and mind, having been to hell and back—quite literally—and survived.

Planting her hands on her hips in defiance, she glared at him. "What are you doing here?" she hissed.

A bark of derisive laughter passed his lips, so different from the warm honey sound his laugh used to have when they were younger. Now it sounded unused, rough, a mockery of what it used to be.

"That is quite the greeting," he said, the words as sharp as a freshly honed blade despite how quiet they were, "considering all you've done."

"All *I've* done?" The man was outrageous, rude, horrible. To think she had loved him once, had promised herself to him, had lain with him. The very remembrance made her ill. "I have done nothing to you," she continued, her voice dripping with disdain. "What of what *you've* done? Or has your ego erased the truth of the past?"

His eyes flared wide with shock. Before he could answer—God knew what rubbish he might have spewed—Mrs. Juniper approached. She eyed both of them with blatant interest.

"Is there a problem here, Miss Athwart?"

Damn it all to hell. That was all she needed, for the woman to begin making up scenarios in her head about her and Iain. *Though any scenario she might make up could not be more outrageous than the actual truth.*

Even so, Seraphina had a reputation to protect, all connected to her sisters and the business they needed for their livelihoods. *Ah, God, her sisters.* Pasting a tight smile to her face despite the panic that surged in her breast, she said in as conciliatory a tone as she was able, "Not at all, Mrs. Juniper."

But the woman did not look the least convinced. She narrowed her eyes as she considered them. "Do you know Mr. MacInnes here then?"

Before Seraphina could answer, Iain spoke up, his voice a veritable purr. "Yes, *Miss Athwart*, do you know me?"

Seraphina ground her back teeth together until she was certain they would crumble to a fine dust. The cur. But she would not be coaxed into revealing more than was necessary to Mrs. Juniper—and thereby revealing to the entire Isle, as that woman would make any slip-up well known before nightfall. Could she hide the fact that she knew Iain? No; she had been foolish enough to violently react to his presence upon seeing him and could not now call it back.

But she certainly would not—could not—reveal the true nature of their past acquaintance.

"I do indeed know Mr. MacInnes," she said calmly. "Though it was long ago."

"Verra long ago," Iain murmured.

"Quite," she replied, keeping her gaze on the too-curious woman beside them lest she give even more away by spitting fire from her eyes at Iain's smug face. In the next instant, however, she realized something horrifying: Mrs. Juniper knew Iain's name.

She swallowed hard. "But is Mr. MacInnes staying at the Master-at-Arms, then?"

"Indeed he is," the woman said. "Arrived just a short

time ago." Suddenly her expression turned crafty. "But we know so little of your time before you moved to Synne. Meeting someone from your past is quite a treat. You must tell me how you know one another."

"Perhaps another time," Seraphina replied tightly. "I really must be getting back."

"Allow me to accompany you," Iain said. Without waiting for her to agree, he offered his arm to her.

He was a blackguard of the first order. From the smug look in his eyes he knew she would not be able to refuse without causing talk. Taking a fortifying breath, she placed her fingers on his sleeve.

Electricity shocked her senses, skittering along her skin, turning her mind to mush. Which only made her more furious, though at herself this time. So much so that, once they were safely out of the inn and turned onto Admiralty Row, she stopped in her tracks, yanking her hand away and turning to glare at him.

"What are you doing here?" she demanded.

"Och, that's an easy one, lass." He took a step closer to her and lowered his mouth to her ear, his voice washing over her. "I want a divorce. And you shall give it to me."

* * *

He perhaps should not have taunted her. He had come here for the express purpose of securing a divorce from Seraphina. Everything was focused on that outcome; it was why he had concealed his title upon setting out to find her, not wanting Seraphina to dig in her heels in an attempt to remain a duchess. Well, he admitted ruefully to himself, that and the overwhelming fact that he finally felt like himself again, now that he had shed the title. Was it temporary? Yes. Would he have to don the yoke of the dukedom once more when this whole fiasco was through? Also yes. But for a short time he could forget that people refused to see the accomplishments he had worked so hard for and only saw his worth in a title he had no control over.

Regardless of his reasoning for keeping it hidden, however, it was of benefit to himself. And if it had the added bonus of punishing Seraphina when she found out the truth, all the better. He set his back teeth together, remembering his fears that he was not good enough for her because of his low status, her insistence that she didn't care for titles or money—and then immediately proving that was a lie by taking her father's offer of riches and the ability to follow her dreams in exchange for leaving him. Despite his anger toward her, however, he had been certain he could remain polite, indifferent, get what he came for, and finally remove her from his life for good.

But then he had seen her, and all the old hurt had come rearing up until it was all he had felt, all he had remembered. How was it that she could be even more beautiful? Oh, she had been beautiful before, of course. From her brilliant red hair that would have done any Scot proud, to her bright blue eyes that spoke of more than her fair share of intelligence, to her strong features that told of a spirit that had drawn him to her like a moth to a flame, he had always found her lovely.

Now, however, there was something more to her that was, quite honestly, stunning. And not just the delicate wire-rimmed spectacles that magnified her striking eyes to an incredible degree. No, there seemed to be a maturity and character that made him realize her hold on him was not yet done. And that realization had enraged him. He should be finished with her. After the hell she had put him through, the heartbreak and grief, he should have written her off years ago.

Yet there she had been, hands on hips, looking as proud and defiant as any Scottish lass, and he had wanted nothing more than to take her in his arms and never let her go now that he had found her again. He had been furious at himself, at her, at the world. And so he had taunted her, and antagonized her. And then, once they were out of sight of that nosy Mrs. Juniper, he had leaned in close to her to finish the job—forgetting for one outraged moment the bright green-and-red bird that sat belligerently on her shoulder.

Seraphina's scent enveloped him, the same lavender that used to make him weak in the knees, and he forgot to pull away. And that was when the bird went in for the kill.

A sharp pinch on his ear had him yelping and rearing back. "Damn and blast," he cursed, cupping his abused ear as he glared at the creature.

It glared right back—if a parrot could glare—and squawked, "I'll gie ye a skelpit lug!"

His jaw dropped open, nearly to his chest. "What the devil?"

Seraphina, however, found much more humor in the situation than he ever would—no matter that the situation should be hilarious, seeing as the bird was speaking in a perfect Scottish brogue and threatening to box his ears. "Funny that," she mused, eyes glittering with a cruel mirth, even as her lips twitched with suppressed laughter. "I have never known Phineas to attack anyone like that. He must truly despise you."

"Like parrot, like mistress, no doubt," he countered,

pulling his hand away, not a bit surprised to find a smear of blood on his palm. "Remind me to find you again should I ever wish to have my ears pierced."

At once her mirth dissipated, replaced with cold anger. "We shall never see one another again after this. As a matter of fact, you shall forget you ever saw me. Is that clear?"

With that she spun about, no doubt intending to leave him right there on the pavement. Without thinking, he reached out and captured her arm in his hand. Her reaction was as swift as it was violent. A low, hissing noise escaping her lips, she yanked her arm out of his grip, holding it close to her body. But it was not the swiftness of her reaction or her defensive posture that had his blood turning to ice. No, it was her face. She looked, quite thoroughly, as if she were a cornered animal.

"I'm sorry," he said, softly and slowly, bringing his hands up palms out so she might see he was not a threat. "I dinnae mean to startle you. It willnae happen again."

Gradually her posture eased, her arm lowering, her expression clearing. Yet she did not take her cautious eyes from him, as if she feared he might spring forward and attack her.

"You are correct," she replied, her voice devoid of emotion. "It shall not happen again. I want you gone from Synne on the next ferry to the mainland."

Instead of feeling annoyance, all he felt was relief. At least she had gotten her spirit back. Anything was better than the frightened, panicked look in her eyes.

Nevertheless, he could not allow her to run him off. "I cannae do that, lass," he replied. "I've come here with a purpose, and I mean to see it through."

A frustrated little divot deepening between her brows, she opened her mouth to speak. Just then, however, there was a swift clatter of feet on the pavement. And then Seraphina was encircled by several women, who separated her from him by sheer will.

"Excuse me, sir," one wee bespectacled miss said in clearly outraged tones, her short curls fairly vibrating in her agitation, "but what do you think you are doing accosting Miss Athwart?"

"I wasnae accosting her—"

But another of the ladies cut him off, this one much closer in height to himself, though still not nearly as tall as he, a full-figured woman with hazel eyes that were pure fire. "We shall not allow you to put hands on her," she snapped, stepping in front of Seraphina like some avenging fury.

And yet a third joined in the fray, this one sporting jet-black hair and a frilly apron and brandishing a teapot as if she would bash him over the head with it. "Go now, and leave Miss Athwart alone, or you shall have us to deal with."

Iain found himself at a loss. He had never been cowed in his life. His great size and rough appearance typically put most people off with a single look.

Yet these three women, surrounding Seraphina and looking as if they would gladly fall on a sword to protect her—not to mention the blasted bird, who had its green wings outstretched menacingly and was looking at his ear once more with a frightening degree of malicious interest— had him stepping hastily back.

"Verra well," he said, before looking at his wife. "Seraphina, I do hope you reconsider talking to me about certain matters. I shall nae leave Synne until you do."

With that he spun about, leaving the four women—and the bird—to stare after him.

Chapter 4

W ho the devil does he think he is?"
"Are you all right?"
"Did he hurt you?"

Her friends' questions came fast as they led her away
from Iain, their concern for her and outrage over Iain's
mishandling of her obvious. Not that his brief hold on her
arm had been rough or cruel. No, it had been incredibly
gentle. But old fears were hard to bury, coming up at the
most inopportune times, and though she had known deep
inside she had nothing to fear physically from this man—
she had never feared him, despite his massive size and
frightening visage—that had not stopped that instinctive
reaction.

Bronwyn, Honoria, and Adelaide continued to fuss
about her like angry mother cats, and Seraphina realized
distantly that she should have been warmed by their worry
for her. The Oddments, the name her group of friends had

given themselves as a kind of retaliation against the ridicule and disdain shown to them by much of society for leading unconventional lives, were some of the most important people in Seraphina's life. Her love for them was second only to the love she felt for her sisters.

Instead, however, she could only feel a strangling panic rise up as they brought her ever closer to the Quayside. Not that Iain was still watching them. And not that it would be difficult for him to find where she lived and worked. If, she thought bitterly, he didn't already know, as it seemed he was fully aware of her presence on Synne and had come with the express purpose of locating her.

But the thought of her sisters, kept safe for so long here in this little slice of England, being found out had that familiar panic rising in her chest, and all she could think about was protecting them at all costs. No matter it had been years since they'd been forced to flee from their father's men, no matter that they were well past their majorities and their father should not have any legal hold over them. She had made a vow to herself to keep them safe, and she would continue to do so until her last breath.

But how to redirect her friends without stirring suspicion? No matter how she loved and trusted these women, she had never been able to confess the truth of her past or the hell she had escaped from. No, not even her sisters knew the whole truth of it.

Just then, however, she spied the teapot still gripped defensively in Adelaide's hand. Miss Adelaide Peacham, proprietress of the Beakhead Tea Room, had no doubt run from her establishment to come to Seraphina's rescue. And that, she decided, was where they would all return.

"Adelaide," she said, loud enough to be heard over

their heated questions, "aren't you supposed to be at the Beakhead?"

The reaction was instantaneous. Adelaide gasped, nearly dropping the plain white ceramic teapot. "Oh goodness. Lady Tesh will have my head."

At mention of the dowager viscountess, the matriarch of the Isle of Synne and one of the most terrifying, strong-willed women Seraphina knew—no doubt a reason she liked the older woman so much—the entire group gave an instinctual flinch and immediately turned about, heading back for the Beakhead. But Seraphina's relief was short-lived. As they entered the cozy tea shop, the bell jingling merrily as they threw the door wide, she realized she would not only have to contend with her friends' questions about Iain and how she knew him, but she would also have to deal with Lady Tesh inserting herself into the conversation as well.

That woman did not waste even a moment before she started in on Seraphina.

"Miss Athwart," she said, raising one silver brow imperiously, "come and sit beside me, and explain just what all the fuss was about that had everyone up and leaving me quite alone here."

As Seraphina sank into the chair beside the dowager viscountess she cast a look about the Beakhead. Alone? Hardly. Half the tables were filled with customers, the two girls who worked for Adelaide busy seeing to them, not to mention Lady Tesh's small white dog, Freya, who was sitting on the chair on the other side of her, looking as imperious and self-important as the dowager herself.

"My apologies, Lady Tesh," Adelaide said, face flaming. "It was horribly unprofessional of me, and shan't happen again."

But the dowager merely waved her hand in dismissal. "Never mind that, Miss Peacham. It is commendable, after all, that you are so very loyal to your friends. And you both as well, Miss Gadfeld, Your Grace," she drawled, looking to Honoria and Bronwyn in turn as they resumed their seats across from her, "no matter that you were supposed to have been my guests for tea."

She turned her piercing gaze back to Seraphina. "What I do wish to know, however," she continued, "is what happened to *you*, Miss Athwart, that caused these three women to up and run out of here as if their skirts were on fire."

Seraphina, face going hot, reached up for Phineas, urging him to step onto her hand with a small nudge under his downy belly so she might have something else to focus on besides Lady Tesh's too-perceptive gaze. She brought the bird close to her face, running her fingers over the bright red crest on his head, down the brilliant green of his back. Phineas looked back at her steadily, his yellow eyes calm, and she took strength from him. He had been through so much—*they* had been through so much. Surely they could get through this, too.

"I merely had a run-in with an old acquaintance," she finally replied, because, really, she had to say *something*. And there was no sense in keeping the pertinent information from Lady Tesh. The woman had ears everywhere and would eventually find out the truth of it—or at least as much as everyone else on Synne already knew. Which was blessedly not much at all.

But the dowager, in her typical quick-minded fashion, would of course recall that Seraphina had been incredibly close-lipped about her past, and so it was no surprise that the woman took that one small morsel of information and held on tight, like a dog with a bone.

"An old acquaintance, eh?" She peered closely at Seraphina. "From your time before you took up residence on Synne?"

But Seraphina had become quite adept over the last thirteen years at deflecting unwanted questions about her past, and no amount of prodding, even by someone as skilled as Lady Tesh, would pry information from her that she did not wish to share.

"What was that? Oh, yes, I suppose so. But are those lemon and lavender biscuits? I do adore them. I don't suppose you would mind if I helped myself to one?"

Without waiting for a response, she reached across the table, snatching one of the biscuits from the plate, plopping it in her mouth. If she had to, she would keep her mouth full for the entirety of her time here, preventing her answering a single probing question.

Lady Tesh, of course, was far from stupid. Narrowing her eyes in acknowledgment of Seraphina's evasion of her question, she turned to spear Bronwyn, who was watching the proceedings with bright eyes behind her spectacles, with a severe glare.

"What was it you were asking me before your unexpected flight, Your Grace?"

Bronwyn, Duchess of Buckley, cleared her throat and pushed her spectacles more firmly up her nose. "Yes, I believe we were discussing Katrina. You said you have received a letter from her?"

Which was the one subject in the world that could succeed in distracting each and every woman present, Seraphina included. Miss Katrina Denby had been not only the fifth member of the Oddments, but also Lady Tesh's companion. Now married to the Duke of Ramsleigh, she was living in domestic bliss with her husband up north. Which made her correspondence to them infinitely precious. While Bronwyn had married her duke and remained on Synne to further her studies of the local insects, Katrina's move had been the first time their closely knit group had been altered. And while none of them would ever begrudge Katrina her happiness with her duke, that was not to say they did not all miss her, dreadfully.

"I will be glad to tell you everything," Lady Tesh said. "Only do sit down, Miss Peacham. You are making my neck ache. Your girls are seeing to your patrons just fine," she continued severely when Adelaide opened her mouth to refuse. "I'm certain they can handle things without you for another ten minutes. Especially considering you ran out of here without a second thought in pursuit of Miss Athwart here and her mysterious acquaintance." Here she pursed her lips and glanced pointedly at Seraphina before, clearing her throat, she opened her reticule, pulled out a letter, and began to read.

Some time later, when Katrina's letter had been read and reread, and the tea had been drunk and the biscuits eaten, Lady Tesh grabbed her cane and pushed herself to standing. The rest of them followed suit, Bronwyn fetching the woman's dog, and they all accompanied the dowager outside to her waiting carriage. There was much fussing on their part over the dowager as they settled her within the equipage; despite her abrasive ways, they all cared for her and had taken to filling in some of the gaping hole that Katrina's departure had left behind. When they would have turned away to go about their days, however, the dowager called Seraphina back.

"Miss Athwart, a word, please."

Seraphina silently cursed herself for letting down her guard. She could pretend she didn't hear the woman, of course, and just keep walking. Or she could claim to have a prior engagement, or that her presence was required at the Quayside.

But knowing Lady Tesh, that would not matter a bit. The woman was frighteningly single-minded when it came to that terrifying curiosity of hers.

Sighing, she turned back around and stretched her lips into a stiff smile. "Yes, my lady?"

She expected a barrage of questions about the mysterious acquaintance that her friends had saved her from. Bracing herself, her mind spun wildly, trying to come up with a believable explanation for it all.

What she did not expect, however, was the look of kindness on the dowager's heavily lined face.

"I hope you know, Miss Athwart," she said in quite the softest tone Seraphina had ever heard from her, "that if you have need of anything, anything at all, I am here for you."

Seraphina blinked in incomprehension. "I'm sorry?"

The woman smiled, an expression not often seen on her face unless it was in mischief or self-satisfaction. Now, however, it was almost gentle. "I know I am harsh and opinionated. That does not mean, however, that I am not the soul of discretion when need be. You are entitled to your privacy and secrets, of course. Not that I won't vehemently deny that should you tell anyone I said that." Here her smile turned mischievous, a twinkle entering her sharp brown eyes before her expression sobered once more. "But should you ever need help, please know you can count on me."

Seraphina was never without words. She prided herself on leaving emotion at the door, at being prepared for just about anything, at moving forward and doing what needed to be done with no help from anyone.

Yet in that moment, confronted with a surprising amount of kindness from the dowager, she found she truly didn't know how to respond.

"Er...thank you, my lady," she finally replied.

Which was apparently enough for Lady Tesh. That woman nodded before, lifting her cane, she rapped sharply on the carriage roof. In an instant the equipage was rumbling down the street, heading back to her home. Leaving Seraphina alone and perplexed, staring after her.

But she was not alone for long. Within moments Honoria was back beside her, tucking a plump arm through hers.

Miss Honoria Gadfeld, eldest daughter of Synne's vicar and currently living above the Beakhead with Adelaide, thrived on gossip. It was an interest her father had tried to break her of for years, an interest Honoria herself had never tried to curb. And so Seraphina tensed once more, fully prepared for a barrage of questions from her voluble friend.

Despite the bright interest in her hazel eyes, however, Honoria merely asked, "The Oddments are meeting as usual tomorrow at the Quayside?"

If Seraphina had been touched at Lady Tesh's kindness, she was doubly so now. Her friend had never been one to hold herself back from getting involved or pushing her nose into places where it did not belong. Yet here she was, doing just that, holding back, though it was all too obvious from the frustrated questions in her gaze that she wanted nothing more than to learn just what was going on with Seraphina.

For the first time in more years than she could recall, tears prickled hotly behind Seraphina's eyes. Not that she would let them loose. No, she had not cried for thirteen long years, and she wasn't about to start now.

But that did not mean the urge was not there.

Squeezing Honoria's arms, she replied, "Yes, tomorrow as usual."

Honoria nodded. "I'll see you then," she murmured before, shocking Seraphina even further, she leaned in and gave her a quick kiss on the cheek. In the next moment she was gone, slipping back inside the Beakhead.

More affected than she would ever willingly admit, Seraphina reluctantly made her way back to Admiralty Row and toward the Quayside. Though she had fought hard to keep her friends and Lady Tesh from probing too much into her distress at having Iain here on Synne, she now knew she had much worse things to contend with: namely, time to think, and to remember. And to figure out what the blazes she was going to do about her erstwhile husband.

Chapter 5

*B*y the time evening came around, Seraphina was faced with the unpleasant realization that there was only one thing she could do regarding Iain: she had to meet with him again.

While she had not seen him in more than a decade, she recalled all too well his drive and stubbornness. She had been drawn to those qualities in the beginning, his focused intensity that, when directed toward her, had made her feel like the most important person in the world. When Iain wanted something, he went after it with his entire soul.

And so she knew he would not just go away, no matter how much she might wish it. No, she had to face him and see to it herself that he left Synne and never returned.

Panic bloomed once more, a poisonous flower in her chest, and the question that had been preying on her mind all that long day dug its teeth into the base of her skull: How had he found her? She had been so careful to erase their tracks. And it had not been easy, not with three red-headed sisters and a parrot. It had taken years to find this place, years of running and dodging their father's men. Only when learning that he had proclaimed to all and sundry that she and her sisters were dead some ten years past had she begun to breathe a bit easier. Having her youngest sister reach her majority had further cemented the idea that they were safe, that they no longer had to worry about what that man might do to them.

Yet there had always been some fear in the back of her mind that this was all too good to be true, that they would be pulled back into that world again if the truth ever got out—and that she would be sent back to hell on earth. And so she had tried to be vigilant, to keep her sisters protected, to make certain they did not experience the same hell she had.

She deposited Phineas on his perch in the corner of their small yet cozy sitting room above the Quayside. Mayhap she had begun to feel too comfortable here. She worried her lip with her teeth as she stroked the smooth feathers along the bird's head. She had to have inadvertently left a trail, like bread crumbs in the forest, for Iain to have located her. She cursed low; why couldn't he have just taken her father at his word, like everyone else seemed to have done, and written her off as dead?

"Seraphina? Are you all right?"

Forcing a smile, though it was the last thing she felt like doing, Seraphina turned to face Millicent. Her middle sister stood close by, her brows drawn together in concern. Millicent had always been the more sensitive of the three of them, ever reacting to others' moods. Seraphina would have to be extra guarded around her, lest Millicent grow suspicious.

"I'm fine," she murmured, linking arms and walking with her toward the small circle of seats. "But you were kept quite busy with Mr. Ronald Tunley this afternoon. Did we not have what he was looking for?"

"Oh, I don't know," Elspeth quipped with a sly smile for Millicent as they settled beside her, "I rather think we had exactly what he was looking for."

"Elspeth!" Millicent exclaimed, batting at her younger sister's arm, her fair skin blooming with bright color as Elspeth laughed.

But Seraphina did not join in on the sisterly banter. Frowning, she adjusted her spectacles and watched her two siblings closely. Had Millicent formed a tendre for Mr. Tunley? As she studied Millicent, at the bright look in her eyes and the small smile that played about her lips, she knew with a sinking heart she had. That was just the expression she used to see peering back at her from her looking glass when she had been foolish enough to fall in love with Iain all those years ago.

Not that it should have been at all unexpected that Millicent had fallen in love. She had to have known that, eventually, her sisters would find someone to care for.

Yet she had not expected it so soon. A foolish thought, she quickly realized. Her sisters were not young girls any longer. They had been fourteen and fifteen when Seraphina had spirited them away from the horrible futures their father had planned for them, and were now in their late twenties. In another life, they would have been several years married, most likely with one or more children at their knees, homes of their own.

And the pawns and chattel of powerful men who would have used them until they were mere husks of themselves.

Now they had a chance to make their own paths, to find their own happiness. And all that would be taken away if Iain made the truth of their past relationship known.

They had been welcomed into Synne society when they had arrived despite having no acquaintances, no family or friends to vouch for them. But Seraphina knew all too well what could happen to a person here if they were the subject of gossip. With a vividness that still managed to enrage her, she recalled what had happened to her friend Katrina not even a year ago before she had married her duke, when she had been the subject of scandal. The "good" people of Synne had turned on her in a moment, making her life hell. Not only that, but they had turned on anyone who remained faithful to Katrina, Seraphina and the Quayside included. What would happen were the truth found out about Seraphina's own past, that she had stolen her sisters from home, that she'd had them all taking on a false last name—that she was in fact married?

Her stomach lurched. Dear God, they would be ruined, chased out of town, on the run again. No matter that they were now all of age, her father was a very powerful man, and no one would be able to stop him if he got it into his mind to make them pay for escaping his rule.

She lurched to her feet. She could not let that happen.

Both of her sisters had fallen silent and were staring at her with worry on their faces.

"Seraphina?" This time from Elspeth.

"I'm fine," she lied. "Truly. I just... need some air is all. Will you watch Phineas while I take a walk down to the beach?"

"Of course," Elspeth replied.

Before the words were out of her mouth, however,

Seraphina was hurrying for the door, pulling her shawl from the hook, making her way down the narrow stairs to the side entrance and out into the warm late-summer night. She had to find Iain and make certain her sisters would remain safe. No matter what it took.

* * *

Iain had expected Seraphina to search him out soon. She had never been one to back down from a confrontation. Mayhap in the next day or two; she had been caught off guard, after all, and would need time to shore up her defenses.

Yet there she was, storming toward him in fiery fury—blessedly without her parrot—while he took the air along the path that ran parallel to the wide band of beach that faced the Master-at-Arms Inn.

"I'm glad I did not have to go to any of the Junipers to locate you," she bit out as she sidestepped an older couple listening to a young singer on the edge of the path. "There will be enough talk from our encounter earlier; I do not want to add kindling to the fire."

Then, without further ado, she grabbed his arm and dragged him to a quiet stretch. Colorful lanterns swung lazily above their heads in the warm summer breeze, the haunting sound of the young soprano's voice and the low rumble of conversation and laughter carrying to them. Yet they were essentially alone in this one small corner of the walkway.

"We will have this out here and now," she said, her voice quiet yet sharp as she turned to face him. Her jaw jutted out, her eyes narrowed to hard slits, her entire body fairly vibrating with anger and determination. She was taller than most women, had always seemed able and willing to go head-to-head with him. Now was no different. If anything, she appeared more of a Fury than ever.

To his surprise and ire, his blood stirred at the glorious sight of her.

But no, he would not be distracted by his seemingly intact desire for her.

"Aye, let's," he replied, crossing his arms over his chest. "The sooner I get off this blasted island and return to Scotland, the better I'll be."

"For me as well." A strange gleam entered her eyes, magnified to a disturbing degree by the lenses of her spectacles. "But before we begin, I want to know how you found me."

The question gave him pause. Not because it was unexpected. If he were in her shoes he would wish to know as well.

But there was something almost fearful in the asking. He was reminded of the last time he saw her, just before her friends rescued her from him. She had been fearful then, too. No, more than fearful; she had been damn near terrified. A disturbing question rose up in his mind: What the hell had happened to her?

A moment later and he pushed the question aside. Now was not the time to be blinded by concern for her. He had a purpose here, months in the making; he would see it through, come hell or high water—or delectable wives who made him remember things he would rather forget.

"To tell you that," he murmured, liking her much better when her hackles were raised, "I must begin with a story."

She scowled. "And if I don't wish to hear your story?"

"Why, then, lass, you shall miss out on just how I found

you. Beginning with how I learned that I wasnae a wid-ower, as I had believed myself to be all these years."

Her scowl deepened—so much better than that fright-ened look in her eyes that had him worrying for her—and she crossed her arms over her chest. "Very well. Have out with it. But quickly, for I haven't got all night."

He leaned against a light post. "You recall Mrs. Mary Campbell, I presume."

The only physical response she allowed to show was a slight flicker of her eyelids. "My father's old housekeeper? Yes, I recall her."

"She wrote to me, told me your father lied about your death. You can imagine my surprise."

"I did not realize Mrs. Campbell was privy to my father's secrets," she replied acidly.

"It has been my experience that most people born into wealth and privilege do not realize that the servants know much more about their lives than even they do."

She pressed her lips tight but did not respond to his little jab. "And where is Mrs. Campbell now?"

"Dead."

He expected a reaction of sorts from her. Maybe a mur-mured word of regret, a slight tilt of her head to acknowl-edge the passing of a woman who had spent the majority of her life serving Lord Farrow and his ilk.

What he had not expected was how deeply his one word seemed to affect her. Her face paled and her arms, which had been crossed belligerently over her chest, slid down to cradle her middle, as if she would hold herself together by sheer force.

But the moment of vulnerability did not last long. Draw-ing in a slow breath, she straightened and turned the full force of her glare on him once more. When she would have spoken again, however, a group of young women came their way. They were talking animatedly with one another but quieted when they spotted Iain and Seraphina off to the side of the path, their eyes bright with curiosity. Though Iain did not know if it was because of him—he stood out, after all, with his uncommon size and quite possibly being the only man in a kilt on the whole bloody island—or Seraphina.

Apparently, Seraphina was not about to wait around and find out. Pointedly ignoring the women, she surreptitiously grabbed his arm and pulled him down the brightly lit path away from the group. Then, giving a quick look around to make certain they were no longer being observed, she yanked him out from under the lights of the lanterns and to the dark beach beyond, behind an outcropping of rocks, until they were quite cut off from the rest of the world.

Out of the circle of glowing lights, everything altered. The laughter and conversation quickly faded, the dulcet sounds of the soprano no more than a backdrop, the hush of the surf watering it all down until he felt as if he had stepped into a completely different world. The sand shifted under his boots, making his feel as unsteady as Seraphina's hand on his arm did, and he was hard-pressed to pull his sleeve out from under her touch. How the blazes could she still affect him?

Blessedly she stopped and pulled away herself, saving him from acting a fool and showing his hand.

"But you have not answered how you located me," she said, her voice haunting in the dark, the husky tones of it wrapping about him like a caress. "I managed to evade my father's men for years. How was it you managed to find me out?"

Pull yourself together, MacInnes. Crossing his arms over his chest, he put all thoughts of his totally unwelcome attraction for Seraphina far from his mind. "Well now, that took a bit of doing. You were not an easy one to track."

"Wholly on purpose, I assure you," she muttered under her breath.

"If I hadnae chanced to see a copy of a particular periodical," he drawled, ignoring her comment, "I wouldnae have found you at all."

She stilled, and even in the dark he saw the glint of knowledge in her eyes. Even so, she would not give in so easily—not that he had expected anything less from her.

"I don't know what that has to do with me."

"Dinnae you?"

Her voice went from flat to vibrating with anger in the space of a heartbeat. "No. I don't."

He stepped closer to her, bending down until his lips were close to her ear, ignoring the heady scent of lavender, which was amplified by the fresh ocean air. "Did you think I would forget how often you talked about selkies, how you dreamed of one day finding the sealskin your father must have stolen from you so you could return to your true place?"

She physically blanched. But, stubborn woman that she was, she clung to her ignorance like a marooned sailor clinging to a piece of driftwood.

"The foolish musings of a foolish girl," she spat. "I do not see what that has to do with anything."

"Dinnae you," he murmured, dropping his voice to an intimate rumble, "S. L. Keys?"

Chapter 6

*H*ow she did not cast up her accounts right then and there she would never know. As it was, her head began to swim, so much so that she took a hasty step back from him, dragging in a deep breath of sea air in the hopes of clearing her senses. But nothing could rid her of the horrible truth staring her in the face, in the form of one over-large, entirely-too-smug Scotsman.

So that was the trail of bread crumbs she had left, was it? Bitterness and self-contempt had her mouth tasting like iron. The one time she had allowed herself to be remotely whimsical, to pay homage to the devastated girl she had been, and she had inadvertently left the one bit of information that could lead Iain right to her.

Even so, it was a flimsy connection, wasn't it? Though they were well in the shadows, and he could not possibly see every infinitesimal nuance of her expression, she carefully rearranged her features to hide her fear and anxiety, aiming for disdain instead. "Come now," she scoffed. "You read a name that sounds somewhat like a mystical creature I used to talk of, and you make a far-fetched connection that it might be me writing some fantastical stories? That is quite the imagination you've acquired since last I saw you."

"Do you honestly believe," he drawled, "that I would traipse all over England searching for you if I dinnae have more to go on than that? Nae, that was merely the catalyst. Once I started reading through your publications, I began to see parallels that I couldnae ignore. An evil, powerful father as the villain. A servant turned hero. And the two younger sisters that the heroine was trying to save."

"All quite common in the genre, I assure you," she dismissed, waving a hand in the air, though inside her stomach was churning. Ah, God, she had put so much of herself into those stories—things she did not want him, or anyone else, becoming suspicious about. Foolish, foolish woman.

"But I am nae done," he continued imperiously. "The most damning by far were the details that only you and I would have known, the things we shared, the secrets we told one another. Did you think I could have possibly forgotten that old ruin and how we climbed to the verra top, how that stone came loose and we found the skeleton of that bird? Or when you wrote to me of the trunk you found in the attic at Farrow Hall and the mirror you pulled from its interior that had a young girl holding a cat painted on the back?" He raised one eyebrow in a cocky gesture that had her temper boiling. "Should I go on?"

She glared at him, even as she silently considered her options. She could continue to claim ignorance, of course, chalk it all up to coincidence, tell him he was deluded to think she was S. L. Keys, and attempt a nimble dance about the subject until the man did not know his arse from his elbow.

But the plan had not fully formed in her head before she realized she was foolish to think something like that would work. Not with Iain, at any rate. He was not some pliable person with soup for brains who would accept anything she chose to tell him. No, he had always been incredibly stubborn, as well as much smarter than even he realized. He had no doubt spent weeks, perhaps months, tracking her down. He would not accept whatever flimsy excuses she might come up with.

And so, knowing she had been backed into the proverbial corner, fully aware that her strongest defense was an impenetrable offense, she raised her chin and met his gaze.

"Are you expecting a trophy then? I assure you, you shall be waiting a long time for one if you are."

The silvery light of the moon shimmered in his eyes, showing the appreciation that her seemingly unconcerned comment had garnered. Not that she cared if he admired her refusal to be cowed. Not one bit.

"Nae going to continue denying it then?" he asked.

She shrugged. "What is the point? It will only prolong my time with you, something I aim to make as minimal as possible. Let us get to the point of your presence here, shall we? The sooner we tackle that, the sooner you may leave Synne. Which is paramount to me just now."

His lips kicked up at one end. "You never were one to mince words, were you?" When she merely glared at him, he nodded, as if he had expected as much. "Nor were you one to speak if silence could do the job just as well. But I have already told you why I have come. I wish for a divorce."

"Surely you don't need me to acquire one," she countered, even as some small part of her mourned. She had gone into their union with her whole heart, certain their love was one for the ages, that they would be together forever.

More the fool, she.

"I'm certain there have been plenty of divorces due to abandonment where the spouse could not be found," she continued. "Simply go to your local commissary or whatever it is you have to do and see it done."

"Ah, but if it was that easy dinnae you think I would have done it already, instead of chasing you the width and breadth of England?" He glared at her, as if she had created with willful intent all of the difficulties he had gone through to get here. "I *did* go to the commissary, as a matter of fact. But they refused the divorce, seeing as you had been legally declared dead. I then went to the Court of Sessions, who also refused, due to your supposed death, even with Mrs. Campbell's letter as proof, stating that the words of a dead woman were mere hearsay. They informed me that if you were truly alive, I must locate you to get the divorce. But you dinnae make it easy on me, lass. After months of searching and failing, it was only by chance that I came upon your stories." He narrowed his eyes, satisfaction fairly oozing from him. "Oh, and you may want to search for another publication to print your tales in. They dinnae hesitate to divulge your whereabouts when I flashed enough coin their way."

Seraphina rather thought that if anger was a physical manifestation, steam would have begun to pour from her ears. She was tempted to rail at him; hadn't he destroyed her life enough? Did he have to ruin one of the few good things she had managed to claim in the years since she had last seen him?

In the end, however, she merely said, "If even the courts believe me to be dead, why fight for a divorce at all? Let me remain dead in their eyes and leave me be." The last came out in close to a pleading tone, despite her attempts to remain cool and collected. Drat the man for dredging up emotions she would keep buried—and a helplessness she had not felt in too many long years.

Fighting to regain control of her composure, she continued. "You can go on as a widower and live your life, and I can remain Miss Athwart of Synne and live mine. It is a simple solution, and one that would have saved you the effort of spending months searching for me."

But he was already shaking his head. "Cunning of you, Seraphina," he drawled. "But I shall nae do such a thing, tempting as it is. Someday down the road, after I have gotten on with my life and married again, you might get it in you to pop your head out of the ground like a badger out of its sett, and then where shall I be? A bigamist. And besides the fact that I shall nae want to go into another marriage with such a horrible secret, I'll nae have the stain of bigamy on me—or the legal repercussions."

Married again. Why did those words tear through her like a bullet? She did not want this man. Not after all he had done to her, how he had betrayed her. What did she care if he remarried?

Yet no matter how much she willed herself to look past it, she could not. Bitterness filled her, that he should move on so completely from what they'd had. And not just the love she'd believed they'd shared, but the friendship as well. For so many summers she had thought they'd had a special bond, one that had grown and blossomed into something beautiful. Until, in the matter of a moment, he'd allowed his greed to win out over any affection he might have felt for her. No, that was the biggest betrayal of all, the fact that he'd turned his back on something she had believed to be so very precious between them, the friendship they had shared for so long.

It was silly, really. It had been thirteen years since then. What did she think he had been about all this time? Of course he would have moved on. And in that moment she wanted nothing more than to move on from him as well—something she had thought she had done but obviously hadn't, if her reaction was anything to go by. A divorce would free her from him completely. It was ideal, really.

Ideal, that is, if she did not have to rise from the dead to do it.

"While I would love nothing more than to be rid of you legally and completely," she replied, "I would rather remain deceased in the eyes of the world, thank you very much. You can be assured your secret shall remain safe with me. You can get on with your life, and I can get on with mine."

He scoffed. "You will forgive me if I don't give any value to your word."

"*My* word?" Once more anger sizzled through her, burning away all her grief and fear.

But he seemed not to have heard her. Or, rather, he was choosing to ignore her, which seemed much more of an insult.

"I willnae leave Synne until you have agreed to help me finalize this divorce," he stated emphatically, crossing his massive arms over his chest. And then he smiled, a deliberate stretching of lips over teeth that had her equally aggravated and wary. "Besides, seeing as we're married, your business and all that you own essentially belongs to me."

She froze. "No," she blurted, an automatic response, even as her mind knew there was no sense in protesting. It was one of the many, many injustices of society, the fact that a married woman owned nothing of her own, that everything went to her husband.

His cold smile widened, the recognition of just how effectively he'd trapped her plain as day in his eyes. "I'm afraid so. And I can see you're aware of it as well." He paused, his eyes narrowing in a kind of victory. "However, if we were to divorce…"

He shrugged, as if it was of no consequence. When in reality it meant everything. Everything she had worked for, spilled blood for, sacrificed for, all to give her sisters security and a good life.

And damn it, he was right. As her husband he could take it all away.

"Fine," she spat. "I will sign what I have to, whatever paper is needed, to declare I am in fact alive. You can take it back to Scotland, and see our divorce is finalized, and we may finally wash our hands of one another for good. In exchange, I insist that you keep the fact that I am alive and well as quiet as possible. I have made a good life for my sisters here on the Isle; I do not want that destroyed."

"Oh, you can be assured I will keep your existence quiet," he drawled, even as a triumphant gleam entered his eyes. "I nae more wish for our union to be made public than you do; you're nae the only one to have made a life for themselves. However," he continued, his voice rising as she nodded and made to turn away, needing to get away from him immediately, now that they had come to their agreement, "I willnae be content with a mere piece of paper from you. After all the trouble I've gone to in order to find you, I willnae be taking any chances. You shall come back to Scotland with me, to declare before the Court of Sessions yourself that you are alive and well and that you agree to this divorce."

She gaped up at him. "You cannot be serious."

"Oh, I assure you, my lovely wife, I most certainly am."

"But...I cannot do that! I have a life here, my sisters, my business. I cannot possibly drop everything and traipse off to Scotland with you."

"You can, and you shall."

The maddening, stubborn, hateful man. Scowling, she jutted out her chin and glared up at him. "And if I don't agree to return to Scotland with you?"

His eyes narrowed. "Then I'm certain I could find the time to remain on Synne and take over the family business."

Rage ripped through her. "That is blackmail," she gasped.

He shrugged. "Blackmail adjacent, at the most."

She let loose a frustrated growl deep in her throat. "You are despicable."

To her frustration, he grinned. "Undoubtedly." His expression shifted, a hard gleam entering his eyes. "Do you agree to return to Scotland with me, Seraphina?"

"Do I have a choice?"

"Nae."

If thoughts had been daggers shooting from her eyeballs, she rather thought she would have killed him on the spot. Unfortunately, however, they were not, and so she was left to deal with the man.

"Very well," she bit out, her mind already spinning. "But it will take me time to prepare for the journey. I have a business to run and cannot be expected to drop everything at a moment's notice."

"Do you think I will allow you time to change your mind?" he demanded. "Nae, we leave at first light."

"First light?" The laugh she allowed to pass from her lips was not complimentary to him, not at all. "You are deluded. Even if I had no other responsibilities, I could not possibly be ready so quickly. I need at least a week."

"Now who is the deluded one?" he countered. "I have responsibilities as well, and I say we leave tomorrow."

But Seraphina was done caving in to every demand he had. Dragging in a deep breath, she jutted out her chin and stared mutinously up at him. "As I have been forced to concede on each and every other aspect of this farce," she gritted, "the least you can do is to give in a small bit. I vow I shall not change my mind, that I shall leave for Scotland to see this done. Now, can you at least meet me halfway?"

He considered her closely. "Verra well," he finally replied. "I'll give you three days to put your affairs in order. Does that work for you?"

"Fine," she spat. She held out her hand. "Give me your direction and I shall meet you there."

But her hand remained empty, hanging suspended in the air like a marionette's. "Oh, nae you don't, my traitorous wife," he drawled. "I willnae gamble on you disappearing again. I'll wait here on Synne until you are ready, and we shall travel north together."

"I would rather eat dirt."

He merely shrugged. "If that is what it takes."

But she pointedly ignored his sarcasm. "I refuse to be

cooped up in a carriage with you for days on end. There must be some other way."

He made a show of considering that for a moment—an insult, really, as she saw from the malicious light in his eyes that he had no intention of reconsidering.

"Nae, I dinnae believe there is."

She blew out a sharp breath, just barely holding back a growl of frustration. "Very well, you beast. Three days from now, at first light, I shall meet you at a place of my choosing. I won't have our leaving together draw any attention; I still have to live here, after all." She narrowed her eyes. "Until then, stay out of my way."

With that she turned and stormed off across the sand— trying and failing not to hear his reluctant, rough chuckle behind her.

Chapter 7

"What do you mean you're leaving?"

Seraphina sighed and glanced about the small circle of her friends, all sitting close together on the compact collection of mismatched furniture, teacups and biscuits suspended halfway to their mouths as they gaped at her. She typically enjoyed the weekly meetings of the Oddments, something that had taken place rain or shine in the small office at the Quayside Circulating Library for years now. But last night's conversation with Iain had effectively soured this week's meeting for her. For she had known she would have to tell her friends that she would be away from Synne for a time, and they would have questions—questions that she was still not ready to answer.

"It won't be for long," she answered instead, trying to redirect them. "A week and a half perhaps. A fortnight at most. But I do hope I can count on all of you to check in on my sisters while I'm gone. They have never handled the

Quayside completely alone before, and while I know they are more than capable, I do worry."

Honoria, however, was not one to be distracted once she sank her teeth into something, just as Seraphina had dreaded. "Of course we will check in on them. You do not even have to ask us to do that, for we all shall, and gladly. But don't think you're going to get out of explaining the reason for your absence. Or where you'll be going."

Before Seraphina could think how to respond—something she had been trying to figure how best to answer since parting from Iain the night before—Honoria's hazel eyes lit up. "Does this have anything to do with that Scotsman we saved you from yesterday?"

"Honoria, hush," Adelaide reprimanded, reaching across the space between their chairs to swat at her arm. Seraphina did not miss, however, that the action was more performative than anything. Adelaide's swat was more a caress than anything, and her eyes did not leave Seraphina. In fact, she leaned closer as she sipped at her tea, as if she did not want to miss even a breath of information.

"I know we vowed not to pry into your past," Honoria continued. "But the Scotsman's appearance yesterday coupled with your news today cannot be mere coincidence."

Coupled. She felt slightly ill at that word choice. *If her friends only knew.*

But they would not know. Not if she could help it. No one would ever learn of that most shameful part of her past when she had been at her weakest. Or what had come after.

"Not to mention the elephant in the room," Bronwyn added, the first she had entered into the fray of this particular conversation. Her gaze, glinting behind her spectacles, shifted to Phineas, who sat happily chewing on a bit of greenery on the perch behind Seraphina. "Or, rather, parrot."

Every eye turned Phineas's way. The creature, traitor that he was, chose that moment to squawk out, "Noo, jist haud on!" before he went back to his leaf.

Seraphina groaned.

"Yes!" Honoria nearly fell out of her chair as she lurched forward in excitement. "You have a parrot that speaks with a Scottish accent. How in the world could we have forgotten that?"

"Well, *I* did not forget, at any rate," Bronwyn muttered from behind her teacup.

A bit of sarcasm that Honoria chose to ignore. More pity, that, for it might have distracted her from Seraphina and her upcoming trip.

But where Honoria was concerned, things were never so easy.

"While we have known you came from 'up north,' I don't think a single one of us suspected you lived in Scotland."

"I did not live in Scotland," Seraphina muttered, knowing she could not keep every bit of information from her friends, now that Iain had come back into her life like a bull elephant at full charge. If she did not say something to pacify them, God only knew how much worse things would get. As it was, she felt as if she were on the other side of a dam, and several spots had grown weak and allowed water to pour through. Right now the only thing she could do was to figure out which breaks she could stop up before the whole blasted thing fell apart.

"I did, however, visit on occasion," she continued in as cool a voice as she was able. "It is where I met Mr. Mac-Innes, the gentleman"—her throat closed at using such a

kind word in relation to Iain, but she pushed through—
"you all saw me with yesterday. He came to inform me that
there are some loose ends I need to tie up, and so I must
leave as soon as I'm able. Now," she finished with a brittle
smile for the group, lifting the chipped teapot in the air,
"does anyone need their drink refreshed?"

If anything, Honoria's expression became more stubborn. "Don't think you can fob us off so easily—" she
began heatedly.

Blessedly, however, Adelaide seemed to have regained
her senses. Placing a firm hand on Honoria's arm, she said,
"Honoria, that's quite enough. If Seraphina does not wish
to explain, that is her prerogative. It is her life, and hers
alone. We must respect her and abide by her wishes."

Honoria stared mutinously at Adelaide for a long
moment, and the rest of them held their collective breaths
as they waited for her response. Honoria was not one to
back down from a challenge.

In the end, however, she seemed to deflate into her seat.
"Very well," she grumbled before shooting a singeing glare
around the room. "But I'll have you know I am not happy
about it. Not one bit."

"Of course, dear," Adelaide murmured complacently,
patting her arm.

"The question now is," Bronwyn joined in, pushing her
spectacles back, "what extent do you wish for us to assist
your sisters? From comments you have made lately, it
appears they have a wish for more independence. If that is
the case, will they resent our presence here?"

"Oh, that is a good point, Bronwyn," Adelaide said with
a frown. "What did Millicent and Elspeth say when you
told them of your trip?"

Seraphina winced. Leave it to her too-astute friends to get right to the heart of the matter. "I, er...haven't told them yet."

As one, three jaws dropped open. Honoria, naturally, was the first to speak.

"What do you mean, you have not told your sisters yet?"

Seraphina, suddenly unable to meet her friends' piercing gazes, took her spectacles off and busied herself with cleaning the lenses on her skirt. She shrugged. "I will tell them. Of course I will tell them. It's not like I *can't* tell them. I mean, I'll be gone for some time, and so certainly cannot hide the fact."

"But...?" Adelaide prompted when Seraphina's voice dropped off into a loaded silence.

Seraphina sighed. "But I don't know what to tell them."

Again a loaded silence. This time, however, it was not Honoria who broke it. It was Bronwyn.

"But they are your sisters. You are closer to them than anyone and share a history with them. Surely they should be the first to know of your plans and the reason behind them."

Again Seraphina winced. "You would think that, wouldn't you," she mumbled more to herself, feeling lower than she had in a long while. She had known since the day she had learned of her betrayal at Iain's hand that she would never again be able to open herself up to another. Not even her dear sisters could know the entire extent of her past.

But she had never felt so completely alone as she did in that very moment, knowing that, no matter how she loved someone and they loved her, there would always be a gaping chasm between them that could never be crossed.

Hopelessness sucked at her, that very same despair that

had nearly destroyed her thirteen long years ago. With incredible effort she battled it back.

"You're all making a mountain out of a molehill," she proclaimed, straightening her back and nodding with much more confidence than she felt. "I simply have not had the time, is all. I'll tell my sisters after your departure."

Bronwyn, however, being of an incredibly agile scientific mind, could sniff out erroneous information much too easily. "You cannot tell your sisters the reason for your departure either, can you?"

Seraphina scowled. "It does not matter."

"Actually," Adelaide said in a gentle tone, "I do believe it matters, very much."

She was right, of course. They all were. But Seraphina was not about to admit that.

"I do believe that's enough on that particular subject," she declared forcefully and with a determined smile. "My largest concern was that you should all be aware of my absence, and to secure your assistance with Millicent and Elspeth, and I have done that. Let us turn our attention now to happier matters. Namely, Bronwyn's upcoming publication. I vow, I am so proud of you. I cannot wait to supply it at the Quayside for our residents, so they might see for themselves that your research has proven fruitful and useful."

Which, of course, thoroughly distracted Bronwyn. No, not just Bronwyn, but all of them. Bronwyn had worked so hard for so many years in studying and illustrating the local beetle population after she had found what she had believed to be a new species. Her upcoming publication was proof that her work was worthy and important. Not that any of the Oddments needed to be given proof. They all believed

Bronwyn was utterly and completely brilliant, no proof needed.

At the end of their scheduled hour—Seraphina had been closely studying the clock above the mantel the whole while, something she had never done for their weekly meetings before—Seraphina stood and motioned to Phineas, who took off from his perch to land on her shoulder. "Well then," she said with a smile that took more than a bit of effort to produce, "that was a lovely meeting. But I really must be getting back to work, as I suspect you all must as well, especially with the end of summer approaching. I will contact you before I depart to provide any pertinent instructions regarding the Quayside and my sisters." With that she began herding her friends from the small office.

Honoria, as expected, proved difficult to maneuver out. Digging in her heels, she threw a mulish glance Seraphina's way. "Now just a moment. I'm certain you can spare another few minutes with your dear friends before we depart. There is so much to discuss still."

But Adelaide, saint that she was where Honoria was concerned, quickly took her in hand. "I'm sure I would love that as well, dear," she said sweetly, grabbing Honoria's arm in a gentle yet firm hold. "But we really must be getting back to the Beakhead. I don't like to leave Gertrude and Juliette alone too long, as you well know. Why, the last time they had the place to themselves, they left the Parmesan ice out and melted the whole lot."

As Adelaide no doubt expected, Honoria was quick to grasp onto that bit of maddening news. "Those girls," she grumbled. "Why you keep them on is beyond me."

"I assume you have someone else in mind to take their places?"

"Of course I do," Honoria declared. With a quick wave goodbye to Seraphina and Bronwyn, she launched into what would no doubt be a long monologue on the importance of good employees—funny that, as she had only been with Adelaide, living above the Beakhead and working with her in the popular tea shop, for three months now. Adelaide, as ever patient, gave Seraphina a conspiratorial wink before ushering Honoria out.

Now that her biggest threat was gone—though she adored Honoria, there truly was no one like her when it came to ferreting out information—Seraphina let loose a heavy sigh. Forgetting, for a moment, that there was someone still with her. Someone who was not as tenacious or outspoken as Honoria, but who was the most brilliant, observant person Seraphina knew. Which could be equally dangerous.

Giving Bronwyn a careful look, Seraphina was about to launch into all the reasons why her friend must have important business to attend to back at Caulnedy Manor, the home she shared with her husband Ash, Duke of Buckley, and Ash's three energetic, precocious sisters. Bronwyn, however, spoke before Seraphina was able to utter a single syllable.

"You've no need to worry that I'll quiz you on your trip. Or your Scotsman," she added with a small smile that lit up her narrow face.

All too soon, however, the smile was gone, replaced with a deep divot between her brows that told of her disquiet with the whole situation. She shifted her bag on her shoulder and reached for Seraphina's hand, gripping it gently. "But just know that we only pester you because we love you."

A lump suddenly formed in Seraphina's throat. Not tears—no, she never cried—but a deep emotion nonetheless that she quickly swallowed down. "As I love you," she replied.

"We know you do," Bronwyn said, squeezing her fingers. "And so I know you will listen when I beg you to be careful."

With one last meaningful look Seraphina's way and a quick pat for Phineas, Bronwyn ducked from the office. Leaving Seraphina and Phineas quite alone. In more ways than one.

But there was no time to be morose. She had much to do over the next three days—no, two days now, as she had already wasted half a day worrying over how she would tell everyone of her upcoming trip—and could not spend a minute more putting off the thing she dreaded the most. Namely, what to tell her sisters about her departure.

But there really was no time like the present. Especially as she had already informed the Oddments that she would tell her sisters immediately upon their departure. And so, straightening her spine, she marched from the office.

Chapter 8

*B*ut *immediately* turned to *soon*, turned to *eventually*. And before she quite knew it, evening had fallen and they were closing up the Quayside. And still she delayed. They were all quite busy, after all, reshelving books and tidying up the reading room and sweeping the floors. Surely she should wait until they were up in their apartment above the circulating library. Though mayhap she should postpone until they had eaten their dinner, she mused, biting her lip as she went over the receipts of the day. Or tried to go over the receipts, as her mind was much too full to pay them the attention they required.

But in a moment she knew that what she was doing—indeed, what she had been doing all day—was only delaying the inevitable. In her mind she saw how it would go if she did not stop herself now: waiting until after dinner would become postponing until after they cleaned up, then waiting until morning, and so on and so forth. At this rate, they would only learn about her departure when she actually departed. And so, depositing Phineas on his perch behind the desk, she expelled a sharp breath and said, her voice warbling in the great gaping silence of the place, "I have something to tell the both of you—"

But her words were cut off as Millicent, in the process of wiping down the front window, gave a little scream. And then she was scrambling toward Seraphina, a look of fear in her eyes that had not been seen there in a blessedly long while.

At once everything else was forgotten in the face of her sister's distress. Seraphina, rushing to meet Millicent halfway, grasped her hands tight, only to find them ice cold. "What is it? What has happened?" she demanded.

"We have been found," she gasped. "We have to leave Synne, immediately."

Seraphina's senses sharpened. This type of thing had been commonplace those first few years after she had rescued her sisters, then fourteen and fifteen and about to be forcibly married off, from their father's home. How hopeless she had been then, how broken, after the year of hell she had been subjected to. That she had not been traveling, as their father had told them, was made obvious when Seraphina had returned home a ghost of the person she had been. But even though Seraphina had adamantly refused to tell them the truth of her absence—she could never tell them of the true horrors of her time away from them—they had trusted her implicitly, begging her to help them escape a fate that to them was worse than death. Seraphina had not hesitated; she may have been broken in spirit, but knowing she could protect her sisters—and that they trusted her to do that for them—had given her life again. She had snuck them out in the dead of night, had them on the run, dodging the men their father had sent off after them. How many times had they found themselves being watched, and how often had they barely escaped capture?

Such a scene had not happened in nearly a decade, not since her father had announced to the world that they were dead and she and her sisters had found sanctuary on the Isle of Synne. Yet the way her body reacted to her sister's panic was all too familiar, falling easily back into the defensiveness that had been so crucial in the beginning: her breathing sped up, her body going cold, her limbs tingling with the urge to act. Releasing her sister's hands, she rushed across the floor to the window. "Found by whom?" she demanded, peering out into the darkening street.

Only to see Iain casually walking down the other side.

She went from cold to hot in an instant. Though whether it was fury at his blatant strolling near her establishment, or her body traitorously reacting to how well he looked with his broad shoulders and strong legs and deliciously arrogant expression, she would never know. And she would not allow herself to figure it out. There was no doubt in her mind she would not like the answer.

But now she had a bigger problem to contend with as Elspeth joined her at the window to see what all the fuss was about and spotted Iain. As she gasped and scurried away to huddle with Millicent, Seraphina let loose a quiet curse. Though it was aimed at herself and no one else. How had she forgotten that her sisters had known Iain? Yes, they had been young when they had gone on their yearly summer holidays to Scotland. More than half their lives had passed since those days.

But Iain was not someone you forgot, even if you hadn't

been head over heels in love with him as Seraphina had been. He was too large, too magnetic, too commanding to be forgotten easily. As was proof in the pale countenances of her sisters as she turned to face them.

"That man," Millicent said, voice shaking. "We know him. Or, rather, knew him. He was a groom at Father's Scottish house."

"Yes," Elspeth replied, her arms tight about her sister. "I remember him as well. Do you think Father sent him after us? And if not, do you think he will go to Father for a reward once he sees us?"

"Oh, I thought we were past all this," Millicent wailed. "And now to have to leave Synne? I don't wish to leave."

"Neither do I."

Ah, God, this was getting out of hand. Millicent and Elspeth were whipping themselves up into a veritable meringue of anxiety. She had to nip this panic in the bud before it turned into something much worse. "There is no need to worry," she declared firmly as she strode toward them. "We shall not have to leave Synne." *I hope*, she silently amended. "He is not here to reveal our location to our father." *He'd better not.*

Too late, however, she realized she had erred, and horribly. Both girls stilled as they stared at her.

"How do you know that?" Millicent asked.

The soothing smile she had been attempting froze on her face as she recognized the dawning realization in her sisters' eyes. "I'm sorry, what?" was her horribly pathetic response.

Elspeth straightened away from Millicent and crossed her arms over her chest. "How do you know the reason for that man being on Synne? In fact, why are you not surprised to see him here at all?" And then hurt replaced her confusion. "You already knew he was here, didn't you?"

What else could she say to that? "I did," she admitted with reluctance.

"When did you learn of his arrival?"

Seraphina winced. "Yesterday?"

"Yesterday!" Elspeth demanded.

"And you did not think to warn us?" Millicent looked wounded in a way Seraphina had never seen directed at her. Which made her feel as if she had kicked a puppy.

She removed her spectacles and pinched the bridge of her nose. "I was going to tell you. But there never seemed a right time."

Elspeth threw her hands up in the air. "A right time? We live together, work together. When is there a wrong time?"

"Especially with something of this nature," Millicent added.

"You're right," Seraphina said quietly, replacing her spectacles and clasping her hands together before her contritely. "Of course, you're right. And I am sorry, truly."

Her sisters looked at each other, in that way they had showing they understood one another better than anyone ever could. Even Seraphina had never been privy to that level of closeness with them. No, that wasn't true, was it? She had been part of that private inner circle once upon a time—before her life had been torn apart and she had closed herself off forevermore to anyone else, even her beloved sisters. One of the many things that had been stolen from her.

"I think we both know you would not purposely put us in harm's way," Elspeth said softly, turning back to Seraphina. "You have done everything in your power to protect us and provide for us in the past thirteen years—even to your detriment."

Was there a mournful bit of knowing in her sister's eyes at that? For a moment anxiety and a deep shame reared up in Seraphina's breast, old companions of hers. Could her sisters possibly know just how detrimental some of the things she'd had to do for their survival had been? Could they know what lengths she had gone to in order to protect them?

She gave herself a little shake. No, she had been careful. They could not possibly know. Her heart thumped heavy in her chest. Yet another thing she had kept from them, all to ensure they were safe and loved and happy. And she would do it again, in a heartbeat.

Elspeth, blessedly unaware of what was going through Seraphina's head, narrowed her eyes in thought, a small line forming between her brows. "You and he struck up a friendship of sorts, didn't you?"

Seraphina was trying to figure out just how to answer that when Millicent chimed in.

"Yes, I remember that as well." She turned wide eyes on Seraphina, who could fairly see memories appear out of the mist of time in her gaze. "Then Father let him go one summer, and you cried. You kept to your room for days. They tried telling us you were ill. But we could hear you sobbing through the door. I think that is the last time we ever heard you cry." Her expression became troubled. "That wasn't long before you disappeared for that year."

Seraphina's head swam as images bombarded her, recollections of a time she had tried so hard to forget. So overwhelmed was she by the sheer number of memories, so dim did her vision go, she feared she would topple over on the spot. Until a sudden rush of wind disturbed her hair, and a warm weight settled on her shoulder, and a small body pressed against the side of her head. Phineas trilled in her ear, the comforting sound he made when she was particularly troubled, and she found her chest relaxing in response, air filling empty lungs, head clearing. Or, if not clearing, at least allowing her to better manage what filled it.

"Yes, we were friends of a sort," she said, purposely ignoring any mention of her crying or of that year apart from them—she involuntarily shuddered—focusing instead on her sisters' memories of Iain. "And you are also correct that Father let him go. So you see, he does not owe Father any allegiance. There is no threat from him in regard to our location or our new identities." *Or, at least, there had better not be.* And she would do everything in her power to make certain that remained true.

But her sisters, who had lately begun to push back against the safe boundaries Seraphina had created for them, adopted now familiar, mulish expressions at her attempt to placate them.

"We should invite him in then," Elspeth said with a determined glint in her eyes, looking to the window, though Iain must be well out of view by then. "We can quiz him ourselves, make certain we're safe—"

"No!" The word burst from Seraphina's lips, sending Phineas launching from her shoulder in a burst of startled feathers. Seraphina leapt forward, sprinting for the door, planting herself in front of it, arms and legs spread like a starfish. It was only as she looked at her sisters' alarmed faces—and Phineas staring in avian effrontery at her from the curtain rod—that she realized how excessive her reaction had been.

And then she hurried to explain the reason for her reaction—and made things so much worse.

"He won't be here for long. We leave in just two days, and with everything that has to be done there isn't time for a visit—"

"We?" Elspeth demanded. "What do you mean, *we*?"

Seraphina nearly groaned aloud. Ah, God, what a bungle. She was tempted to send a curse Iain's way. It was because her sisters had spied him that she was in this particular pickle.

But she knew that was only directing blame where it did not belong. She and she alone was at fault for this mess. If she had not been such a coward, if she had stepped up and told her sisters immediately that she was leaving, she would not now be staring into the hurt eyes of the two people who meant most to her in the entire world.

Exhaling wearily, she let her arms fall heavy to her sides. "I have much to explain, and many apologies to make, it seems. Let us finish up here and head upstairs, and I shall tell you everything."

Or, she silently amended as they quietly put away their things and headed for the stairs that led to the upper floors, *everything they needed to know*.

* * *

As it turned out, needing to leave out so much information led to having very little to tell them. So little, in fact, that in a mere matter of minutes, she was quite done.

Millicent and Elspeth stared at her after she fell silent, obviously expecting more. When Seraphina merely folded her hands tight in her lap, they raised their brows in disbelief.

"That is all?" Elspeth demanded.

"Yes," Seraphina replied, even as she felt her insides burn from how horribly the blatant lie scorched her soul.

"You have nothing more to say?"

This time she could only manage a sharp shake of her head.

"So you mean to tell us," Elspeth continued, exchanging a disbelieving look with Millicent, who was sitting in wide-eyed silence, "that Iain, someone you have not seen in thirteen years, and who has not been involved with any of our family's dealings in all that time, came all the way to Synne to inform you that Mrs. Mary Campbell, Father's old housekeeper, has passed on and that you must travel to Scotland to deal with some issues that had been brought up after her death, and once those issues are taken care of, we will all be much safer?"

"Yes," Seraphina said slowly, though it came out more like a question, the single syllable rising in tone at the end. Dear God, she had lost her touch with this lying business, hadn't she?

Elspeth threw her hands up in the air, frustration and hurt twisting her normally sweet-natured features. "I don't believe you," she cried.

Seraphina clasped her hands so tightly together they began to go numb. "It is the truth," she managed. That, at least, she could say with utmost honesty.

"But it is not the whole truth," Elspeth accused hotly. "I know you must have had your reasons for keeping secrets, for keeping us in the dark about what was going on. We know you must have been through hell trying to keep a roof over our heads and food in our bellies."

Seraphina felt the blood leave her face, and she had to

forcefully remind herself that her sisters were ignorant to what Seraphina had done during those dark years when survival had been doubtful at best. And she had done it willingly. Selling her body had been small in the grand scheme of things, after all, when so much had been at stake.

Even so, she never wanted her sisters to know what she had been reduced to.

Elspeth must have seen some of her emotions on her face. She leaned forward across the small space that separated their seats, mismatched chairs that were worn and faded and had seen better days, and laid a hand over Seraphina's. "We were young, so very young, and we will be forever grateful to you for all you have done for us, for saving us from an abhorrent future and providing us with such a wonderful life. But the days of fear and anxiety are past. We are grown now, and you needn't protect us from the truth any longer. Surely you can let go of some of your burdens and confide in us."

"We love you so much, Seraphina," Millicent joined in, scooting forward in her own chair and placing her hand over their joined hands. "Please, let us in."

Looking at her sisters' earnest, loving faces, she was tempted. Ah, God, she was tempted, after so long, to open herself up to these people she loved so much. The words rose up from the depths of her soul, truths that she had kept secret for what felt a lifetime.

But at the last minute her throat closed up, the thought of the love in her sisters' eyes being replaced with disgust or pity making fear choke her. Or, worse, if in taking on part of the burden she'd shouldered, they were overcome with guilt and hated themselves for it. She could not bear it if the truth of her past changed the way they saw her or altered their love for her.

Stretching her lips into a smile, she straightened and gently pulled her hand out from under theirs. "Truly, you are both making much more out of it than there must be. When Mrs. Campbell died, Iain learned of something that might prove detrimental to us staying hidden. He has promised to escort me north to take care of it. Once that thing is taken care of, we will be even safer than we are now. I will be back within a week, two at most. Now," she continued, rising, "it is growing late, and we still have not had our supper. Let us eat and get a good night's rest. There is much to do before my departure in two days' time."

As they all silently went about their nightly duties, Seraphina knew she would never forget the look of hurt in her sisters' eyes for as long as she lived. But it was a small price to pay to continue protecting them. She only prayed they would one day understand.

Chapter 9

*A*t any other time Iain would have cursed the early hour as his carriage trundled down the still-dark road. The sun was not yet up, the hue of the sky barely past the indigo of deep night. And while he was an early riser—a lifetime of being forced to work just to survive had ensured that—this was bloody early even for him.

But he found that, though he had not slept the night before, though he should by all accounts be dizzy with exhaustion, he had never been more awake. And it was all due to one very particular fiery-haired woman who was waiting for him.

He had received her sharply succinct missive yesterday, which had laid out in steeply angled letters the instructions she'd had for him on their departure. And now here he was, heading for the place of her choosing as she had demanded, some house called *Caulnedy*, a location apparently private enough that no one would witness her climbing into

a carriage with him. And growing angrier at himself with
every turn of the wheels. While he should be approaching this trip with cool satisfaction that he would soon be
legally rid of her, instead his blood pounded hot and his
body thrummed with anticipation that he would see her
again. Damn and blast, he had better get ahold of himself,
and fast. This was no pleasure ride. Nor was it a meeting
of old friends. No, this trip was expressly for the purpose
of lancing Seraphina from his life, like an infection that he
had to purge his body of.

Just then the carriage, in the process of making a turn at
yet another bend in the road—where the hell was this house
he had been directed to?—slowed drastically. The driver
called out to his team, the alarm in his voice clear as the
equipage swayed sideways. Iain's nerves, already frayed
due to his unwelcome thoughts regarding his wife, unrav-
eled further as he grasped onto the wall of the carriage to
steady himself. What, were they being held up by highway-
men now? Which would just be the icing on the cake of
this ridiculously early morning, wouldn't it? Letting loose
a small growl, he threw open the door and leapt down to
the road. He'd be damned if he would just sit and wait for
whomever it was to accost him.

Two women stood in the center of the road like delicate
specters, their slight forms covered from head to toe in
voluminous capes. An alarmed shiver worked up his spine.
He was not one to frighten easily; he was usually the one to
do the frightening, if he was being completely honest. But
the Isle of Synne, from what little he had seen of it during
his wanderings over the last several days, seemed a magical
place, with its secretive forests and undulating beaches, and
rolling hills that resembled nothing so much as slumbering

giants; being waylaid by two figures that appeared like ancient druid priestesses just amplified that.

And then they pushed back their hoods, revealing hair that shone with brilliant red highlights the same hue as Seraphina's in the light of the carriage lanterns, and the breath fled his body entirely. It was like looking at dim echoes of the young woman he had loved so desperately so long ago.

In the next instant, however, reason blessedly took over. There could only be two people in the whole of the world who resembled his erstwhile wife to such a degree, after all, much less in this little slice of Britain. He recalled the small girls they had been, of course, quiet, shy creatures who had adored Seraphina. And she had adored them. To such a degree that she had chosen them over him all those years ago.

And now it seemed Seraphina's sisters had decided a talk was in order before their departure.

He gave a small bow. "Lady Millicent. Lady Elspeth."

Their eyes widened, and they glanced at one another before returning their attention to him. "You remember us?" one of them said—truly, he would never be able to guess which one it was; they looked so alike one would think they were twins. Her voice was tight with tension, her fingers showing white and stark against the bruised purple of her cape.

How could he have forgotten them? They were intertwined with the happiest days of his life—or what had been the happiest. Now those were some of the most painful memories he had.

"Yes," he said low. "I remember you."

She nodded, looking to her sister before quickly returning her wide gaze back to him. Even at this distance he could see her throat work as she swallowed hard. "We were ... surprised to see you on Synne."

"Yes, well," he mumbled. "I would nae have come if it had nae been necessary."

They nodded again, in sync, yet remained silent. He raised an eyebrow. What the blazes was going on here? Did they intend to keep him standing in the middle of the blasted road?

"My ladies?" he prompted.

"Oh, there is no need for honorifics," the slightly taller of the two said—he still didn't have a clue who was who. "We gave them up years ago."

"Yes," he murmured. "So I have heard. Though I have-nae heard the particulars of *why* you gave them up."

They tensed, and in that moment he could see the difference between them. The one who had spoken seemed flooded with anxiety, while the other appeared ready to go to battle.

Despite himself, his lips kicked up in one corner. That would be the youngest then, Elspeth. She had always had a bit more fire than the middle sister.

And then she spoke. "I remember you being kind. But perhaps time has changed you."

"Ah, lass," he drawled, "you have nae idea. But what brings you out here in the middle of a forest before dawn? Shall I assume your sister doesnae know you aim to speak with me?"

She scowled, and he had the feeling that she was about to say something not at all complimentary, when Millicent laid a staying hand on her arm and stepped forward.

"Yes, and we would appreciate it if you did not divulge this talk with Seraphina during your trip north. She has enough on her shoulders; she does not need to worry even more about us and our reactions to this venture you are making together."

"Verra well," he said, nodding once. Was it just him, or did both women sag a bit in relief?

"However," he added severely, casting a look at a sky that was quickly growing lighter, "I would have you make it quick. I'm to meet your sister before dawn, and she'll have my head if I'm late."

Elspeth nodded, drawing herself up and leveling a stern glare on him that did not conceal the worry or confusion in her eyes. "Very well. We do not pretend to know why Seraphina has agreed to return to Scotland with you. But if she returns to us in anything but her usual spirit, or damaged in any way, you shall have us to answer to."

He was tempted to laugh. These wee women were threatening him?

But the laughter died before it could take purchase as the first portion of that little speech reached his brain. He frowned. "She dinnae tell you why we are leaving?"

Twin pain flashed in their eyes. But while Millicent's gaze dropped to the ground, Elspeth raised her chin. "No, she has not," the younger woman replied. "But that does not mean we are asking you to tell us. I'm certain she must have her reasons."

No doubt. More than anything it was shame that she had married someone like him.

Suddenly Elspeth stepped forward. The horses shied to the side, already spooked, but she paid them no heed as she advanced on him. And then she was before him, staring up at him, her eyes glittering like sapphires.

"Just please protect Seraphina," she whispered hoarsely.

"She has given up everything for us and has done all she can to give us good lives, to the detriment of her own. Please, I beg of you, keep her safe for us."

He could do naught but stare open-mouthed at the earnestness and anxiety that stamped her delicate features. What the devil had occurred in the past thirteen years? It was not the first time he had asked himself that, and no doubt it would not be the last.

But now there was a different flavor to the question, as some of Elspeth's anxiety seeped into his chest.

Get ahold of yourself, man, he told himself brutally. No good could come of commiserating with such a woman. Things had been difficult for her? Well, they had not exactly been roses for him either. It was certainly not his fault that her gamble on her father's generosity had not panned out.

But the two women were still looking at him in that earnest way, and he was suddenly transported to a simpler time, when the future had seemed bright.

"Iain, do you think it's hurt badly?"

He looked up from the small bird in the palm of his hand. Wee Lady Elspeth peered up at him in worry, her brow creased, tears welling in her large blue eyes, eyes the same shade as her eldest sister's. Behind her, Lady Millicent was openly crying, tears tracking down her pale cheeks.

"Nae," he said with a small smile. "I daresay it's just stunned. It will be soaring through the clouds in nae time."

"Do you really think so?" she breathed, looking back to the bird.

"Aye," he replied gently.

Both girls smiled at him then, as if he were a giant among men. His chest filled with emotion, though just what that emotion was he wasn't certain. He felt as if he were glowing from the inside out. Confused, shaken, he looked to Lady Seraphina on his other side. It was then, as he was gazing at her sweet face, into her clear blue eyes that were filled with affection and pride and—dare he even think it?—something more, that everything seemed to fall into place. Happiness as he had never known filled him up until he thought he'd burst with it. And he knew, then and there, he wanted to marry her.

The memory swamped him, wrenching him back to a time that he wished with all his might he could forget. Shaken, he took a stumbling step back before getting hold of himself. "Aye," he managed hoarsely, "I'll nae let any harm come to her."

"Thank you," Millicent said fervently, stepping up beside her sister, taking her hand. "But we have delayed you enough. Please remember your promise to not tell Seraphina about any of this. Come along, Elspeth."

With one last long look they moved off to the side of the road and melted into the shadows. He stared after them, feeling as if he was in some strange dreamland. And then one of the horses nickered, the sound echoing back from the thick brush and trees that lined the road, finally waking him from his stupor. Without a word to the driver—God only knew what the man was thinking after that strange interaction—he strode back to the carriage and heaved himself inside.

A mere ten minutes later and they pulled up into the front courtyard of a house. Iain, still shaken by Seraphina's sisters much more than he would have ever admitted, did not comprehend the scope of the place until he stepped down to the gravel drive. Even then, his mind could not seem to fully take in what he was seeing. Sprawling and yet strangely intimate, the house looked like something out of a fairy tale, its brick exterior blending into the surrounding landscape and its many mullioned windows reflecting the blush of the dawn sky and giving the appearance of hundreds of shining will-o'-the-wisps. He looked to the open front door, eager to collect Seraphina and be gone.

It was not Seraphina waiting for him on the front steps, however, but one of the women who had come to her rescue that first day on Synne. The petite one with short curls and spectacles. Alongside her was a lean, dangerous-looking man who was much more awake than anyone had a right to be at this hour. And who appeared as if he would gladly leap down the steps and plant his fist into Iain's face. Iain instinctively widened his stance, as if preparing for that imagined blow.

"Mr. MacInnes, I presume?" the small woman called out in clipped tones, her voice sharp and carrying.

"Aye," he responded, not moving from his spot. "But you have me at a disadvantage, lass."

The man—or, rather, beast—at her side took a warning step toward Iain. With seemingly little trouble the woman held him back with one small hand on his arm. He immediately settled back to his place at her side, though he did cross his arms over his chest, his muscles straining the fine cut of his coat.

"I am Bronwyn, Duchess of Buckley," the woman said, her voice cold. She motioned to the man at her side. "And this is my husband, Ash, Duke of Buckley. Welcome to Caulnedy."

He nearly laughed. There was not a hint of welcome in her. He was damn near tempted to introduce himself by his title. But no, he was not here to have a pissing contest. He was here to make certain he got the divorce he needed. And reclaiming the dukedom now, something he had gladly eschewed upon leaving Scotland, would not help him one bit.

Instead of acknowledging their titles, Iain looked to the bright open doorway behind them. "Is Seraphina here then? Or are we to glare at each other for the foreseeable future?"

As he expected, the duke once more reacted, this time with a low growl. But he was not the one to move forward this time. No, his petite wife did, stalking down the steps, across the drive, until she was nearly toe to toe with Iain. Craning her neck back—truly, she was a tiny thing, barely coming up to the center of his chest—she glared up at him. Despite himself, he felt the stirrings of admiration. Most men quaked in their boots when they saw him. But this wee thing looked ready to do him harm, and happily at that.

"Mr. MacInnes," she said, her mouth forming his name as if it were something disgusting and slimy, "we do not know exactly what you and Seraphina are to one another, or what the details of this trip north are. But whatever it is, it must be incredibly important to our friend. Therefore, we support her judgment implicitly. And we want you to know that Seraphina is very dear to us. She is fierce, and brilliant, and you shall rue the day if she is not returned to us as her fierce, brilliant self."

"A common theme this morning, it seems," he muttered to himself.

Her eyes narrowed behind her spectacles. "What was that?"

"Nae a thing, Your Grace," he said smoothly. "I shall return her in one piece, I vow it."

Her expression said she did not believe him one bit. But

she nodded sharply and, her lip curling as if she could not wait to get away from him, she made her way back to her husband. That man gazed at her as if she were the most beautiful, precious person in the world and wrapped his arms about her.

"Wife, you never cease to leave me in awe," he said.

Her expression changed, a softness taking over her narrow features. "Liked that, did you?" she asked archly, her arms going about his waist.

"Oh, yes."

"Good." She grinned, her gaze drifting to the duke's lips.

Was it just Iain, or did the two look as if they were about to kiss? Face heating, he loudly cleared his throat and was about to demand where the blazes Seraphina was—God knew he had no wish to watch these two go at it—when a clattering trailed out from the open doorway behind them. He had not thought it possible to feel relief at seeing his estranged wife again. And so it was almost with eagerness that he turned to greet her.

Which was not the wisest mentality to have when dealing with his wife, a fact that was proven as his body reacted in a wholly unwelcome manner to the mere sight of her. His heart leapt in his chest, his breath stalled, and his legs tensed, as if they meant to stride toward her. And every inch of skin went electric, aching to touch her.

Which is probably why, when he finally managed to gain control over both his mental and physical states, his fury at himself was even stronger than before. Well, no more, he vowed as their eyes met. He'd be damned if he allowed her to catch him off guard again. No, they would get through this damned road trip, he would get his divorce. And then he would never have to see her, ever again.

Chapter 10

Well, doesn't he look ready to explode?

Seraphina hid a smile as she hefted Phineas's cage and the bag with her things more securely in her arms. She had not planned on being delayed in meeting him, especially after she had been so adamant that they meet before dawn. But Phineas had balked at being secured in the brass cage and had required a bit of bribery—and more than a bit of cuddling—before he could be persuaded to enter the contraption. She could not blame him. He was hardly ever secured in such close quarters, after all, typically given full freedom to stretch his wings and move about at will. She eyed the black lacquer carriage with trepidation, an equipage she would be confined to as surely as her bird would be confined to his cage. "I know how you feel, darling," she murmured in commiseration.

But if the delay had been the thing to put that ferocious scowl on Iain's face, she decided with smug satisfaction it had been well worth it. After the last two days, dealing with her sisters' hurt and her own anxiety over this upcoming trip, she was in no mood to be kind to him. No, not at all.

"It took you long enough," he grumbled, shifting from foot to foot in agitation.

Ignoring him, she made her way to Bronwyn's side. Her friend took her bag and tucked an arm through hers.

"You are certain?"

"Yes, of course." She forced a smile. "Don't fret. I shall be back before you know it."

"You had better," Ash muttered, casting Iain a dark look before moving forward to kiss her on the cheek. "If you are not, you can be certain I shall come after you. And believe me when I tell you, there are plenty of ways I learned to deal with blackguards while running a gaming hell back in London. Some of them are quite imaginative." He grinned. "Or perhaps you would like me to implement those particular talents now?"

Despite the strain of the situation, Seraphina smiled. "That shall not be necessary. Though I do appreciate the offer."

"I havenae got all day," Iain barked from his place by the carriage, aggravation plain in his grumbling tone.

Ash's grin melted away, dark shadows falling over his face that would have been terrifying if Seraphina had not known him better. "You're certain?" he asked her as he glared at Iain.

"It is tempting," Seraphina drawled, "but yes, I'm certain."

Bidding him a fond farewell, she walked with Bronwyn toward the carriage—still pointedly ignoring Iain. She was going to be cooped up with him for the next four days or so; she would delay interacting with him as long as she possibly could.

"You will take care, won't you?" her friend asked, looking at Iain askance.

Before she could answer, Iain was beside them, his outraged gaze snagged on Phineas in his cage.

"You are nae bringing that creature with us."

Fury sizzled along her skin. "I cannot leave him behind."

"You certainly can." He cupped his ear as if to protect it from further damage. "I'll nae have pieces of me nipped off at every turn. That bird is a menace."

"Now listen here, Mr. MacInnes—" Bronwyn started, her small frame vibrating in anger.

But as much as Seraphina would have loved to have seen her friend rail at Iain, she was too incensed to sit back and let another do it for her.

"I refuse to leave Phineas behind. He has dealt with enough in his life, and I shall not have him anxious over my leaving when he cannot understand that I will return." And then, in case he did not quite understand what she was getting at, she said, clearly and distinctly, "There is no bargaining in this matter. Phineas comes with us, or neither of us does."

His eyes sparked with his ire, and even Bronwyn, brave and fierce Bronwyn, made a small sound of alarm. But Seraphina was not about to be cowed. She stood straighter, leveling a return glare his way.

Finally he pressed his lips tight and nodded sharply. "Verra well," he grumbled, before adding, "but if it takes one more bite out of me, I shall have it put into a stew."

Rolling her eyes—there was no doubt in her mind he was all bluster—Seraphina turned back to get her bag from Bronwyn. Her friend handed it over readily enough, a fair amount of admiration in her gaze as she kissed her goodbye. "Never mind then," her friend murmured. "I see you have things in hand."

Seraphina gave her a surreptitious wink before, ignoring Iain's outstretched hand, she passed her bag to the waiting groom and climbed into the carriage, settling Phineas in his cage on the seat beside her. Her pet gave a low trilling, his nervousness apparent as he took in the dark interior of the equipage.

"It's all right, darling," she cooed, focusing her entire attention on the bird—though whether that absolute focus was completely due to her concern for Phineas, or partially due to wanting to distract herself as Iain entered the carriage, she did not wish to know.

But that did not stop her sharp awareness of Iain as he stepped up into the vehicle. Though the interior was spacious—incredibly spacious, really—that did nothing to detract from how utterly and completely his presence filled it. This trip, she thought a bit wildly as he settled himself across from her—and his bare knee came indecently close to her own—was going to be the longest four days of her life.

* * *

This was going to be the longest four days of his life.

Iain shifted in his seat as the carriage trundled down the clifftop road. It had been several hours since their departure from Caulnedy, and with the ferry trip to the mainland now behind them there was nothing to do but sit back and wait for the next stop on their journey. The sun had crested the horizon some time ago, and warm golden morning light spilled into the carriage, bathing Seraphina's forest-green covered lap, highlighting the bright auburn braid that circled her head, glinting off her delicate spectacles, bringing life to the smattering of freckles across her pert nose...

He swallowed hard and tore his gaze away, shifting once more. Blasted idiot, that he was unable to stop from glancing at her.

They had not spoken a word to one another since leaving her friend's home. Well, at least he and Seraphina had not spoken. Once the blasted bird had settled in, it had started up a constant stream of Scottish insults that would have made any Highlander proud. And each one seemed aimed toward Iain.

Like now, as it cocked its gaudy head to the side and speared Iain with one bright yellow eye. "Ye scabby bawbag."

He glared at it. So now he was a scrotum, was he?

"Where, for the love of all that is holy, did you find such a creature?" he growled.

Seraphina, who had kept her gaze firmly out the window, turned to him with a scowl. "Phineas is not a creature," she snapped. "He is a parrot. A red-crowned parrot, to be precise. His particular species is from Mexico."

"Which doesnae answer how you came to be in possession of him." He crossed his arms over his chest, a bit less on edge now that the awkward silence had been gotten out of the way. He would take incensed, vocal Seraphina over quiet Seraphina any day. "In fact, it creates more questions than answers. Such as: How does a parrot from Mexico wind up in England talking like a blasted Scot?"

The change in her was swift, and not at all how he had expected her to react. Pain flashed in her bright blue gaze and she seemed to draw into herself. "He...belonged to a dear friend of mine who sadly passed away." She looked to her pet. "She gave him into my keeping. And we have been together ever since."

Suddenly her voice turned contemplative, almost soft. "He grieved when she died, and it took him so long to recover. He has developed a fear of being abandoned because of it. So now you know why I could not have possibly left him behind. Where I go, he goes."

There was a beat of silence as she pressed her fingers to the bars and the bird gently nibbled at them, a surprisingly deep affection in the act. Well, damn and blast, he certainly never expected to feel compassion for the creature.

Nor, he thought with no little bit of frustration, had he wanted to feel compassion for the bird's mistress. Scowling, he looked out the window to the horizon. The Isle of Synne was a distant thing now, slipping away from view as the carriage worked its way up the coast. Out of the corner of his eye he saw Seraphina crane her neck, leaning farther and farther out the window until she could see the Isle no more. Then, with a defeated little sigh, she slouched back against her seat, the color seeming to have been drained right out of her.

And there went that twinge of sympathy again, as well as more than a fair bit of disgust. At whom? Himself? Because he had forced her to leave her little island to make things right?

Yes, you damn blackguard. The voice whispered through his head, setting his teeth on edge. Forcibly turning away from the sight of Seraphina looking so dejected, he squashed that small voice like a bug beneath his boot. He would not allow himself to feel compassion for his wife.

* * *

By the time the carriage stopped for the night, Seraphina ached from the top of her head to the tips of her toes. There had been moments of respite, of course. They'd had to stop the carriage to change the horses and eat. And Seraphina had made certain that extra time was given so she might let Phineas out of his cage for a bit of flying time. The poor dear would go mad if he had to spend every moment in that blasted cage.

But they were few and far between. The rest of that day had been one long, torturous affair; between Seraphina holding her legs as still as possible to prevent her knees from knocking into Iain's, craning her neck at an unnatural angle to keep from looking Iain's way, and keeping her hands looking as relaxed as possible in her lap to prevent Iain from seeing how much this whole ordeal affected her, she was an absolute wreck. So much so that, upon stepping from the carriage into the busy yard to the inn, she nearly tumbled to the ground as her legs screamed. It was only through sheer stubbornness that she kept her feet under her, waving off Iain's offer of help with a dark scowl before storming inside the whitewashed, timber-framed structure. *Just let me make it to a room*, she bargained with herself, even as she hid a wince from a particularly painful cramp in her thigh. *Let me make it to a room, and a bed, and away from Iain's gaze*.

Blessedly they did not have to wait long; the moment the proprietor caught sight of them he was scurrying forward, his eagle eyes taking in not only Seraphina and Phineas, but Iain behind her as well.

"Welcome to the Boar's Head," he said with a wide smile. "Do you require rooms for the night?"

Seraphina cast a quick look about her, noting what she

had not seen before, namely, the cleanliness of the place and the quality furnishings. Damnation, couldn't Iain have chosen a place a little less high in the instep? She had limited funds, after all, and while she could afford a decent room, she had certainly not budgeted a room at one of the higher-end inns in the area. She opened her mouth to say that no, they would be taking their business elsewhere—preferably an inn that would not cost her a month's worth of earnings to stay in—but Iain was there before the first syllable emerged.

"Aye," he said, "your finest pair of rooms for my wife and me, as well as soft beds and good food for my men."

But Seraphina hardly heard the innkeeper's response for the roaring in her ears. His *wife*? The blasted idiot. It did not matter that it was true—much to her disgust. The whole purpose of this trip was so they might dissolve their union, not tell everyone from here to Scotland that they were indeed wed.

But she could not very well reprimand him in full view of everyone. And so she waited. And waited. Finally, when their cheery back-and-forth was done with and the book was filled out—dear God, he was writing *Mr. and Mrs. Iain MacInnes*—and the innkeeper led the way up the stairs, Seraphina was at Iain's side. Her hand on his arm pulled him back just far enough so they were out of earshot of the overeager innkeeper. "What the devil do you think you're about?" she whispered furiously. "You should not have introduced me as your *wife*." The word came out like a curse, her lip curling as if possessed of a life of its own.

He raised a brow. "Why nae? It's true enough."

"Not for long." Thank God.

His gaze said he thought the same. But, stubborn man

that he was, he would insist on defending his decision. "And what would you have had me introduce you as?" he demanded. "I dinnae think these fine people would look kindly on two unmarried people traveling together."

"I don't know," she replied hotly. "Introducing me as your sister would have sufficed. Anything but as your wife."

A low, rough laugh burst from his lips. "I hardly think that would work. Though your hair is as red as any Scot, you dinnae have our lovely accent."

But to no one's surprise she was as stubborn as he. While she grudgingly admitted to herself that he was right, she found herself declaring mutinously, "I can speak in a Scottish accent."

Apparently they were no longer even attempting to follow the innkeeper, for Iain stopped on the landing and stared down at her, massive arms crossed over his chest. "Is that so? Well then, give it a go."

And because she could not back down from a challenge, she did, using some of Phineas's more colorful phrases.

"Noo jist haud on. I'm fair puckled, ye ken?"

For a moment he stared at her, and she was certain she had bested him. But in the next moment he threw back his head and let loose a laugh so long and loud it would surely draw the attention of every person in the place. Not to mention the furious heat it caused in Seraphina's cheeks.

"Ah, lass," he chortled, wiping at his eyes. "I truly needed that."

She glowered at him. "It wasn't that bad."

"It was so bad," he said with a patronizing smile, "that I am surprised Saint Andrew dinnae rise from the grave to smite you on the spot. Though maybe I should have your bird speak for you. His Scottish is a sight better than yours."

The innkeeper approached then, a puzzled frown on his face. "Is something amiss, sir?"

"Nae a bit, my good man. My apologies for the delay. Lead on."

In a matter of minutes, they were shown to their rooms. The innkeeper swung the door wide with a flourish, revealing a space filled with decadent furnishings and expensive fabrics. Seraphina took one look around and blanched. She may be exhausted, and stiff, and in desperate need of a bath and food, but there was no way she could stay here.

"Mayhap," she ventured, holding Phineas's cage in front of her like brass armor, "you have something a bit smaller. I do not require so much space, I assure you."

"Nonsense," Iain said in his booming voice before the innkeeper could react. "Nothing but the best for my wife. This room will do just fine."

The innkeeper's expression, which had begun to fall in dismay, brightened considerably. "Wonderful, wonderful. And your room is just through here, Mr. MacInnes." So saying, he moved into the room, heading for a connecting door hidden in the dark wood paneling.

As Iain and the innkeeper talked in the other room, Seraphina reluctantly stepped over the threshold. She used to live in such opulence; as daughter to an earl, she had been constantly surrounded by richness and excess.

But it had not brought her happiness, she reflected morosely as she deposited Phineas's cage on a table. In fact, it had done the opposite, stripping her of every freedom, making her feel as caged in as Phineas no doubt was. She opened the door to the cage then, and her pet stepped out onto her hand eagerly enough, stretching his wings, his low chittering telling her he was not happy, not at all.

She stroked her fingers over his head and back, talking in a soft, soothing voice until his feathers unruffled—quite literally—and he busied himself with taking in his new surroundings. She had opened her own cage long ago, had escaped from her gilt prison. She clamped her teeth together hard. And she'd be damned if she was pulled back into that world of titles and self-importance and cruelty.

Iain came back into her room, looking entirely too smug for her liking. "Hot water for a bath and a tray of food will be sent up for you posthaste. It has been a long day, and I dinnae think you wished to eat in the dining room."

But she was beyond being grateful for these small kindnesses. She scowled at him. "You should have consulted with me regarding our lodgings. I cannot afford such luxury."

"You do nae have to afford such luxury," he stated. "I am paying for it."

"You?" When he nodded, she narrowed her eyes. "You have the means to throw money away on something of this sort? Come to think of it," she continued, growing more incensed with each second that ticked by, "that was your own carriage, wasn't it? Am I now to assume you have the means to afford such a lavish lifestyle?"

Any good humor still in his eyes was gone in an instant. "Aye," he replied, his voice gruff and almost hostile. "I have nae been idle in the past thirteen years, lass."

No doubt. Acid filled her mouth. Especially as his sudden bounty of funds had originated with her own father, and the fortune he had thrown at Iain to drive him away.

But it had never been about her father throwing money at him, was it? No, it had been all about Iain actually accepting that money.

Suddenly tired beyond bearing, feeling every mile of their journey so far, Seraphina closed her eyes. "If you don't mind, I would like some time alone to rest."

When he did not immediately move away, she opened her eyes to see him staring at her with an inscrutable look. Finally, after what seemed an age, he nodded once and, turning about, quietly slipped through the connecting door, closing it behind him.

Chapter 11

*I*ain had thought that, when Seraphina finally realized he was not the poor fool he had been, it would be a satisfying thing. God knew it had taken her long enough to come to that conclusion. Truly, she must have been incredibly distracted all that long, horrible day to overlook the fact that they had not been traveling in a post chaise, but in his own private carriage.

Finally, however, she had deduced that his financial standing was quite different from what she had known. And it *had* been satisfying to see her reaction.

For all of a second.

But then the suspicion and outrage in her wide blue eyes had turned to a pain and hurt so deep it had shocked him. It was almost as if she had felt betrayed somehow. Why? It was not as if he had been the one to leave and throw what they had away.

Yet she had looked, quite honestly, as if he had broken faith with her—and broken her heart in the process.

Sighing deeply, he tore his gaze away from the thick wood panel that separated their rooms. He had struggled enough on the Isle of Synne when he had known she was just a short distance away. Then, with her back in the land of the living—and back in his life—it had felt as if his entire world had shifted. Sleep had not come easy, his mind as restless as his body.

Now, however, with only a single barrier between them, it was so much worse. Every noise had him unconsciously straining to hear more. Was she even now sitting and eating the fare he'd had sent up to her, or talking to that blasted bird with a softness she never showed toward him—or sinking into the bath he'd ordered for her? That last was the worst; such thoughts inevitably led to his imagination taking over—an imagination he had not even known he possessed, much less in such vivid abundance. Images of Seraphina swamped his mind then, of her submerged in warm water, her skin glistening wet, the soap sliding between the valley of her breasts as she washed herself, her hand dipping beneath the water...

He groaned and pressed his fists hard into his eyes, as if he could banish the rogue thoughts by sheer will. What the devil was wrong with him? Yes, he had loved her and wanted her desperately when they had been younger. Yes, his body had burned for her. Yes, that one time they had lain together as man and wife still seared his brain even now, thirteen years later.

But that did not mean he wanted her *now*. She was nothing to him, merely a problem to be gotten rid of at the earliest convenience. A fact that, no matter how reasonable, his cock could not seem to understand. Glaring down at the tent it made of his kilt, he let loose a low curse and pushed to his feet. He would go for a walk, he decided brutally, stalking toward the hallway door. A nice long walk in the cool evening air would be just the thing to clear his head—as well as to purge Seraphina from his bloodstream.

But as his hand fell on the latch he heard a heavy thump and crash, then a cry of pain. Acting without thinking, he sprang for the connecting door to Seraphina's room. Bursting through, he was halfway across her room before he realized what was before him.

Seraphina, in nothing but a towel. But no, she wasn't *in* the towel at all. Rather, it dangled from one fist, held at her throat, draping across her pert breasts and down the length of her front. The fire behind her created a golden halo around her body, highlighting her long legs, the flare of her hip, the swanlike curve of her neck. Every inch of exposed flesh glistened, droplets of water catching in the light and shining like a hundred diamonds.

"By all that's holy," he muttered hoarsely, unable to help the words from slipping out. Dear God, she was even more delectable than when she had been, oh so briefly, his.

Her jaw hung open and she stared at him in unmitigated horror. "Iain!" she squeaked. Her fingers turned white-knuckled as she fumbled with the towel, trying to cover herself more fully.

All at once he realized what a perverted arse he was being, standing there staring at her in nothing but what she'd been born in. Blanching, he closed his eyes tight and spun around.

"What the hell are you doing in my room?" she cried.

"I heard you cry out," he hurried to respond. "I thought you were in some trouble, and so I came to offer my assistance." But even in his agitated state he could hear how feeble that excuse sounded. He could have knocked first, verifying through the door that she was well before barging in like a stampeding bull.

She seemed to think the same. There was a heavy, disbelieving pause before she choked out, "I stubbed my toe."

"Oh, I'm...sorry." Really, could this moment get any worse? But as the seconds passed in horrified silence it did get worse. Apparently his mind had been wiped clean when he had witnessed the glory of her glistening body nearly uncovered, and he hadn't left when he should have—which was bloody *immediately*. He continued to stand there, his back to her, the only sounds the crackle of the fire and their own harsh breathing. *Move*, he ordered himself with no little desperation. *Walk forward, one foot after the other, through the damn door, and leave her be.* His feet, however, felt nailed to the floorboards.

Then her voice rose up, high and strangled. "Can you please leave so I may dress?"

That finally did it. He bolted for the connecting door without another word, closing it behind him with a bang. As he stood against it, chest heaving and body still at painful attention, he looked at his own bed and groaned. With this new image of Seraphina burned into his brain, so much more delicious than the brief memory he had of her from their youth, he knew he would not get any sleep this night. Desperation coursing through his tense muscles, he headed for the hall door and that walk. And did not return for a very, very long time.

* * *

Seraphina had not thought that anything good could have come out of the debacle of Iain walking in on her the night before. It had been a nightmare of the worst kind, after all. She already felt horribly vulnerable on this ill-conceived trip north, what with all the emotional baggage that was wrapped up in the maddening Scot she was forced to travel with; being exposed physically had only worsened that feeling. Add into that the expression on Iain's face when he had looked on her unclothed body, the heat in his eyes that had seared her from the inside out, the rough sound of his voice, as if he were speaking a benediction, and she had not slept a wink that whole night long for thinking of it—nor had she stopped cursing herself for her body's very visceral reaction to that hot gaze, a desire awakening in her that had been dormant for so long.

But at least not sleeping had meant no nightmares, something she dreaded nightly. To be thrown back into that worst time of her life while she was already feeling as brittle as the shale cliffs that housed Synne's impressive collection of fossils would have been devastating.

Her night of non-sleep had also provided her ample opportunity to decide how to proceed on this trip, especially after the disaster of the first day. She was through with sitting silent and awkward. No matter that she was not pleased with her publisher for revealing her location to Iain, she had a serial to continue writing, and had been given the unexpected gift—if one could call it that—of plenty of idle time, as well as being in the company of someone whom she did not have to hide her secret occupation from. She would use these next days to the fullest and write as much as she was able to. And if in writing she was given the means to continue her pointed ignoring of her travel companion, so much the better.

And so she had taken her small portable writing desk

into the carriage, and had set about getting as much down as she could. And she had managed beautifully...for all of five minutes.

"I'm sorry again about last night."

Seraphina's pen scratched a long, jagged line on the paper at the unexpectedness of Iain's voice, overloud in the close confines of the carriage. Pressing her lips together, she tightened her fingers on her quill. "Please, don't mention it," she bit out, dipping her head lower, hoping he would take the hint that she did not wish to converse further—and especially about something so distasteful to her.

But apparently Iain was not in a hint-taking mood.

"I just wanted you to know," he continued before she had gotten two words written, sounding gruff and uncomfortable. "I dinnae purposely barge into your room. I reacted without thinking."

"I understand that," she gritted, dipping her head even lower, until the stray tendrils of her hair brushed the paper. The quill trembled in her hand, sending a small drop of ink to splatter the page.

"I certainly dinnae intend to see you bare arsed—" he went on, like some mindless runaway horse.

"Iain," she interrupted with a tight voice, finally looking him in the eye, though her cheeks felt about as hot as the entrance to Hades, "if you say one more thing about last night, I swear I will hit you over the head with this blasted writing desk."

At which point, of course, Phineas decided to join in.

"I'll gie ye a skelpit lug," he squawked, before letting loose a cackling laugh, head bobbing up and down, yellow eye on Iain.

As if in some strange pantomime, Iain turned slowly

to stare at the bird. His eyes tightened at the corners as if in pain, his lips twitching, and Seraphina wasn't certain if he was trying to stop from laughing or attempting to keep himself from murdering Phineas. When he turned back her way again, his gaze didn't give away his thoughts about her pet. But that did not mean there was no emotion in his eyes. They were so intense, so focused, Seraphina felt as if they were magnets drawing her in. The tension between them expanded with each passing second until it was almost a tangible thing. Finally, when she was certain she would scream from the strain of the moment, he nodded sharply.

"My apologies again," he mumbled before, shifting his massive body so it was more or less reclining across his seat, he propped his head against the seam between the squabs and the wall of the carriage and closed his eyes. Within a matter of minutes, soft snores filled the interior.

But no matter that she had finally been released from his gaze, that did not mean she was any less a prisoner. Helplessly she studied his face as she had not dared to since they had reunited. There was still that new harshness of countenance that made her heart cry out; no amount of relaxing would ever take that completely away.

But in this reposed state, with his features softened in rest, there was something of that boy she had loved shining through the rust of anger and cynicism he had taken on in the years since. And seeing that made her heart ache worse than when she had thought that boy gone forever.

Seraphina sighed, finally tearing her gaze away from him and looking down to the damaged page of disjointed writing with disgust. Whatever momentum she had managed to claim had been thoroughly trampled. She took out a new paper, stared down at the blank page with pen poised, willing the words to come back to her. But after some long minutes she was finally forced to admit that she would get no more work done this day. Letting loose a low growl, she packed up her things and placed the writing desk on the floor. It would appear she was in for another long, tense day.

A yawn rose up then, one she valiantly tried to hide behind her palm. Or perhaps she might catch up on the sleep she missed last night. Sudden exhaustion pulled down on her. Unable to keep her eyes open a moment longer, she rested her head back against the seat and allowed her lids to drift closed...

...and woke up on the floor of the carriage.

Panic tore through Seraphina as a cacophony of sound invaded her ears: men shouting; horses neighing; Phineas screeching; the carriage groaning as it shifted under her. And above it all—or rather, above her, for he was lying half atop her—were Iain's curses, rough and loud.

But they did not last long. In a moment his hand was on the side of her head, his gaze scouring her face.

"Seraphina, are you hurt?"

Why, she wondered a bit wildly, did he look so worried for her? It was almost as if he cared.

But he didn't care, she reminded herself brutally. Just as she did not care about him. The whole point of them being together, after all, was so they could separate for good.

Yet that realization did not stop her heart from twisting as the worry in his eyes appeared to grow.

"Seraphina? Seraphina!"

His voice was growing more desperate, calling to something in her. And then his hands began to work over her limbs. There was nothing sexual in it at all, of course. Deep down she recognized it for what it was, a means of determining if she had any broken bones.

Yet combined with the weight of his body over hers, his thick thigh between her legs and pressing to that most intimate spot, his warm breath washing over her face, it was like a spark set to dry kindling.

She gasped, her hand trapping his against her leg, preventing it from traveling farther down. "I'm fine," she croaked.

The relief on his face as he glanced back at her, the softness in his eyes, turned that small spark in her belly to a bonfire. Did he have to look at her that way, as if she were important to him, as if her safety were paramount? Blessedly Phineas announced his outrage just then, his mad squawking and flapping halting whatever it was that had passed between Seraphina and Iain in its tracks.

With a grunt, Iain planted his hands on the benches and pushed himself up until he was perched on one seat. "Stop your complaining, you damned pigeon," he growled, apparently back to his grumpy self as he helped Seraphina gain her own seat—no easy thing, she soon learned, as the carriage seemed to be listing in a pronounced way toward one side.

Finally free of Iain's body on hers—though, regrettably, not free of the aftereffects of said body pressed to her own—Seraphina busied herself with Phineas. "Are you all right, darling?" she cooed as she righted his cage. The accident had sent Phineas sprawling along the bottom of the brass structure in an inglorious heap of feathers and outrage.

But the parrot was not to be soothed. He screeched, fumbling about, wings flapping. Finally, knowing he needed much more than mere platitudes, she opened the small door. Phineas scrambled out immediately, climbing his way up her arm until he was perched just where he liked it, on her shoulder. Even then he was not a bit happy. Low trilling sounds issued from his throat as he swung his head back and forth, an obvious sign of distress.

"Oh, my poor dear," she crooned, running her hand over his head and his back, pressing her cheek to his warm body.

"Your Grace," the driver called out, his face appearing in the window, "are you and Miss Athwart all right?"

Iain, who had been watching Seraphina, nodded sharply. "Aye, we're well, Jones. And you and Kenneth and the horses?"

"We're fine, sir. Though the carriage isn't. The road is blasted steep, and with a rut at the bottom. I'm afraid the wheel is badly damaged. Seeing as how violently we listed to the side, we could be looking at a broken axle as well."

"Damn it all to bloody hell," Iain muttered. "Was the drag not properly set?"

Jones's face heated. "I'm sorry, sir, that would be my fault."

Heaving a beleaguered sigh, Iain ran a frustrated hand over his face. "As long as no one was hurt," he said to the man in a far gentler voice than Seraphina expected. Then, pushing open the door, he maneuvered his way to the road as best he could before turning back to offer a hand to Seraphina. She took it with alacrity, not wanting to spend a moment more in the cockeyed interior, scrambling out of the carriage with Phineas attached firmly to one shoulder and her bag hastily slung over the other.

Iain moved to the far side of the conveyance and bent down beside his men to peer beneath the wreckage.

The man named Kenneth grunted before spitting off to one side. "It'll take a good half day to fix, I'm thinking."

A half day extra on the road with Iain. Seraphina bit back a groan. Of all the bad luck.

"And how far to the next town?" Iain continued, his brow dark as he looked up and down the road.

"That there is Sunderland Bridge," Kenneth replied, gesturing to the stone bridge just up ahead that spanned a wide river. "Durham must be some three miles up the road. Perhaps four."

Seraphina's muscles seized, her stomach twisting until she was certain she would cast up her accounts. Durham? She had known they would pass the village, of course. She did not have an idle mind and had not wished to put herself entirely in Iain's hands without at least educating herself on the path they would be taking north. The name of the place had jumped out at her from the maps she had pored over, not because she was familiar with it, but because it was so very close to Lanchester—and her father's main residence, Farrow Hall, her childhood home.

Pressing a fist to her stomach, she forcefully swallowed down the bile that rose in her throat. They were not supposed to have stopped for any length of time anywhere near that place. Perhaps a change of horses, a quick meal in Durham, and then onward to the next stop on their journey. She had attempted to comfort herself with the fact that even if she were to run into her father or someone in his employ while passing through the town, she was well past the age of her majority; he no longer had any power over her.

But as had been proven by her sisters' reactions to seeing Iain on Synne, as well as her own instinct to protect them at all costs when she had seen them in distress, they all still carried too powerful an echo of the old fear of being found to ever let it go. And now here she was, forced to remain in this town mere miles from her childhood home. Her vision went dim at the edges.

Suddenly a warm hand on her elbow jarred her, bringing the world into focus again. She looked up blearily to see Iain's face close to her own, that concern that had touched her so back in place.

"Mayhap you are nae as well as you thought you were," he murmured, his gaze scouring her from head to toe. As if what ailed her could be seen with the naked eye.

"I'm fine, truly," she mumbled, pulling her arm from his grip. Or at least attempting to. He was having none of it.

"You may have hit your head during the crash," he replied grimly. "I'll find you a place to sit. I'll nae have you keel over and hurt yourself worse."

"I'm fine, I tell you," she insisted, scowling. "And I shan't sit idle. I wish to help."

But it was not Iain who answered her.

"There's nothing for you to do, miss," Kenneth called out from his place beside the carriage. He kicked at the damaged wheel with his boot. "Only a blacksmith can repair this, I'm afraid."

Mayhap if the man had not used such a blatantly patronizing tone, or smiled in that small, condescending way men had when talking to a female, Seraphina might have nodded and sat down on the side of the road and allowed them to do what needed to be done.

But he had used those time-honored signs of patriarchal superiority. And in Seraphina's agitated state, anxious over being so close to her father's home and angry at herself for even caring, she could not let it go.

Not that she could have let it go in her normal frame of mind.

"Then I shall fetch a blacksmith," she declared. She pointed up the road. "Durham is that way, you say?" Without waiting for an answer, she stormed toward the bridge.

There was a beat of charged silence behind her, followed by a rumble of low male voices in a highly perturbed state. Then, suddenly, the fall of footsteps, and Iain was at her side, his long stride matched to her own.

"You are not going to change my mind about going," she bit out, keeping her gaze straight ahead as she kept on her course.

"Oh, I wasnae going to even attempt it, lass," he drawled. "I am fully aware that you are even more stubborn than you were in our youth, and I've nae wish to waste my breath. Besides," he continued, stretching his arms from side to side, "I need the exercise after being so long cooped up."

Seraphina breathed deep and slow, praying for patience. "I wish to go alone," she gritted. "I do not need your protection."

Out of the corner of her eye she saw him look at her. And then his voice, softer than she ever expected, "Oh, I know you dinnae."

Her breath caught in her throat. There was almost a tenderness or sadness in the words that she felt deep in her soul. In the next instant, however, he ruined the effect spectacularly.

"You have your pigeon for that. And seeing what he did to my ear, I know he's perfectly capable and willing in his bodyguard duties."

She rolled her eyes, strangely relieved that they were back to sniping at each other. "And he will gladly do the same to the other ear if you do not leave me be."

"Attacks on command, does he?"

Was that a smile in his voice? Whatever it was, it caused her lips to soften. Not a full-blown smile, of course. She did not like him enough for that. In fact, she did not like him at all.

Nevertheless, the tension around her mouth eased. And not only that, but the muscles in her back loosened as well. She sighed, dropping her shoulders for the first time in what felt like hours.

And immediately felt a twinge in her neck. Wincing, she reached up and rubbed at the spot.

He moved a step closer, his gaze sharp on her now. "I knew you were injured," he muttered. And then his hand was on her bag, taking it from her shoulder.

"I can carry my own things," she grumbled, making a halfhearted attempt to keep hold of it. But in the end she let it go. She would never admit as much, but it truly did feel much better to have that weight no longer pulling on her neck.

"I would take your pigeon from you as well if I thought he would allow it," he murmured.

"Even to the detriment of your ears?" she asked, glancing his way for the first time since they had set off.

His lips curled upward, a faint humor dancing in his eyes. Once more Seraphina felt as if she were looking at the boy he had been, the boy she had loved. Shaken, she hastily glanced away. Best to remember him as the boy who had betrayed her. For she would not be taken in as a dupe again.

Chapter 12

*T*here it was again, that ghost of grief in her eyes. He frowned as he followed her example and looked ahead. Why grief? She could not possibly regret what they had lost. She had been the one to leave him, after all, proving what he had always known, that he was beneath her and would never be worthy of her.

Anger attempted to boil up in him, to burn away the worry and compassion he had begun to feel for her. But it was a weak thing. After the past week, she was no longer the evil woman who had betrayed him and broken his heart. At least, he reflected ruefully as he sidestepped a rut in the road, not completely. He had seen too much of the residue of pain and fear in her eyes to compartmentalize her so severely now.

Which, of course, only made him furious at himself. What did it matter what had happened to her in the intervening years since leaving him? After all, she had been the one to throw their future away. There should not be a single part of him that cared what had befallen her since.

Yet that hadn't stopped him from panicking when he had woken and found himself atop her in the carriage. The very idea of her being injured had revived something in him he had thought long dead, a need to protect her as he had always wanted to. And then after, when they had been looking over the carriage and she had paled and swayed on her feet, his certainty that she was in truth injured, his concern for her well-being, had overtaken everything else. It was the main reason he had not wanted her going off alone to fetch a blacksmith. Head injuries were stealthy things, after all, and he did not want her to be alone should something occur.

Now that he had a moment of quiet to think, however, something tickled the back of his mind, unrelenting. Something about the timing of her reaction, right after mention of Durham . . .

In a flash it came to him, just why Durham was so important: it was close to Lord Farrow's seat.

At the reminder of that man, Iain's anger sizzled and sparked back to life. How could he have forgotten? Farrow Hall had been the place Lord Farrow and his family had called home for the majority of the year, the place where Seraphina had grown up.

Common sense, of course, told him that something horrible indeed must have happened since their separation for Seraphina to have run away with her sisters and changed their surname and hidden from their sire. Yet common sense could not get through his blind anger at the thought of that man who had destroyed Iain's one chance at happiness.

"You do nae wish to take a detour from our travels to

visit your father?" he snapped before he could call the words back. Not that he wished to call them back. The dam of emotion that had begun to crack from the pressure of his arrival on Synne seemed to crumble, and he knew, with a focused clarity, that this moment was the culmination of thirteen years of tension and pain. It was time to have things out, here and now.

She stumbled, and it took everything in him not to reach out for her. But her moment of shock was quickly gone as she turned to face him. Even in his fury-fueled mind he recognized that an anger almost equal to his own blazed from her eyes, the clear blue at the center of a flame.

"Visiting my father is the last thing I wish to do," she bit out. "Though perhaps you don't feel the same. After all, a trip to see him could prove beneficial to you. It is not as if you're a stranger to such tactics."

He narrowed his eyes. It felt, quite literally, as if every piece of his body stilled and focused to a pinpoint. "What the blazes are you talking about, woman?" he growled.

"Only that mayhap the money you took from him all those years ago needs to be replenished. And giving me up to him could do just that."

Money? Was she blaming him for accepting payment for his job in Lord Farrow's stables now? "I never took a penny from that man that wasn't owed me."

"Owed you." Her voice seemed to strangle in her throat, and again that look of hurt in her eyes.

But he would not be drawn into feeling pity for her again. "Aye, owed me," he replied. "Though even that was a paltry amount. But men of his ilk are forever underpaying—"

Her hand connecting with his cheek cut his words off. The parrot spread its wings in its agitation, and for a moment, with the bright feathers framing her face, Seraphina looked like an avenging faerie about to wreak havoc on his head.

"I've known all these years you were a bastard," she choked. "However, this is low even for you."

But he hardly heard her. The slap, as little as it had hurt him, had jarred something troubling in his brain, and he suddenly had the very uncomfortable feeling that they were talking about two very different things.

"Seraphina," he said, his voice slow and cautious, as if he feared she might tear him limb from limb should he speak too loud, "you do recall that I worked for your father, dinnae you? And I was paid a wage by him?" *Until he went and sacked me for caring for you.* But that was something else altogether.

The harsh laugh that escaped her lips was grating to his ears and altogether unexpected. "As if that was what I was referring to."

More confused than ever, he threw up his hands. "I never took a penny from him otherwise."

Again that sharp laugh, almost manic. "You must think me stupid."

"On the contrary, I've always believed you to be one of the smartest people I know," he replied without thinking. A moment later he cursed himself for showing even that small bit of feeling for her. But he would not linger on it.

"Are you saying," he said, his voice sounding distant to his own ears, "that you believe I took money from your father for something other than my position in his household?"

"You think to deny it?" she asked, her voice threaded with equal parts disbelief and contempt. "Do you honestly

believe that I would not find out? That I would remain ignorant of the reason why you left me?"

His jaw dropped to his chest. "Why *I* left *you*?"

But she seemed not to have heard him.

"I should have known," she spat, stalking toward him, her
willowy form vibrating with rage, "that your need to revenge
yourself on my father for letting you go without a reference
would be paramount to you, that it would even overshadow
anything we might have had. And I, stupid girl that I was, fell
for it. I let you dupe me, let you make me think that you loved
me, gave myself to you body and soul—"

Her voice cracked, and she pressed her lips tight. The
bird, visibly agitated, lifted off from her shoulder and flew
to a nearby tree.

The change in her was instantaneous. Clamping her
hand over her mouth, eyes wide, she turned away from
Iain and went to just below where the parrot perched. "I'm
sorry, darling," she cooed. "Please come back down. Come
along, love. There's a good boy."

But the parrot merely swayed from side to side, eyeing
Seraphina, letting loose random screeches that echoed
through the brush.

Iain watched this whole thing with a kind of numbness,
his mind still trying to understand the accusations she had
thrown at his head. Revenge himself on her father? Dupe
her? She could not be serious. When had he ever given
her cause to think he could be capable of such a thing? No
doubt this was some redirection on her part, a way to make
herself feel better about leaving him.

But baffling slices of the last week came back to him
now, random comments and reactions and looks connecting like pieces of a puzzle. She truly believed he left her all

those years ago. With every fiber of her being, she believed it. Which, if it was true, meant she had not left him. At least not willingly.

Dear God.

In two strides he was behind her. Spinning her about, he barely registered her gasp of surprise before he spoke.

"Did your father tell you I received money from him to leave you?" he demanded.

The shock and worry in her eyes melted away, replaced with pain. Ah, yes, she believed it, down to her bones.

"That fucking bastard," he spat before, taking a deep breath to calm himself, he looked Seraphina in the eye. "I dinnae take money from your father," he said, slow and distinct lest she mishear him.

"You lie," she replied, her voice a hiss of sound.

"I swear, it's the truth."

She pressed her lips tight, her chin jutting mutinously. It was all too obvious she didn't believe a word he said.

Letting out a harsh breath, he bent his head until their eyes were level. "Your father never offered me money. But even if he had, I wouldnae have taken it. I swear it."

Something in his voice must have finally broken through her anger. Her eyes clouded, a frown marring her brow. And then she said the thing that nearly broke him.

"Then why did you leave me?"

"I dinnae leave you lass," he managed. "I was told *you* left *me*."

I was told you left me. It frightened her how deeply she wished to believe him.

For so many years she had thought this man, a person she had befriended, had fallen in love with, had trusted with her entire self, had betrayed her for money. And it had destroyed her. Now here he was, proclaiming with an earnestness that she felt down to the depths of her soul, that he had not, in fact, done as she'd been told, that he had been made to believe she had been the one to leave. A kind of relief and joy blossomed in her breast, that the person she had trusted most in this world had not let greed turn him from her.

But had she learned nothing over the years? Was she really so desperate to turn her back on the caution she had so carefully cultivated, to leave herself raw to more pain and betrayal?

Apparently so, for she had the sudden aching desire to close the small distance between them and bury herself in his embrace. How wonderful it would be to let down her guard for once, to lean on someone. To feel that same safety and security she'd felt in his arms so long ago.

"Seraphina," he said then, the one word almost pleading as it escaped his lips, drawing her further into the pull of him.

Blessedly they were interrupted just then by a man on horseback passing them on the road. Had she truly been so focused on Iain and her wildly inappropriate desire for his arms about her that she had been completely oblivious to the rider's approach? She quickly extracted herself from Iain's loose grip and stepped back, the better to put some much-needed distance between them.

"I don't believe you," she said when they were alone again. "I saw the evidence with my own eyes in the bank drafts made out to you, heard the proof in a witness who saw the whole transaction."

He narrowed his eyes, his hands closing into white-knuckled fists at his sides. "All provided by your father, I'd wager."

She stared mutely at him. What else could she do? It was true.

His gaze scoured her face, as if seeing her for the first time. "Do you wish to know what your father told me, Seraphina?" he asked hoarsely.

She shook her head, for some reason frightened of what he might say. But he plowed on regardless.

"Your father told me that he had finally given you your dearest wish, that he had offered to send you away to travel the world. And that you had taken him up on the offer."

She gaped at him. "That makes no sense. Why would I do that? I loved you, was willing to leave everything behind, even my sisters, for you."

But she knew the answer to that question the moment it passed her lips. She saw, with a clarity that stole her breath, that same vulnerability that had been in his eyes when they'd parted all those years ago, the same sense of unworthiness she had been unable to erase. It was faint, and quickly covered up. But to Seraphina it was as good as a shout, telling her the truth of what had happened: her father had used their weaknesses against each other to separate them.

"Oh," she breathed before, her legs crumpling beneath her, she sank to the road in a heap.

He was beside her in an instant, his hands on her arms. "Seraphina—"

But whatever he had been about to say was lost as an ear-piercing screeching started up, bundled within a great flutter of wings. And then Phineas attached himself to Iain's head, talons gripping onto chunks of hair, wings flapping.

"Holy hell!" Iain shouted, trying in vain to extricate Phineas from his hair. But every time his hand got close to her pet, the bird snapped at his fingers. "Ow! Damn it all to ever-loving—"

Mind still spinning, Seraphina scrambled to her feet and hurried to Iain—no easy thing, given the man was stumbling about in the road.

"Phineas!" she called, reaching up for him. "Let Iain go. Phineas, no. You're a very bad parrot. Come here now."

Phineas finally seemed to hear her. Half hanging down the side of Iain's head with wings outstretched, he stopped and cocked his head at her. Whistling low, he let go of his unwilling perch and climbed onto her outstretched hand.

"That's it, darling," she crooned as she helped her pet onto her shoulder. "Enough of that now."

Iain stared at her in disbelief. "That's all? You are nae going to punish the beast?"

She blinked. "Punish him? Of course not. He believed you were harming me. Besides, what would you have me do? I cannot very well give him a spanking."

He gaped at her, motioning toward his tousled hair with an outraged hand. "He nearly took my eye."

She was tempted to shrug off his concerns, or laugh, or roll her eyes. In her right frame of mind she would have done all three, with a sprinkling of condescension for flavor.

But she was suddenly and overwhelmingly tired beyond bearing as she gazed at him. Wrapping her arms about her middle, she could do naught but stare mutely at him.

He sighed, all the fight seeming to go out of him. "Regardless of what a menace your pet is"—he ran a hand through his hair to smooth down the worst of it—"we have more important things to discuss, it seems."

Which was something she was not ready for. Dear God,

to relive all that, but now with the knowledge that her father had lied to them both?

"Later," she said. He frowned, opening his mouth, no doubt wanting to have it out here and now. But she held up a hand, stopping him in his tracks. "I need time to process what you have revealed to me. Let us get through today and all that needs to be done. Tonight, after I have had time to come to terms with this news, we can talk."

Never one to retreat when he was set on something, he scowled. In the end, however, he must have seen something in her to make him back down. He nodded his head, sharply.

"Very well," he replied gruffly. "Tonight."

Chapter 13

Once again Iain found himself unable to keep his gaze away from the door connecting his room to Seraphina's. Though this time the reason for his focus was much worse than imagining her naked in her bath.

Sighing heavily, he gripped tighter to the arms of the chair he sat in. Or, rather, perched on. There was no lounging back in comfort for him just then. With his entire body equal parts anxious for and dreading the discussion that was to come, he could not relax even a bit.

Their entire focus throughout that long day had been directed to seeing that the carriage was mended and the horses cared for and his men seen after. And thank God for the distraction of it all. He'd needed to concentrate on something besides the devastating truths they'd unearthed during their argument. Even so, he felt equal parts eagerness and dread about the coming conversation with her, one that would finally provide them with the answers both of them needed.

Now, knowing the time for talk was nearly upon him, he felt as if he would vibrate out of his skin. His ears strained for every hint of sound. Was she waiting for him to go to her? Should he rise and knock on the connecting door?

Finally, unable to take the uncertainty a moment longer, he pushed to his feet and strode to the door. Just as his hand raised to rap on the heavy panel, however, a tentative knock sounded.

His heart stuttered in his chest, his body freezing up. Before he could recover, a soft voice sounded, muffled through the wood.

"Iain?"

In a moment his hand was on the latch, pulling the door wide. And there stood Seraphina. He sucked in his breath at the sight of her. Why? It was not as if they had not seen one another just an hour ago. She was the same woman he had been traveling with these past two days, after all. She was even still wearing the same clothes.

Yet something momentous had shifted in him where she was concerned. She was not the woman he had been manipulated to see her as. That false Seraphina had been burned down to a cinder, everything he had believed and held to be true burning with her, and he was only now beginning to see her for who she truly was.

She shifted from foot to foot in front of him, glancing at the room behind him, his shoulder, his neck, basically anywhere but his face. "May I come in?" she asked, her voice as hesitant as he had ever heard it.

At once he realized he had just been standing there like an imbecile, not speaking, barring her way. His face flushing hot, he quickly stepped back, motioning with one arm for her to enter. She did, moving past him swiftly, the faint scent of lavender drifting after her like a veil and tickling his senses.

"I've settled Phineas in his cage and covered him for the night," she said, going to the hearth, looking down into the flames. "I thought it best that we talk in private."

Without realizing it, his hand went to his head. He could still feel the damn pigeon scratching at his skull. He would be surprised if he didn't have a bald spot after that attack.

Not that he could blame the creature. At least, not now that he was able to think more clearly on the matter. The moment had been charged, tense. The bird had already been agitated; it was only natural that when it had seen its mistress on the ground with someone leaning over her, namely the person she had been quarreling with, its protective urges had been awoken.

But he was beyond grateful that he did not have to deal with the beast tonight. He would rather not have to worry that he would once more fall victim to the creature's claws. And it was all too obvious that he would need his full focus for the conversation to come.

Seraphina spun about then. She held aloft a liquor bottle and two sturdy glasses, something he had not noticed upon her entrance.

"I also thought this would not go amiss," she continued, cheeks bright pink, though whether that was from the warmth of the fire or any emotions she might feel was hard to say.

"Oh, God, yes," he said, suddenly needing alcohol more than he needed breath, hurrying forward and dragging a small table between the two overstuffed chairs by the hearth. She placed her treasures down and sat, busying herself with opening the bottle and pouring generous portions into the glasses. Her hands, he noticed as he sat across from her, were trembling. Much like his own were, he reflected wryly as he clenched his fingers into fists in his kilt.

"I'm not planning on getting drunk, of course," she babbled as she handed him a glass. "I would much rather go into this with a clear head. But I thought a bit of liquid courage would help."

"Aye," he agreed gruffly. He watched as, belying what she had just proclaimed, she downed the entire glass of liquor as if it was necessary to her survival. An impressive feat, truly, as now that he'd had time to take a proper look at the bottle, he noticed it was a good strong Scottish whiskey. Swallowing hard, he did the same, reveling in the burn of it through his chest and into his empty stomach. He had a feeling they were going to need this even more than either of them believed.

She slammed the glass down. "There," she proclaimed. Her eyes glittered with purpose behind the lenses of her spectacles, and for the first time since she entered his room she looked him in the eye. "I'm ready now. Shall we get started then?"

Why did it sound as if she was girding herself to talk with a solicitor in preparation for a particularly unwelcome bit of business? But perhaps, he reasoned as he placed his own glass down, it was best to go at it that way. This subject, after all, would not be pleasant, and could prove to be incredibly emotional.

Sitting straighter in his chair, he nodded. "Verra well. Do you wish to begin?"

"Yes." She cleared her throat and folded her hands in her lap, looking for all the world like a governess. A delicious, utterly gorgeous governess.

"Let me preface this all by saying that I am not naïve,"

she said in clipped, no-nonsense tones. "I shall hear what you have to say on the matter and consider it carefully. As, I expect, you will do as well. We have spent nearly a decade and a half believing one truth; I think you can agree with me that we must go into this with caution."

He nodded again, which seemed to please her if the satisfied look in her eyes was any indication. But when she opened her mouth to continue, nothing came out. She frowned, blinking several times as her jaw slowly closed. Then, letting out a short burst of air through her nose, she opened her mouth and tried again.

But once more, nothing emerged. Looking troubled, she chewed on her lip.

"Maybe I need more whiskey," she mumbled before, reaching for the bottle, she said to him, "and mayhap it would be best if you begin."

"Verra well," he replied, watching as she downed another glass of the heady, smoky liquor. But when he tried to speak he found himself struck with the same malady Seraphina had been struck with: which was, namely, he didn't know how the blazes to start. How did you begin to untangle such a mess? It was strange that, in the hours that had led up to this, impatiently waiting for them to be done with the chaos of the day so they might finally get everything out in the open and clear the air, he had not even considered how he would say what he had to say.

Finally, deciding there was no better place than when the whole heartache started, he began.

"I waited for you at our assigned meeting place for what felt like hours," he said quietly, feeling out the words as the memory fell over him, dank and heavy. "But you never came. I was certain your father must have done something to stop you, so I went to his estate. He knew I was coming and was waiting for me. He informed me that he had finally relented to your wishes and would nae force you to go to London for the season, but instead would finance your much-desired travels, with the condition that you leave immediately. And that you had agreed."

She stared at him, the glass cup halfway to her lips. "And you believed him?"

"Nae without proof." He sighed and scrubbed a hand through his hair, the devastation of that day coming back to him with a clarity that cut. "I went to Mrs. Campbell for that. And she verified that what your father told me was the truth, that she saw you leave with her own eyes. She had physical proof as well, a package she said was from you." He could still feel it in his palm, the weight of it so slight yet so very heavy for how completely it had crushed him.

"It was the ring I had placed on your finger just that morning," he continued, his voice hoarse even to his own ears. "And the scrap of my tartan I had pinned to your dress."

She was silent, not even a breath coming from her direction, and he chanced a glance up at her. She looked quite literally as if she had been struck.

"But I never would have parted with your ring, or your tartan," she rasped. "I swear it."

Despite the fact that he knew better, anger rose up in his breast. "Then how do you explain this, Seraphina?" he demanded. Reaching into the sporran at his waist, he yanked out the very same scrap of tartan he had given her, opening it to reveal the simple silver ring within. He had kept them with him all this time, as a reminder that he should never again trust another.

But once more her reaction took him by surprise. She

stared at the scrap of metal as if it was the most precious thing in the world.

"I did not give it up to anyone, Iain," she said, her voice quiet, nearly swallowed by the snap and spit of the fire in the hearth. "When I awoke, I noticed it was gone. But I swear I did not remove it myself."

"Awoke?" His every sense homed in on that one word. It could very well be nothing, of course. So she had fallen asleep somewhere and woken to find it gone.

Yet he could not shake the feeling that there was something more to it. That feeling only grew as she paled and clamped her lips shut. What the devil had happened?

"It does not matter," she said. "The fact is, I did not remove it."

He wanted to hold on to the familiar heartbreak, to keep it between them like a shield. But despite himself, he believed her. And it frightened him silly. Who was he, if not the man he had become after she had torn out his heart and stomped on it? Or rather, he reflected wryly, after he'd been led to believe she had betrayed him. But the reality pointed to that being a malicious lie, used to separate two people who had loved one another.

Blessedly there was still one thing that stood between him losing himself and staying strong against the pull of her.

"But the housekeeper vowed she had seen you climb into a carriage with your sisters. She said you were wearing the same green dress with the violet flowers at the hem that you had worn to wed me."

"A ruse," she explained quietly, bitterly. "My sisters told me of that day, how my father gave our lady's maid my gown to wear and sent them all away unexpectedly. I suppose it was his way to give credence to his lies, that anyone watching from the house might have assumed it was me leaving with them." She gave him a pained look. "Including Mrs. Campbell. Who then confirmed for you that she had indeed seen me leave."

His breath left him, taking with it the remnants of his outrage. He ran a hand over his face, his head spinning. Ah, yes, Seraphina's father was more than capable of creating such a deception. Sighing, he took hold of the bottle of whiskey and poured generous amounts of the amber liquor in their now empty cups. From the tightness about Seraphina's mouth and her pallor and the way she watched her cup with almost desperation, she looked as if she needed it nearly as much as he did.

"And now it is your turn," he said, raising his glass to her in a toast before taking a long draught. He let out a satisfied grunt and wiped the back of one hand across his mouth, bracing himself for what was to come. Blessedly, with his stomach empty from being unable to eat a bite of his dinner for the anxiety that plagued him, the whiskey was affecting him much quicker than he had anticipated. Already his head was feeling decidedly fuzzy.

"Your father told you that I accepted money to leave you, you said," he prompted.

She took a long swallow of her own drink before, closing her eyes slowly and shivering as it worked its way into her stomach, she spoke. "Yes."

"And you saw the proof of these transactions with your own eyes, heard the proof with your own ears."

"Yes," she answered again, this time quieter. "Or what I thought was proof."

He leaned forward in his chair, ignoring the way his head swam. "I dinnae take money from your father, Seraphina," he said, a repeat of the very same words he had said to her that afternoon.

Though now she actually seemed to hear him. Yet that did not mean she automatically took him at face value. His lips quirked. Not his Seraphina.

He froze. *His* Seraphina? Where the hell had that come from?

"But you are wealthy," she pointed out almost defiantly. Her arms swept out to encompass the room, the best the small Durham inn had to offer. "You have a carriage of your own, something only the wealthiest can afford. And I imagine it does not stop there."

He shifted in his seat. "I'm comfortably set," he hedged. Another lie. Or, if not a lie, then a wild underestimate. "It is the product of years of effort. I was nae idle these past thirteen years, you know." His lips kicked up at one end, though not in humor, more an ironic tilt. "Mostly fueled by anger, I suppose."

Her lips, glistening as she swiped a stray drop of whiskey with her tongue, slid upward as well. "That I can well believe."

They sat there for a time, gazing at one another. As Seraphina's lips slid down into a frown and her lovely blue eyes softened in a kind of sadness and acceptance, Iain felt a shift in him as well, a realization that, against his better judgment, there was not a bit of doubt that what Seraphina had told him was true and that everything he had believed had been a lie. And anger boiled up in his gut.

"If your father was here," he growled, his fingers tightening on the glass in his hand, imagining it was Lord Farrow's neck, "I would make him rue the day he set his plan into motion to separate us."

But wasn't the man close? He stilled, looking down into the shifting amber light of his drink as the fire fought through the dark liquid. Farrow Hall was but a short distance from them. He could be there in no time at all, and finally collect his pound of flesh from a man who had taken everything from him. Or, rather, he thought as he looked Seraphina's way, everything that had mattered.

Before he knew what he was about, he'd downed the rest of his drink and was on his feet. Seraphina must have seen something alarming in his eyes, for she stood as well, swaying slightly before quickly catching herself.

"What are you about, Iain?" she demanded. Was it him, or was there a slur in her voice? Or mayhap it was his ears; everything sounded incredibly off just then.

Perhaps it was the drink going to his head, but he did not even consider lying to her about his plans. "I am going to visit your esteemed sire," he said, striding for his coat, which he had left draped across the end of the bed, "and I am going to make him pay for what he did to us. And you are coming as well. You can do more damage than even I can. If it got out that you were alive, and he lied, he would be ruined." He reached for the coat, missing it on the first try before, narrowing his eyes in concentration, he managed to get ahold of it.

Seraphina, however, was suddenly there before him, her hands on his outerwear as he tried to shrug into it. Why, he thought as she ripped the material from his grip, was she so blasted strong?

But then he didn't care, because suddenly they were in each other's arms.

God, there had never been anyone like Seraphina for him. It was like she had been made for him. So damn tall and strong, yet her body a veritable map of curves that were even more pronounced now with her maturity, and all so soft he ached to sink into her. Her arms clung to his waist, even as he gripped her about the shoulders, and he had the vague impression that they were holding one another up. Silly, that, as he wasn't *that* drunk. Certainly not enough to have lost his head and his balance at the same time.

"You cannot go to my father," she said, the words muffled against his chest.

Her father? What the devil was she talking about? He didn't want to see her father. He wanted to stay right here with her. He pulled her closer, burying his face in her neck, his heart stuttering as she seemed to sink into his embrace. She smelled so damn good. He wondered if she would taste good as well...

In the next instant she gasped and pulled out of his grasp. "But let's not talk further about leaving tonight," she said, the words high and breathless and tumbling from her lips like chimes in a breeze. "There is still a bit of whiskey left and I've a mind to finish it."

So saying, she dragged him back to the chairs before the hearth, and poured them each another generous draught. And that was the last thing he remembered.

Chapter 14

*T*he first thing Seraphina noticed when she woke the following morning was the faint headache behind her eyes, her body's typical response after the rare occasion when she spent a night over-imbibing. The second thing she noticed was that, for the first time in what felt forever, her night had been blessedly blank, no nightmares marring the expanse of dreamless slumber she had somehow been gifted.

The third thing she became aware of—which should have been the first, she realized as she gradually grew more aware of her surroundings—was the incredibly broad chest beneath her cheek, and the strong arm about her shoulders...

...and the thick, decidedly bare leg between her own. Immediately the lethargy of a moment before disappeared. There was a man in her bed. Worse, she was wrapped around him like a squirrel climbing a tree. And even worse than that, she thought with no little horror, she was wearing naught but her chemise.

"Gah!" she cried, an instinctual, guttural sound that tore through the quiet of the room, even as she desperately attempted to disentangle herself from the man's arms. No easy thing, considering the weight and strength of said arm, as well as the length of sheet that seemed to have wound itself into a veritable knot about them.

Unfortunately, the combination of her outburst and thrashing were not conducive to keeping the man blissfully asleep and unaware of her position atop him. He startled, his large body jerking, even as his voice, deep and gruff with sleep, rumbled through the room.

"By all the saints! What the hell?"

She froze at that familiar Scottish brogue, one hand on the mattress beside his head, the other gripped about the sheet that had somehow anchored her to him...and her thigh, pressed indecently against that most private part of him, something that was not remotely concealed no matter the layers of her chemise and his...kilt? He froze as well, gaze clashing with hers. And then her confusion dissipated, like a warm breath on a pane of glass, and the realization of just where she was, and whom she was with, came to her like a bolt of lightning. She was with Iain, on the road to Scotland, to secure a divorce. A goal that did not seem as imperative as it had just yesterday, considering how absolutely right it was beginning to feel being pressed up against him.

But why was she in *bed* with him? Her brain, thankfully, was now fully awake, and not about to let her suffer unduly, as the memory of the evening before came flooding back. They had drunk whiskey, had learned the truth of their separation, and when Iain had made to go off after her father, she had enticed him to drink even more whiskey in an effort to keep him with her. When they had become sleepy and she should have retired to her room she had not wanted to leave him. She had told herself it was to make certain he did not sneak off in his inebriated state to confront her father. But the truth of the matter had been that she had not wanted to be alone. So they had climbed into the massive bed together and had immediately fallen into quite the most peaceful slumber she could remember ever having.

Iain, still several long seconds behind her in understanding what was going on, frowned up at her. "Seraphina?"

His voice was a deep rumble, vibrating his chest. That very chest that the tips of her breasts brushed against. Electricity shot through her nipples, and quite against her better judgment she let out a little gasp. His eyes zeroed in on her mouth at the small sound. And suddenly his confusion was gone, replaced with a heat that caused her body to burst into flames. When he began to stir against her leg, his cock hardening and pressing into her thigh, she was finally prodded into movement. Quite literally.

Rearing back from him, simultaneously breaking the hold of his arm about her shoulders and the sheet about their entwined bodies by sheer force, she tumbled from the bed, just barely staying on her feet as she scuttled across the room. But then she made a nearly fatal error: She glanced back at Iain. He was sprawled on his back in the bed, white sheets like a cloud about him, his shirt gaping at the neck and highlighting his strong throat and the dusting of fine hair across the massive breadth of his chest.

His kilt tenting over his erection.

Ah, God.

Her mouth watering in the most baffling way, she hastily looked away, only to spy the rest of her clothes in a messy heap on the floor. Grasping this distraction for all it was worth, she lunged forward, gathering the articles into her arms—and sending a dark glare to the empty whiskey bottle, now on its side on the small table before the cold hearth, as she did so.

"I'll just go ready myself for the day then," she said, her voice much louder and higher than warranted. She did not look Iain's way again as she hurried for the connecting door, but that did not stop her from being achingly aware of him, seemingly carved in stone—*no, do not think of that particular body part of his as stone*—not having moved a single muscle since she'd lurched from the bed. Blessedly she soon had the door between them, slamming it with much more force than she should have. She leaned back heavily against it, closing her eyes in mortification, clutching the mass of wrinkled clothes to her chest.

She was an idiot. An absolute idiot.

Phineas chose that moment to make himself known. He squawked impatiently from behind the cloth cover of his cage in a tone that indicated it was not the first time he had done so that morning, the sound of his beak and claws clattering against the brass bars muffled by the sheet. Seraphina hurried forward, lifting off the cover and opening the cage door. But no matter how she focused on talking to her pet and feeding him and giving him plenty of pets and love, nothing could distract her from the voice inside her head telling her to go back through the connecting door and return to Iain's bed and arms—this time for more than sleep.

Which was absolutely ridiculous, she sternly told herself, face heating as she took a small knife to an apple and cut a slice off, passing it to Phineas. They were going to get divorced. They were most certainly not on this trip to renew their relationship. Yes, their separation had been based on a lie––or, rather, several lies, all put about by the same evil person. They should never have been torn apart.

But that did not mean they could just pick up where they had left off. They had their own lives to lead, ones that did not include reclaiming a past that was well and truly gone. No matter how utterly delicious Iain had become in their years apart.

Flustered as an image of that delicious body filled her mind, she rose, leaving Phineas happily eating his breakfast, and made her way to the basin in the corner of the room. Pouring a quantity of cool water into the bowl, she quickly removed her chemise and took up a small washcloth, washing her face before rubbing the damp fabric over her arms, her chest, her stomach. And then, hesitating just slightly, she dipped the washcloth between her legs.

How would it feel, she wondered as her eyes drifted shut and she slowly dragged the washcloth against her sensitive flesh, to open her legs to him? How would it feel to take him into her body again? When they had first lain together, they had been young and inexperienced, with stars in their eyes. Now, with years between then and now, they would each bring something new to the table—or, rather, bed. She was certain he had not been a monk in the years since. There would be no green boy fumbling and eager. And she had been with others as well. Granted, most of her encounters had been for survival, a way to support her sisters in their darkest days, but she was not ashamed of those occasions.

She had done what she had to do and would do it again if need be. But how would it be with Iain now, when she was so much more aware of what her body liked—and what Iain might like as well?

This line of thinking, however, was not doing her any good. Frustrated, she blew out a sharp breath before, throwing the washcloth down on the stand, she stormed to where she had deposited her balled up clothes from the previous day, jerking them on. No matter the truth that had come out, no matter that they now knew neither of them had betrayed the other, their time had passed. There was no reclaiming even a small portion of what they'd had.

Yet that did not stop her mind from conjuring images, quite against her will, of what it might be like to lie with Iain. She had seen enough of his body upon leaving the bed that it did not take much of an imagination to wonder. Dear God, he was finely formed, even more so than he had been when they'd been young. Of course, she had not fully appreciated his body then. She'd been so innocent, and while she had enjoyed their lovemaking to an extent, she had been too overcome with nerves to properly experience it.

Now, however, older and much more experienced—and with his half-clothed form still bright and fresh in her fertile mind—she couldn't help but imagine what it would be like to lie with him. How would his large hands feel on her bare skin? Would they be as gentle as they had been when they'd been young?

And was he wondering the same about her?

That final question had her blanching. Ah, God, what if he was? She recalled the feel of his cock against her leg, how it had grown hard, how he looked as if he might kiss her...

She blanched again, even as that place between her legs turned molten. Surely his physical reaction to her had been as natural and unintended as hers had been. He could not possibly wish to renew things between them, even if it was only physical. But then an even worse idea came to her: What if he believed something had already happened between them?

She moved about the room in agitation, packing up her things and setting the room to rights, though she had not so much as slept in the bed. No, of course he did not think anything might have occurred. And, of course, he didn't wish for anything between them. She slammed the door to the empty armoire closed with more force than needed. But in the slight chance he did, on both counts, she had best set things straight between them, and the sooner the better.

* * *

As it turned out, however, making certain Iain did not have any expectations for something between them was the last thing on her mind when she saw him next.

He'd had breakfast sent to her room, with a good quantity of strong coffee, so she'd not had to enter the dining room for sustenance—and been forced to see him for the first time in a public setting since waking nearly naked in his arms. No, she had not had to contend with that uncomfortable moment until she appeared in the busy yard for their departure. She'd stepped into the late-morning sun, breathing in deep of the fresh air, ready to finally see Iain and get past that first uncomfortable moment.

At the sight of him standing beside the equipage talking to his men, however, she instantly forgot all about remaining distant and cool. His shoulders were broad under the snug fit of his black coat, his legs strong where they peaked out beneath his kilt, the hair atop his head catching the sunlight and transforming to a myriad of browns and golds and auburns. A shiver of electrical awareness skittered through her body, her mind emptying. Her steps slowed, her gaze traveling over him from the top of his head to the tips of his boots. Remembering all too well what he looked like beneath those clothes.

Phineas, secure in his cage once more, must have sensed the change in her, for he ruffled his feathers and called out, perturbed, "Noo jist haud on!" Which, of course, caught Iain's attention. His head jerked up, his gaze snagging on her.

It was as if time froze. For the barest moment, she felt as if the entire world had been encased in amber, achingly still, only she and Iain seemingly aware of one another.

And then a horse neighed, and a man laughed, and the spell was blessedly broken.

Face hot, Seraphina raised her head and stormed forward, determined not to show a bit of her nerves. "Good morning, gentlemen," she said as she approached Iain and his men, nodding her thanks as the groom took her bag from her. And then, without another glance Iain's way, she climbed up into the carriage with Phineas. She had been so determined to make certain he understood that nothing happened between them and that there could be nothing physical between them, she had not considered how painfully awkward it would be to do so. But no matter how uncomfortable she felt in his presence now—something that should have dissipated after their conversation the night before but which their climbing into bed together had completely negated—she was determined to get through today, even if it killed her. Which, she thought as her eyes once more traveled to Iain standing just outside the carriage door—only to see his gaze quite firmly on her, though he talked to his men, a new awareness in his eyes that had her skin pimpling—it just might.

Chapter 15

*I*ain had no sooner hefted himself into the carriage and settled across from Seraphina before he began speaking, determined to tackle the elephant in the room...er, carriage.

"About last night—"

Unfortunately, she chose that moment to speak as well, and not only that but the exact same words, her voice at once echoing and clashing with his in the close interior. Which caused them both to lose whatever momentum they had managed. They fell into a charged silence, staring at each other, uncertain how to continue.

It was only when the carriage jolted forward that Iain finally reclaimed some ability to think. He cleared his throat. "Nothing happened last night," he finally blurted, needing to get it out in the open, needing her to know. After witnessing the horror in her face when he had woken and how swiftly she had torn herself from the bed and his arms,

God only knew what was going through her mind. He could not have her questioning what had occurred between them.

"Yes, I'm aware of that," she replied with a quickness that told of relief.

He let loose the breath he hadn't known he was holding as his own relief coursed through him. Thank the saints she had not been torturing herself with questions about what might have happened. But when her expression suddenly shifted, tension bracketing her mouth in a frown, his muscles seized once more. Whatever else she felt she had to say, it was not pleasant.

"What is it?" he demanded, wanting to get it over with—whatever *it* was—quickly.

Gripping the seat beneath her as if to anchor herself to the spot and keep from spinning off in a blur of agitation, she blurted, "I want you to know that, no matter the state we happened to wake in this morning"—her cheeks blossomed into a hue so vibrant it battled with her hair for attention—"nothing will happen between us."

It took him some seconds to understand what she was saying. But when he did, he couldn't help but gape at her. "I would nae ever expect that, Seraphina." No sooner were the words out of his mouth, however, before he remembered his body's reaction to her atop him, how his cock had sprung to life. Right against her leg.

He cleared his throat. "I assure you," he said, his voice strangled, "that part of me has a mind of its own but in nae way controls me."

She nodded, her gaze dropping from his, as if she could no longer stomach looking at him—or was just too damn embarrassed. He winced. That he could understand only too well.

"That's…good," she finally managed. "I'm glad we have gotten that out of the way then."

They fell into silence once more. The carriage rocked beneath them, the jangle of the tack and the steady and unrelenting pounding of the horses' hooves on the road muted inside the plush interior. Phineas, that damned pigeon, made a few low, trilling sounds. And he was left wondering what the devil he could say after such awkwardness.

Which was ridiculous, considering the revelations of the day before. They now knew that neither of them had betrayed the other. Their animosity and unease with one another should be gone, banished along with the lies they had unearthed. But things were no easier between them than they had been. In fact, they seemed so much worse, each of them seemingly unable to comprehend how to act with the other.

Suddenly she spoke again, her husky, uncertain voice filling the interior of the coach. "And…you are still intent on securing a divorce?"

He blinked. Perhaps that was the source of unease then. He had not even thought to question their determination to continue on with their plans to divorce. But it made sense, didn't it? Everything they had been led to believe about the other leaving had been a lie. It was only natural that one of them might wish to take up where they had left off.

He nearly snorted at that. As if the past thirteen years, more than a third of his life, could be so easily brushed under the rug as if it was of no significance. As if he could forget all the heartache and life-changing events that had transpired in that time.

Even so, it took some effort to reply to her. The words he knew he must say, that they needed to move forward with the divorce, stuck in his throat, refusing to budge for several long, agonizing seconds. "Aye," he finally managed, forcing the words past the strange lump in his throat, "I am still determined to divorce you."

She nodded again. "Good. I am as well." She looked at him then, the bright blue of her gaze seeming to hide some deep emotion he could not name. "After all, we are not the same people we were, are we?"

"Nae," he replied quietly, even as his chest ached with the truth of it. "That we are nae."

Something in his tone must have affected her, for her eyes suddenly turned unbearably sad. It was quickly gone, however, as she turned away to busily smooth her skirts over her lap. "I'm glad to see you've given it as careful consideration as I myself have," she said, her voice brusque. "I would have us on the same page where something so momentous must be accomplished."

The moment of their shared grief, as if they both mourned what might have been, had been brief. Yet it had shaken Iain to his core. As it did to her, if her trembling hands were any indication. Forcing a bark of laughter in an attempt to dissolve the loaded emotion of the moment, he said in a careless way he knew would rankle her, "Oh, there was nae careful consideration on my part. Rather, it was the decision of a moment."

As he'd hoped, Seraphina quickly took the bait. All hint of vulnerability vanished as she turned a scowl on him. "But that's pure carelessness."

That familiar, mulish glare had relief coursing through him. An uncertain, nervous, and most importantly sad Seraphina he did not know how to handle. But here was proof she was as ready to go to battle as she had ever been.

It righted his off-kilter world. Or, at least, made it a bit more level.

"I dinnae see why I need to carefully consider anything," he replied offhandedly. "I've lived the majority of my life being led by my instincts, and it has rarely let me down. In fact, it has led me to becoming a verra wealthy man. Why should now be any different?"

Her scowl deepened. "It is a rash way to live. One should be methodical and precise, looking at each option carefully before committing."

He grinned, unable to do anything but, in the face of the utter absurdity of her argument. "Seraphina, are you seriously attempting to dissuade me from divorcing you?"

She stared at him mutely for a moment, all emotion vanishing from her face at his question, like a slate wiped clean. Then the mulish expression was back in place. Not that he had expected her to let down her guard and laugh. No, that would not have been his Seraphina at all.

He paused. *His Seraphina* again? Oh, no, there would be no thinking like that. No matter how very *right* those two words sounded...

"I believe," she said slowly, blessedly breaking him from his wholly foolish musings about laying claim to Seraphina in any capacity, "that as we have decided the quest for a divorce shall continue, there is nothing further to say on the matter. Now, if you will excuse me," she continued, reaching for the small travel desk she had brought with her, "I have work to do." And with that, she lowered her head, effectively ending their conversation. And Iain did not know whether to be grateful for it or not.

* * *

By the time they reached Morpeth, the stop for their third night on the road north, Seraphina had written what felt to be reams of pages. Though whether those pages had anything on them that was fit to be printed was another matter entirely.

She flexed her hand several times, wincing as the muscles refused to completely extend, locked in rebellion for the hours of punishing work she had forced them to do. Several of the fingers were stained with ink, and she rubbed at them as she bleakly considered the mess of pages piled on the seat beside her. Somehow her heroine had found herself locked in a room and in a very compromising position with the mysterious groom, who had reappeared after so long being gone. Here was the bit where she had found herself in bed with him, there the two pages she'd had to cross out when things had gone a bit too far. Her cheeks burned when she recalled just where her imagination had taken her after their stop in Newcastle, when the sight of Iain, looking like a Scottish warrior of old against the ancient stone castle that had given the city its name, had done things to her insides she had not been able to control. Even now, exhausted and sore in every muscle of her body, she felt the stirrings of heat between her legs at the remembrance of it.

Which was ridiculous. She was a modern, independent woman. She was not one to swoon at the sight of a powerful, confident man. In fact, she had no need of a man at all for even the most basic human requirements, much less for those that were decidedly private in nature. God knew she had been taking care of her own desires for years and had never felt any lack in the act.

Iain shifted in his seat, and she realized it would not take much for him to crane his neck and read those incredibly detailed passages. Blanching, she hurriedly gathered them up, stuffing them in the small writing desk with more force than necessary. When she chanced a glance up at him, he was watching her with hooded eyes.

She cleared her throat. "Shall we secure our rooms for the night?"

"Aye," he said, his voice a deep rumble she felt clear to her toes.

The inn was busy and cheerful, the innkeeper even more so as she bounced up to them. "Good evening," she said with a wide smile, pushing a stray lock of straw-colored hair from her eyes. "Are you here for the wedding?"

"Is that what all the fuss is for, then?" Iain asked. "Nae, my wife and I are merely passing through and require a pair of rooms for the night."

Wife. There was that word again. She frowned, shifting Phineas's cage more firmly in her arms. Though she must be getting used to him using it, for it didn't annoy her nearly as much as it had.

"Oh, I'm terribly sorry, but I'm afraid we're nearly full up and haven't a pair of rooms," the innkeeper said, her satisfied tone belying her words. "We do, however, have one room left, spacious accommodations with a splendid view of the river. I'm certain you and your lovely wife would find it more than satisfactory for the night."

Seraphina froze. A single room? To share? Immediately her thoughts went to just that morning and waking in Iain's arms half-clothed. He must have been recalling that very scene as well if the sudden flush staining his cheeks was any indication. Which affected her in places she would rather not think of just then, considering they were standing in the main room of a bustling inn surrounded by strangers.

"Mayhap," he mumbled to her, "we should look for another inn."

"Oh, you won't find another inn with two rooms available," the innkeeper said with a smile, ignoring the fact that Iain had not been speaking to her to begin with. "In fact, we're lucky we have even the one. All of Newcastle is fairly bursting with revelers for the wedding tomorrow. It is Sir Robert Henry's eldest son, you know," she said in an aside to Seraphina, "and they are throwing quite the to-do."

The woman could, of course, be lying through her teeth in an attempt to rent them her last room. But taking a look about at the other patrons, all of whom were unusually cheerful, each seeming to know the other, and Seraphina knew with a sinking heart that the woman was telling the truth. Damn it all to hell.

And when her gaze snagged on another carriage entering the yard, obviously just arriving and no doubt carrying someone else in need of a place to stay for the night, Seraphina reacted without thinking.

"We'll take the room," she blurted.

"Wonderful," the innkeeper exclaimed, beaming at them.

Ignoring Iain's horrified look—really, did he think she wanted to share a room with him?—Seraphina followed the innkeeper, determined to get through this night even if it killed her.

* * *

The *spacious accommodations with a splendid view of the river*, however, proved to be anything but.

Seraphina surveyed the room as the innkeeper, having

taken Iain's instructions to bring up a good quantity of food, took her leave and closed the door behind her, the unoiled hinges making an ungodly noise in the small space. Ah, yes, small, for that was the only word to describe it. Even with just a bed—which wasn't overlarge by any description— and a table with two chairs, it felt cramped, unable to hold a bit more furniture, much less two taller-than-average people and a parrot. The promised *splendid view* might have helped relieve some of the cloying closeness of the space— except for the fact that the window was a single, narrow thing, and the only view of the river it could claim was if a person angled themselves far to one side and used a hefty dose of imagination.

"Damn it all to hell," she muttered.

"Well, this is a fine mess," Iain grumbled as he tossed his bag in the corner. "Why did you nae allow me to go searching for other accommodations? I'm certain I could have found something for us."

She glared at him, placing Phineas's cage on the floor and opening the door. Phineas scrambled out, climbing up her arm to her shoulder with alacrity, as if he could not get out of the tiny space fast enough.

She definitely knew that feeling.

"Do you think I want to share a room with you?" she demanded. "And more specifically, this room, where I shall be in danger of bumping into you every time I turn about? While I would love to believe the innkeeper was lying through her teeth, all signs point to her being truthful regarding accommodations in this blasted city. And with night fast on us, and more people arriving, I did not want to waste a chance on something uncertain when we had a certain outcome before us."

He considered her closely. "Nae, you never were a gambler, were you?" Then, quieter, "All but for that one time, when you took a chance on me."

And look what happened after. The sentence remained unsaid, yet loomed between them, a near physical manifestation.

Feeling decidedly bruised, and not just in body, Seraphina busied herself setting out a small feast for Phineas on the table. "And you always were, weren't you?" she said. "A gambler, I mean." At his grunt—which she took to be an answer in the affirmative, though they both knew her question had been merely rhetorical—she glanced sideways at him. He had sat on the bed and was shrugging out of his coat. A disturbingly intimate action that set her stomach to doing somersaults.

"Like I said," he replied, "I've made a good living for myself because of it."

Her lip quirked as Phineas took a nut from her fingers. "A good living that includes a private carriage and the best rooms as you travel."

"Present room excluded," he remarked with a rough chuckle.

To her surprise, an answering laugh spilled from her lips. "I would never disparage such spaciousness, and especially not with such a scenic view."

He chuckled once more, and a lightness came over her body at the sound, shocking her, releasing some of the tension in her shoulders. Phineas looked up at her, tilting his head, his curiosity palpable. And no wonder. Seraphina had held herself rigid for so long he must think it had become part and parcel with her.

Iain rose and made his way to the table, sinking into the

chair across from her. "I still cannae believe that bird of yours is so tame," he said, eyeing Phineas carefully. It did not slip her notice that he kept his hands firmly in his lap.

Nor did it slip her notice that she did not feel an immediate agitation at his closeness. Rather, she was happy he had joined her. Why happy, she didn't have a clue.

To cover her confusion, she shrugged. "Phineas was well trained before I took him in," she replied.

"That's right. He had a prior owner."

For a moment she remembered Bridget, the one person who had been kind to her in that horrible place. The older woman had protected a frightened Seraphina as best she could, had given her comfort and hope where there had been none.

But then Bridget had gotten sick—as so many of the poor women there had—and she'd needed comfort herself when her end had drawn near. And the one thing she had fretted about when the fever had driven her out of her mind had been Phineas. How she had worried for him, locked up in that horrible house with her family. How she had cried out when her time was drawing near, begging for someone to save her beloved pet. And Seraphina had promised she would save the bird and care for it, giving her friend peace in her final moments. It was a vow she had made certain to keep, retrieving Phineas once she had been able to, caring for him with as much love as Bridget would have, healing his body and his heart as best she could.

Shaking her head to dispel memories that brought so much grief, she turned her attention back to her pet. "His previous owner was a wonderful woman," she continued, "brave and strong. And she loved Phineas dearly, just as he loved her. They were all the other had in the world, and he mourned her dreadfully. It did not help that he had been treated abominably by her family. It took some time for him to trust me. But I think the effort was worth it. Now I cannot imagine my life without him."

He was quiet for a moment, watching Phineas intently as he cracked into a nut with his sharp beak, using his talon to hold it steady. Was that a wince she saw? No doubt Iain was thinking of his own beleaguered ear. When his hand jerked up seemingly of its own accord toward his ear, she found herself grinning. To think that this massive, strong man was terrorized by a small bird.

He glanced at her and flushed, no doubt guessing why she was smiling. Clearing his throat and lowering his hand once more to his lap, he said, "Tell me more of this friend of yours. She must have been quite a woman to have tamed this pigeon from hell."

Still smiling, she ran a finger over the top of Phineas's smooth crown. He turned his head, nibbling affectionately at her finger before resuming his meal. "Her name was Miss Bridget Gunnach," she replied softly. "She was an older woman, small but commanding, with the most beautiful long silver hair you've ever seen. And she was unfailingly kind and generous. She took me under her wing when I was feeling quite hopeless, and gave me strength, and kept me going when I believed I could not..."

Her voice trailed off as she realized she had said much more than she had intended to. It had been so long since she had talked of Bridget, the words bringing back too many emotions, the grief of her passing, of the loss of her, as deep and unforgiving as a bottomless chasm. And to her dismay, the talking of her dear friend dredged up disjointed images that she tried valiantly to keep buried: a small cell; the weight of iron about her wrists; low moans and incoherent babbling.

And pain. So much pain, both of body and mind, until she thought she truly was as mad as they all claimed.

But Iain was gazing at her with a troubled frown, more questions in his eyes than she could ever answer—and certainly ones she never wanted to hear. To keep him from giving voice to those questions, she held out a slice of apple to him. He started, looking at it in confusion.

"What, do you want me to share the pigeon's dinner?" he asked gruffly. "I doubt there is enough for us both."

"No, I want you to feed him."

The confusion in his eyes was replaced with horror. "I have nearly lost an ear and a good quantity of hair to that creature," he declared. "My fingers will nae be the next piece of me it attempts to remove from my person."

Relieved that their conversation had turned to calmer waters, Seraphina rolled her eyes. "Phineas is not the evil demon you seem to think he is. He is quite sweet, actually."

"Sweet!" His lip curled in disbelief as he considered her pet. "That is nae the flavor I would give to him. Nae, I'd more likely describe him as sour. Or spicy. Aye, he's definitely spicy, with a bit of tartness thrown in for good measure."

"Oh, don't be such a child," she said, grasping hold of his hand and drawing it to her.

Which may have been a mistake. The feel of his strong fingers in hers, the warmth of his skin and the calluses that roughened his palm, sent a shiver of something deep and primal through her. And he felt it, too, if his sharply indrawn breath was any indication. His fingers curled around her own, gentle for all their strength, and she could do naught else but stare down at their entwined hands. While hers was an almost translucent paleness, with light blue veins and faint white scars, his was large and rough and tanned, the dusting of hair on his knuckles and the crisscross of veins and tendons strangely thrilling. As she watched, his thumb dragged with gentleness over her knuckles.

It was the lightest of touches, something without any meaning, a mere caress. Yet it touched Seraphina in a very visceral way. She felt it from the roots of her hair to the tips of her toes and every inch in between. Was she so starved for touch, then, that such an innocent contact of skin could affect her so deeply?

Shaking, confused, she pulled her hand from his. He released her immediately, not a hint of pressure in his fingers to keep her trapped in his grip. Which should have brought her relief. And it *did* bring her relief.

Yet there was also a hint of disappointment as well. Why? She chewed on her lip as he hesitantly held out the slice of apple to Phineas, who took it without hesitation. She didn't want anything to do with Iain, after all. They were on this trip to secure a divorce, to legally end whatever it was they had shared all those years ago, and to go their separate ways. And that was all.

Wasn't it?

Chapter 16

*T*he remainder of the evening was spent in silence, each of them keeping to themselves—not an easy thing in so small a room—some seemingly insurmountable wall having gone up between them at that innocent touch of their hands. And, as baffling as it may be, Iain found that he missed Seraphina.

Not that she wasn't there just feet away from him. No, there was no escaping her physical presence in this cramped space. But after that short moment of connection, when they had talked and laughed together in a faint echo of what they used to have, he was left feeling strangely bereft when it abruptly ended. Which was probably why he had forgotten what was to come when the time to sleep was at hand.

Seraphina, who had been interacting with her bird in a sweetly intimate way that had him simultaneously liking and feeling jealous of the creature, suddenly cleared her throat and stood. "I suppose it is time to sleep if we're to get an early start tomorrow," she said pointedly.

Sleep. Which meant sharing the single bed. Which was suddenly looking much smaller than it had when they'd first entered the room. Iain, who had pulled one of the uncomfortable wooden chairs as far across the room as he had been able and had been pretending to read for the past hour—when all along he had been watching Seraphina and her pigeon out of the corner of his eye—swallowed hard. "I'll leave you to change then, shall I?" he asked as he rose. Then, before Seraphina could reply, he was out the door, closing it firmly behind him.

The hall was dark and narrow, yet for the first time since closing himself in that room with Seraphina, he felt he could breathe. He dragged a breath in, closing his eyes and leaning back against the wall. Though as the sounds of her moving about the room drifted out to him, making him realize just what she was doing in there—and how close he would be lying next to her in a short while—his chest began to close up again. And when he recalled, quite against his will, the scene from just that morning when he had woken to her over him, her luscious body pressed to his, his cock against her thigh, he found himself gasping to force air into his starved lungs. Perhaps it would be better if he were to sleep on the floor. Yes, the boards were rough and bare. Yes, it would be incredibly uncomfortable, and he would no doubt rise in the morning with aches in places he did not even know he possessed.

But he would be no better lying next to her, that was certain. In fact, he rather thought he would be much worse off after a night of holding himself stiff as a board—in more ways than one—afraid to move an inch or even close his eyes lest he find himself tangled in her arms once more.

By the time Seraphina opened the door to let him back in the room, he had convinced himself that sleeping on the floor was quite possibly the best decision he had ever come up with. And apparently Seraphina was of the same mind, if her relieved expression was any indication when, without a word, he stripped the bed of half its pillows and blankets and began forming a makeshift pallet on the floor.

Even so, she was not without politeness—albeit grudging politeness. "Are you certain you do not wish to share the bed?" she asked, in a tone that said loud and clear she hoped he would refuse.

"Nae, I'll be fine; I've slept on worse," he mumbled, trying not to notice how delicious she looked in her prim nightgown, a plain thing with nary a bow or flounce, that covered her from neck to toe yet made him all too aware of what was underneath.

So saying, he lowered himself to his sad excuse for a bed. Should he remove his kilt? Perhaps. But there was no way on God's green earth he was going to strip in front of Seraphina.

That woman, after speaking to her pet in that husky voice of hers that had parts of him stirring to life, put the bird away in his cage before, hurrying to the bed on bare feet, she quickly climbed beneath the covers. There was much fussing as she adjusted her blanket and pillow, the bed creaking beneath her the whole while. Iain pressed his back molars together until he was certain they would crack from the pressure, closing his eyes tight, holding himself as still as possible. She would soon settle, he told himself. And once she did, he could pretend she was not there and finally fall asleep and put this whole horrible night behind him.

But once she quieted, once he could no longer hear her body shifting on the mattress, he was in for another type of torture. It began as a low murmuring, someone from one of the adjacent rooms no doubt talking, an occasional laugh breaking through. He focused on the sound as if it were a lifeline, something to concentrate on instead of the sound of Seraphina's soft breathing. That soon backfired in a spectacularly horrendous way, however, as the murmurs transformed into low moans. When those moans grew louder, then were quickly accompanied by a rhythmic creaking and thumping, his fears that they were to be the unwitting auditory audience to a vigorous bout of lovemaking were realized.

And then, to make matters so much worse, he instinctively glanced at the bed—only to find, in the dim light of the low fire, Seraphina's wide eyes on him.

They stared at each other for a long, agonizing minute. All the while the sounds on the other side of the wall continued, growing in enthusiasm.

When a particularly energetic bout of moaning ensued, Seraphina sat upright in bed, as if shocked with a jolt of electricity, fumbling her spectacles back onto her face and hugging her knees to her chest.

"Talk to me," she demanded, the words quick and frantic.

Iain leveraged himself up on one elbow, desperately glad for the distraction. Even so, he could not seem to form a coherent-enough thought to figure out what he could talk about that was not centered around the noises bombarding them. "About what?"

"I don't know. Something. Anything." She waved an

impatient hand in the air, her voice rising as the moans on the other side of the wall gained in volume. "Tell me how you made your fortune."

Relief coursed through him, as well as a healthy wish to tease her from her anxiety. "Are you admitting that I did not take money from your father then?"

He was rewarded with her dark frown. "You know very well it would be stupid of me to continue believing his lies. Now, are you going to tell me or not?"

He fought back a smile. "Very well," he said, lying back down, pillowing his head in his hands and looking up at the ceiling with its dark beams and thick plaster. "After I was told you betrayed me, I was quite heartbroken, as you can imagine. But I did nae allow the heartbreak to remain for long. I had my pride, after all. And so my mind turned to revenge. But I was a nobody, with nae money or power over an English peer."

The bed creaked as she shifted, making him pause. And then her voice, soft and husky from the shadows, drifted to him. "You were never a nobody to me."

He exhaled a soft breath at the confession. When he glanced her way, he expected her to blanch and declare she had misspoken. Instead she stared steadily and somberly at him. Clearing his throat, more affected than he could admit, he continued.

"With revenge against your father out of the question— or, at least, immediate revenge—I set my sights on using what few skills I had against other English usurpers, those bastards who had swooped in like vultures and taken possession of the homes of good Scots families simply for the crime of defending their country. I was always good at cards, you may recall." He grinned her way.

She smiled, fond remembrance in her eyes. "Yes, I recall. You won my pin money off me more times than I can count."

He chuckled. "Though you would insist on having me believe that you lost on purpose, wouldnae you?"

"You will allow me my pride," she quipped. "I had to save face somehow."

They gazed at one another across the distance between their beds, and Iain's breath caught in his chest. Maybe it was the shifting shadows of the low fire, or the glint of faint light on her glasses, but there seemed to be a decided softness, almost affection, relaxing her features. And it touched him in a very visceral way.

In the next instant, however, more vigorous pounding started up, this time hitting the wall at Seraphina's back. Gasping, the alarm back in place in her eyes, she scooted forward farther on the mattress and prompted him to continue. "And so you found those English men and fleeced them to within an inch of their lives."

"Aye." His voice cracked on the one word. Clearing his throat, he tried again. "Aye, and it was nae difficult. They are a cocky lot, those English. And they believe to a one that an overlarge Scotsman is a stupid brute who can easily be taken advantage of."

"Which you gladly disproved," she murmured, almost admiringly.

"Aye," he repeated with a grin, then continued with more enthusiasm. "Soon I was accepting their stolen Scottish houses as payment, taking back some of our heritage. I returned them to the families they had been stolen from, when I could."

"And so you became some type of Scottish Robin Hood."

He thought on that for a moment, liking the sound of it. "Aye, I suppose so," he mused.

"And you've been alone all this time?"

The question took him aback, but more for the fact that she sounded so very sad asking it. So surprised was he that she could feel any type of grief for him, he replied without thinking, wanting to console her.

"Nae any longer. Nae now that I have my gran and cousin."

She stilled, her eyes widening behind the glittering lenses of her spectacles. And he very nearly cursed himself aloud for his mistake. When she had known him, he had been an orphan, with no known family, alone in the world. Now he was revealing that he had relations, ones who were part of his life.

Of course, when he had first decided to keep knowledge of his family, and especially his newly acquired title, from Seraphina, he had been determined to divorce her. She had no right to that information, he had told himself, and might use it against him or refuse to assist him in their permanent and legal separation if she knew.

But everything had changed now that he knew she was innocent and had been as duped as he in their forced parting.

It shook him, that knowledge. What did he expect would happen, that they would abandon this goal he had been working toward since learning she was still alive and well? That they would remain married, would see this coming together as a second chance to have the life they had wanted all those years ago, would forget everything that had come between them and live happily ever after?

And why the hell not?

His entire body seized at that, not so much a whisper as a shout in his head. No, he could not think along that vein.

Too much was changing, and much too fast, the very foundation of what he had built crumbling beneath him. Who was he, if not the angry, driven man who had taken his heartbreak and crushed it in his hands, becoming a kind of alchemist as he turned that lead weight of grief into a cloak of gold? It meant everything he had known, everything he had become, was a lie, a mere mirage.

Seraphina remained silent across the small room, questions loud in her gaze, though her lips remained pressed tight. She had always been insatiably curious, her fertile mind like a sponge for information; she would no doubt wish to question him extensively on his unexpected revelation that he had family. And suddenly he was exhausted beyond bearing. How could he possibly respond to her when he was so uncertain of both his past and his future... and had no idea what her place in it was any longer?

To his shock, however, no question passed her lips, only a softly spoken statement that shook him down to his soul.

"I am glad you found someone, and that you are not alone."

And then, in a room that was finally silent, their neighbors apparently finished with what they were doing, she gave him a nod and, placing her spectacles back on the side table, rolled on her side, her back to him. Iain, for all he had been exhausted just moments ago, found he could not so much as close his eyes, his gaze anchored firmly to the graceful line of her back, certain he would not be able to sleep a wink...

...Until he awoke to a soft whimper filling the room.

Disoriented, he cracked open his eyes and peered about. Where the devil was he? And why the hell did his entire body ache? He winced, trying to roll on his side—only for his hip to come up against the unforgiving wooden floor beneath him. All at once it came rushing back to him: the solitary room at that blasted inn he'd been forced to share with Seraphina; the electric touch of her hand on his that had spurred such discomfort between them; the noises from the room next door and the conversation they'd shared to drown it out.

But what had woken him? A faint rattle of metal brought his attention to the shadow of a cage in the corner. The bird gave a soft trilling beneath the cover. Ah, of course. Phineas must have called out. Damn pigeon. Glowering at the cage, he resolutely closed his eyes, determined to claim a sliver more of sleep.

Just as he was drifting off, however, the strange noise reached him again, prying him from Morpheus's arms. Or, rather, wrenching him from them, for the noise was coming not from the cage, but the bed—and was decidedly human.

He tensed, suddenly wide awake, his senses honed down to a sharp point as he focused all his attention on Seraphina in the bed. There was the creak of the bed frame, the soft rush of her breath growing fast, another low whimper. Was she having a nightmare? *Stay in your place*, he told himself severely. It's just a dream; nothing to fret about. She'll be fine in no time.

But her movements only grew more agitated, pale limbs flashing in the faint moonlight as her legs worked free of the covers. The bird's agitation seemed to grow in concert with Seraphina's, the tinny sound of its talons and beak on the metal bars as it moved about, a disturbing accompaniment to his mistress's unintelligible mumbling. Iain's muscles trembled as he held himself still, not knowing what to do, what she needed from him.

Then, suddenly, she cried out, her words frighteningly clear.

"No! Please, I swear I'm sane. Let me out!"

He lurched to his feet, bounding across the room in two strides. Seraphina thrashed about on the bed, the covers tangling about her, her face contorted in a panic so severe it sent ice through his bones. Dropping to the mattress, he gathered her in his arms, alarmed at the cold clamminess of her skin.

"Seraphina." He brushed a hand over her forehead, pushing loose strands of hair from her face, wiping the sweat from her brow. "Seraphina, can you hear me?"

She opened her eyes, but though she looked at him, he knew she did not see him. Her gaze was flat with fear, her hands gripping tight to his arms with unimaginable strength.

"Please let me go," she pleaded, her voice hoarse and rough. "I don't belong here. I need to get back to my sisters."

By the saints, she was still dreaming. Worse, she thought he was whoever was hurting her in that dream. With infinite care, he released her, placing her against the pillows, hoping she would somehow sense by his actions that she was safe. Instead she scrambled back against the headboard, as if she could not get far enough away from him.

His heart cracked. What torment was she trapped in? And why the hell did it seem as if it was the echo of a very real event?

"Seraphina," he said, soft and low, praying he could reach her, "you are safe."

She shook her head, eyes wild, her knuckles white as she gripped the headboard.

"Seraphina," he tried again, "I vow it, you are safe." And

then, the two words dredged up from the very depths of his soul, "Mo bhean."

"Mo bhean."

The words reached out to her, remnants of a happier time, breaking through the thick fog that strangled her. *My wife.*

The stark cell she was trapped in melted away, the manacles about her wrists dissolving, the twisted face before her changing. And there was Iain, his beautiful visage contorted with worry as he gazed at her.

She blinked, looking wildly about, disoriented. Yes, the cell was gone, the putrid stink of feces and vomit and the cries of the other women gone with it. The room she was in was small and dark, the mattress beneath her soft, faint moonlight shining through a window devoid of bars.

"Iain?" she asked hoarsely, looking back to him, blinking to disperse the last fragments of the dream.

Relief washed over his face. "Aye, Seraphina, it's me."

It came back to her then in a flood, the trip to Scotland with Iain, the overcrowded inn, being forced to share one small room. And Iain, telling her of the past thirteen years, revealing he had found family, sleeping on the floor so they did not have to share a bed...and the worry on his face that had transformed into relief as she woke, with those two achingly gentle words extracting her from a nightmare that had been all too real and consuming.

He watched her carefully now, the low fire catching in his irises, his hands clenched tight in his lap, as if he feared to move too quickly and frighten her. "Do you know where you are?" he asked quietly.

She nodded, releasing her grip on the headboard, hands

shaking as she smoothed her rumpled nightgown. "Yes, I know," she replied, the words a mere whisper of broken sound.

He exhaled, the rigid lines of his shoulder relaxing. One hand came up, as if he were about to brush it against her cheek, but he quickly corrected himself and returned it to his lap.

"I'll just leave you to your sleep then," he said, making to get up.

Panic tore through her, that she might find herself back in that place once he returned to his makeshift bed. Without thinking, her hand shot out and gripped his arm. He stilled, staring down at it, white-knuckled fingers against the pale white of his shirt.

"Seraphina?" There was confusion and what seemed to be longing in his voice.

"Stay here with me," she choked out.

His gaze flew to hers. "What?"

Her cheeks burned hot at what her request might imply, and what he might think about her bold invitation, but she could not back down. Her fear was too great.

"There's room enough on the bed," she said, the words coming fast and desperate. "I'm not asking for sex, of course. And I know after last night you cannot want to be near me. But I think I will sleep better if you're in the bed. I don't often have such violent nightmares. And I am sorry I woke you because of it. But I think if you were to stay in the bed with me it might help."

She was beginning to babble, her tongue tangling as she attempted to persuade him to remain with her. Before she could draw breath and continue in what would have no doubt proven to be a humbling example of bruised pride, he took hold of her hand. His fingers were warm about her own chilled ones, sinking into her bones, stopping her desperate words in their tracks.

"Let me fetch my pillow and blanket," he replied softly.

She swallowed hard and nodded, forcing her fingers to release his sleeve. He moved quickly, gathering his things, returning to her. Yet every second was like an eternity. Finally he slid in beside her, his large frame taking up a good portion of the sparse mattress.

She had never been so happy to be crowded in her life.

They lay quietly beside one another for a time, not speaking, his bulk warm and comforting against her side. But as the minutes ticked past, she still found herself afraid to close her eyes. What if it all came back, that horror that had been her truth? She ached to curl into his side, to feel his arms about her. Yet pride kept her mouth closed tight, even as her lids remained open, and she stared with stinging eyes at the faint outline of dark beams on a pale ceiling. Just when she felt she would twitch out of her skin, he spoke, his voice a soothing balm on the rawness of her soul.

"Do you wish me to hold you, Seraphina?"

In answer, she rolled onto her side, curling her body against his. His strong arm came about her, holding her tight, his heart beating steady and sure under her ear. And as exhaustion finally claimed her, relaxing her body and dragging down on her eyelids, she thought maybe, just maybe, he could chase the demons away.

Chapter 17

*F*or the second time in two days Seraphina woke to find herself wrapped in Iain's arms, though each experience was as different as night and day. While that first morning had been filled with horror and embarrassment, this morning she woke to quite a different set of feelings.

There was no panicked urge to extract herself from his embrace for one. No, she rather thought she would be quite happy to remain curled up against his large body for the foreseeable future. She rubbed her cheek against his chest, sighing contentedly, letting the deep, even sound of his breathing lull her. She could not recall a time when she had felt so protected and safe. At least, not in the last thirteen years.

She should perhaps feel shame after the scene she had made last night. It was not often she allowed herself to be so vulnerable, and especially in front of others. She was the strong one, the one who kept her head even in the direst of circumstances, the one others looked to when times were hard. She was certainly not the one to receive comfort. And she had prided herself on that. How else could she have protected her sisters when all seemed lost, keeping one step ahead of their father when he hunted them like dogs, building a life for them out of nothing but pure determination? If she had shown a bit of weakness, if she had allowed even a moment of uncertainty or fear, everything would have crumbled out from under them.

Yet here, in Iain's arms, it felt so very right to let her worries go, even for a short time.

He stirred, his body shifting against her own, his arm tightening, and she tensed. It was one thing to find comfort in his presence when he was asleep; it was quite another to let down her guard when he was fully conscious. What would be his reaction to finding her in bed with him again? Yes, he had come willingly last night, had even been the one to offer to hold her so she might sleep. But mayhap he would see it differently in the light of day. Would he look at her in aggravation that she had ruined his sleep by making a spectacle of herself? Or, worse, would he pity her for losing control? When he stilled, then pulled back, no doubt due to the unexpected realization of how entangled their bodies were, she was certain her fears were about to be realized.

But she could not have been more wrong. Leveraging himself up on his elbow, he gazed down at her. And there was nothing but worry on his face.

"You are well?"

The concern in his voice had her eyes itching in the most baffling way. Not from tears, of course. She never cried. Nevertheless, she blinked furiously to alleviate the feeling.

"Yes, I'm well," she whispered. "I'm sorry about last night."

"You've nae need to be sorry about anything," he replied. Then, reaching up, he brushed a stray tendril of hair from her cheek, his fingers caressing her skin.

She shivered from the tenderness in his touch, which transformed to waves of sensation that rolled through her body. Why? Because of one gentle brush of fingers on her skin? Was she that starved for human affection? Not that she had ever been without it. She had plenty of people in her life who would offer it to her, and gladly; her sisters and her friends were affectionate creatures to a one.

No, they had always been ready with open arms for her; she had been the one brushing off physical affection, seeing it as a weakness, something that she could not indulge in lest she let down her guard and with it her armor against the world. But after her vulnerability of the night before, something had shifted, and she recognized the yearning she had kept buried for so long. Yes, she had been starved for physical touch. But it was no one's fault but her own; she had been the one to starve herself, until her soul was emaciated from it. And she found she was hungry, so very hungry.

What would it feel like to let go of her tightly held control, just a bit more, with this man she had loved so long ago, the one man who had ever shown her gentleness? And then, because she could not stop herself if she tried, she wound her arms about his neck, and raised her head to brush his lips with hers.

It was the barest of touches, as light and delicate as a flower's petal. Yet his reaction was deep and real, his entire body jolting as he drew in a sharp breath. When she raised her lids to look at him, his eyes seemed to have claimed all the brilliance of the rising sun.

"You dinnae have to show your gratitude that way, Seraphina," he said, his voice hoarse.

"It was not gratitude that had me kissing you, Iain," she replied softly.

He swallowed hard. "What was it, then?"

In answer she pulled his head down and claimed his lips with her own.

By God, she was like heaven in his arms.

Did confusion still run rampant in his whirling mind? Yes. But he was not a fool. He had seen the desire in her eyes, in the faint curve of her lips. She wanted him, perhaps even akin to how desperately he wanted her. If that wasn't enough, the feel of her hands in his hair as she pulled his head down to kiss him within an inch of his life would have certainly done the trick.

And he wanted her, so badly his soul ached with it. He groaned as her tongue delved into the recesses of his mouth, tangling with his own. She had always been a passionate creature, eager and enthusiastic, their furtive kisses having driven him wild with desire for her in their youth, culminating when they had consummated their secret marriage. But there had always been something nervous in her then, an uncertainty that had no doubt been brought about by her innocence.

Now, however, she was certain, confident, taking control as she shifted their bodies, pushing at his shoulders until he fell on his back with her atop him. He went willingly, eagerly even, following her lead in this new dance. She gripped his head with both hands, as if to hold it still for her onslaught. Her body pressed into his, strong and lithe, and he ran his hands over the flare of her hips, trailing up her spine, across the muscles of her back until he was cupping the back of her head. The soft, silken strands of her hair threaded through his fingers, drifted down over his forearms, brushed his cheeks, carrying with it the heady scent of lavender and soap and *Seraphina*. He dragged that scent into his lungs, so she was not only above him but within him as well, and his head spun from the joy it brought him.

This is how it should have always been for them. This wild desire, this need for one another that had not dimmed over years of forced separation and perceived betrayal and God knew what else that had been thrown in their paths. They had found their way back to one another again.

All so they could drive the last wedge between them by securing a divorce.

No! It was wrong; he felt it in his bones. This thing he had worked toward for so long, had traveled the width and breadth of England for, had forced Seraphina into doing, had become in the last day and a half the very last thing he wanted.

Gasping, he broke the kiss, staring up at Seraphina with new eyes. Damn but she was beautiful, her bright eyes heavy-lidded, her pale skin stained pink, her lips swollen from kissing. And then she smiled, and his heart somersaulted in his chest.

"Do you think I'm through with you?" she murmured, the huskiness of her voice like a physical caress.

"God, I hope nae," he groaned as she lowered her head again. The kiss was harder now, her teeth coming into play as she nipped at his bottom lip, dragging a low, pleading moan from his chest. When her hands worked under his shirt, skimming over his stomach, playing him like the finest instrument, he lost the ability to think at all.

"Mmm," she murmured, the sound a purr, her lips trailing from his mouth to his jaw and down his throat, "you were always finely formed, but these muscles are a lovely addition."

A strangled laugh burst from his lips. "I could say the same about you," he managed as one of his hands brushed the sides of her breasts. When she took hold of that hand and formed his fingers around the soft plumpness of her, he groaned. "Lass, ye shall kill me."

"Surely you're made of sterner stuff than that," she teased, even as her teeth nipped his collarbone.

"Nae when it comes to ye," he choked out. "I've always been weak when it comes to ye."

She made a soft, needy sound in her throat at that, her touch becoming a bit more desperate, a bit more demanding. He willingly gave himself up to her, each trip of her fingers over his skin making him wilder for her. And when she pushed his shirt up to his neck and began kissing his chest, he thought he might combust from the fire it ignited in him.

"Do you want more, Iain?" she murmured, her lips dragging back and forth across his skin, her breath hot.

"God yes," he groaned. He wanted more, not only of this physicality between them, but a life with her as well. The life they'd planned all those years ago, the life that had been robbed from them.

"We'll return to Synne," he gasped as her tongue did wicked things to his nipple. "We'll gather your sisters and return to Scotland. They can live with us if they wish. I shall protect them as fiercely as I protect you."

She stilled and raised her head. "Live with us?"

He should have perhaps paid better heed to the strange tension in her voice. But he was awash in sensation, and for the first time in a very long time hopeful for the future, and so did not heed the faint alarm pealing in the back of his mind.

"Aye," he replied, running his hands over the smooth length of her thighs where they straddled his leg. "You dinnae think I would forget them, did you? Of course they shall live with us."

She pushed away from him, scooting back across the bed until she was well out of reach. "But there is no *us*, Iain."

He frowned. Something was wrong, very wrong.

"Of course there is," he declared, sitting up. "There is no reason to divorce now. Not after learning the truth of why we were separated."

But she shook her head, even as she pulled her night-gown over her legs. "The truth changes nothing."

"It changes everything," he insisted. He reached for her, certain it must just be nerves that had her talking that way. But she slipped from the bed, standing at the foot of it, as if in preparation to bolt.

"No, it does not," she replied firmly. "I have no intention of remaining married to you, Iain."

Confusion gave way to frustration. "What was all this then?" he demanded, indicating the bed and his disheveled clothing and her kiss-swollen lips. "Did you lie then, and it was all due to gratitude for last night?"

She flinched, but glared at him, planting her hands on her hips. "I can desire you and still wish to divorce you," she snapped. "Physical passion is not necessarily incumbent upon deeper feelings. And my body has urges, as I'm sure yours does."

"So this was merely physical to you?"

"Yes."

The blunt answer stunned him mute, more for the fact that it actually pained him. *Damned fool.* He had been in the throes of deep emotion, and she had been quite the opposite.

But she was not done with him yet. No, she still had some flaying to do.

"What did you think would happen between us, Iain?" she asked. "Did you think we could pretend the last thirteen years never happened, that we could go back to when we were young and in love and live out the simple dreams of those two naïve fools?"

"We were nae fools," he growled, swinging his legs over the side of the bed and rising to face her. "We were naïve, yes. You have that right. But we were nae fools. We were forcibly separated by your father."

"Which is something we cannot change," she replied firmly. She moved to the covered cage in the corner, where Phineas, the damn pigeon, was beginning to make his presence known. "But you have your life now, and I have mine," she continued, lifting the cover and opening the door so the bird could scramble out. "I worked hard to build my business, and I refuse to give up control of it. And you went through an incredible amount of trouble to find me in order to secure a divorce so you might remarry. That cannot have changed in the past days."

But it had changed. And he was furious at himself for allowing it to have.

She must have seen the frustration in his face when she

glanced up from her pet, for her tone gentled. "We cannot go back in time, Iain. I am sorry for making you think otherwise. But you will thank me for putting an end to those thoughts, you'll see."

But as she turned away to ready herself and her pet for the day, and Iain mechanically followed suit, he knew it would be a very long time, if ever, that he felt gratitude for losing the dream of her again.

Chapter 18

*B*y the time they reached Alnwick for their afternoon stop, Seraphina thought she might shatter from the determined unconcern she had adopted since the disastrous kiss with Iain that morning.

That man, however, had never looked so dour. Had he really expected them to pick up where they had left off, to not only remain married but to build a life together? Yes, the truth was devastating; it was heartbreaking to know they had been fooled, that they had spent the past thirteen years hating one another when all along they had both been victims of her father's cruelties.

But that did not mean they could ever go back to those people they used to be and live happily ever after.

Didn't it?

The traitorous words whispered through her head, like the threat of a storm brewing on the horizon. Seraphina, in the process of removing Phineas from his cage in the busy

yard of the White Swan Inn so he might have his afternoon
exercise, blanched. No, it most certainly did not, she told
herself fiercely as she helped the parrot to her shoulder and
stepped away from the carriage. She was happy in her life,
having built a prosperous business with her sisters and in
possession of a wonderfully tightly knit band of friends.
She was independent, and free, and did not have to answer
to anyone. If she gave up this plan to divorce Iain—one
that she had balked at from the first but now saw the wis-
dom in—she would be forced to concede everything she
had worked for. And after all she had endured, she was not
about to allow any man to have power over her. Not even
one as delicious as Iain.

And he was delicious. For a moment she was overcome
with memories of how wonderful he had felt under her, the
taste of him on her tongue and the way his large hands had
roved her body. But no matter how desperately she wished
for a repeat of that morning—and then some—she knew
they could never indulge in that again. Not if it caused him
to change his mind regarding their permanent separation.

Iain, who had disappeared inside the inn while she saw
to Phineas, reappeared then, a basket hooked over one arm.
He considered her for a moment with an unreadable expression before, holding up the basket, he said, "I know your
bird has need of exercise. And I suspect you and I do as
well. I thought a picnic would be just the thing. The innkeeper directed me to a grassy spot with a fine view of the
castle. It is a bit of a walk, but I dinnae think you would
mind it."

Which shouldn't have softened her as much as it did. Yet
his thoughtfulness, coupled with the tic in his cheek that
told of an uncertainty that was altogether endearing, did

much to crack the protective layer she had built about her heart. Or, rather, crack it more than it already was, though she had tried with all her might to keep it in one piece.

"That...lovely. Thank you," she replied quietly, stepping back and indicating he should lead the way.

Heading out onto Alnwick's busy main thoroughfare, they walked in silence. Well, except for Phineas, who was busy whistling and chirping and swiveling his head this way and that as he took in the new sights and sounds. All the while Seraphina's mind was busy, comparing the quiet man beside her to the one who had been her companion these past days of travel.

Not that he had been particularly verbose along the way. Yet there was something subdued about him today, morose, contemplative. It wasn't until they turned down a quieter side street, and then one even farther on that led to a wide swatch of green lawn, that he spoke at all.

"We'll stop in Berwick-upon-Tweed tonight," he said quietly. "Scotland is just beyond that."

Her stomach dropped. Why? It was not as if she wished to continue with this farce longer than necessary. Especially since things were so strange between them now. Or, rather, stranger than they had been.

"Yes," she replied evenly, though her insides felt anything but. "And then a long day's journey to Edinburgh, correct?"

"Aye." He paused for a moment before continuing. "Though perhaps it would be wise to rest for the night in Haddington before heading on to Edinburgh. If you're amenable, that is."

"Yes," she blurted before the words were fully out of his mouth, then silently cursed herself for her eagerness. Which was ridiculous. She could not want to travel nearly

sixty miles in one day, after all, which they would be doing
if they tackled the entirety of the trip from Berwick-upon-
Tweed to Edinburgh. No, her eagerness had everything to
do with comfort for them and Iain's men and the horses,
and nothing at all to do with the fact that she would be
claiming an additional day of travel with Iain by postponing. Certainly not.

They found a flat, shady spot near an oak tree and busied themselves by laying out a soft blanket and emptying
out the contents of the basket, a quantity of paper-wrapped
goods that revealed bits of cheese and bread and meat pies
still warm from the oven. When Seraphina got to the last
parcel, she paused as it fell open to reveal a quantity of
fresh fruit and nuts.

"For the bird," he explained gruffly when she gave him
a quizzical glance.

Which should not have further softened her heart. Yet
it did.

"Thank you," she managed, lowering Phineas to the
blanket and laying the open parcel before him. He made
a swift beeline for it, reaching in immediately with his
beak, taking hold of a nut, using his talon and his tongue to
open the shell and extract the tender insides. He gave a few
contented little chirps, bobbing his head up and down.

Seraphina, watching him, smiled for what felt the first
time since leaving Morpeth. "And it seems Phineas thanks
you as well," she said. She glanced up—only to find Iain
watching the bird with fascination.

"I never actually watched the beast eat before," he said.
"But it is an incredible sight, isn't it. His tongue is like a
finger the way it manipulates the food." Phineas reached for
another nut, cracking into it with his beak, and Iain visibly

winced. "Though I already know what damage that part of it can do."

She laughed softly. The sound drew his attention to her, but there was no answering amusement on his face. And when he spoke, her amusement faded as surely as the morning fog on the sea that kissed Synne's shores.

"I am sorry about this morning," he said gruffly. "I suppose it was nostalgia, that kiss reminding me of what we used to have."

She swallowed hard, taking hold of a soft roll and breaking off a piece, crumbling it in nervous fingers. Phineas, sensing another treat, waddled over and began picking the pieces off the blanket.

"It did feel nice to experience that again," she agreed softly. "It brought back so many memories I had purposely forgotten. Not that it can truly bring those times back," she hurried to say. Dear God, she didn't want to renew his interest by some thoughtlessly spoken words.

"Aye," he replied. "I know that now."

She nodded, expecting relief, troubled when only a soft sadness fell over her.

They ate in silence for a time, making quick work of the food. Seraphina's stomach rebelled against it; her emotions were much too volatile for her to eat with any ease. But she had long learned that you ate where you could and did not pass up a meal. Too many times in those uncertain years when she and her sisters had first absconded from their father's house they'd had to go to bed hungry, and she'd trained both them and herself to never forgo sustenance.

But eventually the time came when she could not get a morsel more of food into her roiling stomach. Sighing, she rose to her feet, bending down to retrieve a curious Phineas as he hunted insects in the grass.

"Come along, love," she cooed. "Let's give your wings a stretch."

Just as she was moving off, Iain called out to her. "I dinnae suppose you could use my assistance, could you?"

Blinking in surprise, she looked back at him. He had risen as well and was brushing out his kilt. But it was his eyes that arrested her attention. They appeared uncertain, almost sheepish.

"I know I am nae that pigeon's favorite person, of course," he said wryly, tilting his head in Phineas's direction. "But I am willing to hold out a figurative olive branch to him. If," he added forcefully, "he can keep from biting any more of my appendages."

She cocked one eyebrow at him, suppressing a smile. "If you're certain," she murmured. "He's such a bloodthirsty thing, after all."

He glowered at Phineas, but there was no malice in it. "That I know fair and well. But I refuse to be cowed by a bird."

She nodded. "Very well. Stand over by that tree there," she said, indicating a large oak some thirty feet away. "And hold your arm out at your side."

He did as he was bid, lifting his arm straight out beside him, a look of grim determination on his rugged face, even as he leaned his head as far to the opposite side as he was able.

She couldn't help her grin then. Nor could she help the way her heart pounded at the endearing sight of this large, strong man trying so valiantly not to be afraid of a small bird.

"Now say, firmly, *trobhad, Phineas*," she instructed.

He blinked, his barely hidden anxiety replaced by bemusement. "You must be joking," he said. "Just how Scottish was this friend of yours?"

"Oh, she was very Scottish," she quipped. "I daresay she would have even put you to shame."

But she hardly heard his feigned scoff at such an idea. For the first time since Bridget's death, she had thought of her friend with a soft happiness instead of grief.

Iain must have sensed the change in her, even at thirty paces away. He stilled, his arm lowering slowly. "Seraphina, are you well?" he called.

Forcing a smile, she waved a hand in the air. "Of course I'm well. Now then," she continued, adjusting her spectacles to hide her disquiet before raising the hand that held Phineas, "lift your arm and speak firmly."

He did not look convinced by her act. But he nevertheless did what she bid, raising his arm perpendicular, a look of fierce determination on his face as he said in a booming voice, "Trobhad, Phineas."

That bird, as well-trained as he was, first by Bridget and then by Seraphina's own efforts, took off immediately, bright green wings flapping and tail flared as he flew toward Iain. For his part, Iain tensed as the parrot made its swift way to him, yet he kept his arm out straight, a firm perch. When the bird landed, Iain grunted slightly in surprise, then held as still as any marble statue, seemingly hardly daring to breathe.

The sight was so comical, so ridiculous, that Seraphina could not help the laugh that bubbled from her lips. He glared at her before returning his side-eyed glance at Phineas, who cocked his head and considered Iain with his bright yellow eye.

"Just what is so hilarious about this?" he demanded through gritted teeth, in a singsong voice that was completely at odds with his words.

Which, of course, sent Seraphina off into further gales of laughter. "You look as though he is ready to attack your jugular," she sputtered.

"I wouldnae put it past him," he grumbled as Phineas moved farther up his arm—toward said jugular. "Staaay," he said in a low voice. "There's a good parrot."

Finally taking pity on Iain, Seraphina said in as firm a voice as she was able, considering how overcome with laughter she was, "Trobhad, Phineas."

The bird lifted off in a flutter, coming to land on her hand. Extracting a seed from the pocket at her waist, she offered it to him. Voracious thing that he was, he eagerly accepted it.

"Do you wish to try again?" she called across the grassy expanse of lawn.

"Aye," he said, his voice firm, his expression determined. "Trobhad, Phineas," he called, with only the slightest tensing when the bird, as ever obedient, landed on his arm.

They worked with Phineas for some minutes, and with each recall of the bird Iain seemed to grow more confident, more relaxed until, watching her pass a seed to Phineas for the dozenth time, he surprised her by declaring, "I wish to reward the pigeon as well."

She pursed her lips. "If you're certain."

"Aye, I am," he declared before, stomping over to the picnic, he retrieved a strawberry. Then, taking his place once more, he called the bird to him.

Once Phineas was on his arm, Iain paused and gave Seraphina an uncertain glance, as if to seek reassurance. And her heart swelled. Damn the man for being endearing. Wishing she could be annoyed at how swiftly he was burying himself under her skin, she found she could only smile.

"He won't bite," she called out in encouragement. "I swear it."

Pressing his lips tight, he nodded and held the strawberry out for Phineas.

The parrot cocked his head before, reaching out, he took a delicate bite of the fruit. And the delighted look Iain shot her way had her body going soft and warm all at once.

More than that, however, was the tingling in her chest, as if something had been awoken in her that was both foreign and achingly familiar.

Flustered, she called Phineas back to her. "Mayhap it's time to leave," she mumbled. Then, turning to Phineas, she ran a finger over his crown before saying, "Fly free, love."

Giving a gentle nibble to her finger, Phineas eagerly took off, making for the clear blue sky above their heads. She watched him go, heart aching with envy as it did every time he soared for the clouds, as if there was no care on earth that could touch him. She never failed to wonder what it would be like, to leave everything behind, for there to be nothing but open space between you and the earth, to feel the wind in your face, to defy gravity and just *be*.

So engrossed was she in watching Phineas and wishing she could join him, however, she did not immediately hear Iain sidle up beside her.

"What an experience that would be," he murmured. "Would that us humans could have such freedom."

She glanced at him—more from shock that his words so clearly mirrored what was in her own heart—and was in no way prepared for just how close he was. Which, of course, threw her completely off-balance. She reached out to catch herself, grasping onto the nearest solid object—which happened to be his chest.

Of course it was.

To make matters worse—so much worse—he reacted automatically as well, his arms snaking around her waist to steady her. Her body came up flush against his, her breasts pressed into the broad expanse of chest that just that morning she had run her fingers and mouth over. In her shock she did quite possibly the stupidest thing she had ever done: she glanced up, her gaze clashing with his.

Eyes the color of misty moors were no longer cool but unbearably hot, causing that private juncture between her thighs to turn molten. She forced herself to breathe, trying with all her might to dispel the sudden aching desire that permeated every inch of her body. But it only managed to increase her awareness of him as the heady, spiced scent of him filled her up, bringing her back to that early-morning kiss.

"My God," he breathed, his heavy-lidded gaze snagging on her mouth.

"My God" indeed. She swallowed hard, her fingers unconsciously clenching around his lapels, as though some part of her dreaded him trying to pull away. And no logical voice in her head could impel her to let go. Probably because that logical part of her was growing weaker and weaker the more he held her against him. Perhaps if she had not given in to desire for him that morning she might have been able to fight it better. But as it stood, the memory of being held in his arms was too fresh, too potent for her to brush it aside with any ease.

But brush it aside she did, though it was quite possibly the most difficult thing she had ever done.

"Your men must be waiting for us," she managed, forcibly straightening her fingers and taking a purposeful step back. She cleared her throat, wiping her hands on her skirts, trying not to notice the way his arms remained outstretched, as if beseeching her to step back into their embrace. "We'd best gather up these things and return before they come in search of us."

"Aye," he mumbled before, giving her a long look, he turned to pack up the picnic things. And as Seraphina assisted him, she sent up a silent prayer that they did not find another full inn at the end of their day's journey. She did not think she would have the will to ignore her body's urgings again, no matter she knew better.

Chapter 19

*B*ut no matter her prayer was somehow answered—an impressive thing, truly, as her faith in a higher power was horribly lacking—there was no relief for Seraphina. Rather, she felt only a vague sense of loss as she stood with her back to the closed door of her room at the Berwick-upon-Tweed inn later that evening and stared about an interior that seemed lacking for all Iain was missing from it.

It was not as if they did not share a space, of course. Iain had secured a suite of rooms this time, larger even than her home back on Synne above the Quayside, with a spacious shared living space bookended by two well-proportioned bedrooms. Yet she felt as if an entire continent stood between her and Iain. Especially as she had no intention of leaving her room all night long.

Busying herself with seeing that Phineas had a bowl of clean water to wash the dust of their travels from his feathers, she then did the same for herself, undressing and sinking into the copper tub that had been set up before the cheerful little fire. She was sorely tempted to lose herself in the warmth of the water and let it ease the soreness from her muscles and her heart. God knew she needed it. But after that first night on the road, when Iain had unexpectedly walked in on her *au naturel*, she was not about to chance it again. It was difficult enough keeping herself from going to him while she was fully clothed; the temptation was so much worse with nothing at all between them but charged air.

Finally clothed again, this time in her modest nightgown, she sat before the fire, brushing her damp hair out to dry. Phineas, done with his own bath and dry himself, rolled and hopped about on the coverlet, wrestling with small bits of felt and bells she had sewn together for him, the cheerful jangling and squawking at complete odds with the turmoil within her. She knew what had to be done, of course. They had to continue on, head for Edinburgh and proclaim to the Court of Sessions that she was alive and well so the divorce could go through. They had to finish what they had started and release themselves from this lodestone that was pulling them under with each passing day that they spent together.

Yet she could not help the part of her that mourned, especially now that the truth was out and she had gotten a bit of Iain back again.

For a moment fury and heartbreak overtook her. Her father had stolen so much from her and her sisters. He should have loved them, cared for them, and instead had treated them as no better than the bitches in his kennel. For her own sanity and her sisters' happiness she had done her best to put him behind her; it was the only way to move forward, leaving the past horrors in the past, spending most of her energy on the future. It was bad enough that her father infiltrated her nightmares; she would not allow him to steal any more of her life from her.

Now, however, she was forced to confront the true extent of her sire's cruelties. Iain had been a victim, too, as well as the future they might have had together, the life they might have lived, the children they might have had... She had grieved before, of course, when she had believed Iain had betrayed her. The grieving now, however, was so much different, so much sharper, the blade of injustice fairly slicing her to ribbons.

She pulled harder than necessary with the brush, yanking on a particularly stubborn snarl of hair until tears came to her eyes, as if the pain of it could replace the pain in her heart. They could not return to that time, she told herself fiercely. No matter how cruel that truth was, there was no denying it. She knew that, and he finally accepted that. Which, of course, should make it easy.

Yet it didn't. In fact, now that he was not opposing her, she found it was so much harder to keep heading for that horizon.

Her hair just about dry, she began to wind the long tresses into a thick plait. Which, of course, snagged Phineas's attention. Flying to land on her knee, he played his usual cat-and-mouse game with her hair, reaching for the strands as she wound them about one another. She laughed softly at his antics before, smile falling again, she sighed heavily.

"I thought this trip would be so easy, Phineas," she said softly as she took up a piece of ribbon and tied the end of her plait together, then pushed it over her shoulder.

His favorite plaything out of sight, he turned his attention to her face, cocking his head. "Noo jist haud on," he said with a severe look and several sharp clicks of his tongue.

She sighed. "I cannot slow down and take my time. For then I shall be forced to think about every aspect of this mess I've found myself in. Of course I did not think it would be easy. But I believed any difficulty would be from how much Iain would vex me, not because..."

"Gie it laldy," Phineas squawked when her voice faltered.

She glared at him. "You wish for me to be passionate about it then, you devilish thing? Very well. I thought this trip would prove difficult because of how much Iain vexed me, not because I would want him again, so much I can barely breathe."

Phineas ruffled his feathers, giving a particularly high-pitched squawk. She rolled her eyes at his bit of attitude. "You were not around when we were young," she scolded him. "You would not know how wonderful what we shared was. Why, he was my very dearest friend. And then, later, the very first man I ever loved." She gave a humorless chuckle. "Or, rather, the only man I've ever loved."

And just like that she was awash in memories: when she'd snuck from her rooms at midnight and met him in the woods behind the house; when they had let her sisters ride ahead and he had kissed her behind the hedgerow; when he had left small bouquets of wildflowers on her windowsill. And the one that brought the most painful ache to her chest, when they had met at the peak of the highest hill on her father's property at sunrise and he had dropped to one knee in the dew-covered grass and had asked her to share her life with him always.

Fury and grief and a pain so bitter she could taste it on her tongue filled her again, even more potent than before. Damn her father for tearing them apart. She could have been happy with Iain, could have made a life with him and had children with him. Her breath caught in her chest at that *if only*. She had believed the heartache was well and truly behind her. Now here was Iain, come back into her life like a hurricane of regret and grief and hope and want. And she was cruelly reminded of that loss all over again, all that had been stolen from her. From *them*. And she wanted to curse and howl and, yes, even sob. But she could not. No, she had to remain strong, ever unwavering and steady in the face of adversity and hardship.

But she was so tired of it all, of the constant need to remain aloof and resilient. For once in her damned life, she wanted to let down her guard and lose herself in passion. To give a proper farewell to that poor, naïve girl who'd had such hope in her heart for the future, instead of leaving her unceremoniously buried in the dank cells of that asylum among the cries of the other inmates.

She was on her feet before she knew what she was about, gathering a quieting Phineas up and helping him into his cage in the corner for the night. Turning, she looked at the door to her bedroom, imagining Iain in his own room across the way. Then, heart beating madly in her chest, she made her way to him, knowing that, for tonight at least, she would gladly lose the battle to stay away from him.

* * *

Iain put aside the latest issue of the *Gaia Review and Repository*, heaving a sigh and running a hand over his face.

As he'd sat silently across from Seraphina in that blasted carriage—which had suddenly felt so much smaller than in the previous days of travel—a disturbing idea had begun to take shape in his head that he had not been able to shake. Something horrible had happened to her in the years since they'd married and parted, a trauma that had her shrinking back from an unexpected hold on her arm, that had her crying out in terror in her sleep and begging to be released from some place only she could see. Though with how closely Seraphina guarded her inner self, he could not see a way to learn what that thing might be.

But after they'd retired to their suite of rooms at the inn that evening and he had opened his bag to extract his things for the night—and spied the pile of periodicals he'd carried the width and breadth of England as he'd searched for her—he'd begun to realize that the answer to all of his questions might very well be right under his nose.

He'd never thought, however, that he might come away with more questions upon skimming through Seraphina's writings as the mysterious author S. L. Keys. Yes, those very same writings had led him to her. There had been too many similarities between the story and what they'd shared all those years ago: the disparity between their stations in life; the cruel guardian and sweet younger sisters; the dawn-bathed proposal on a hilltop; the secret marriage and dreams of a simple life in another country.

But now that he read with new eyes, he found even more similarities. Could the bits of her life that she remained stubbornly close-lipped about be there as well?

He focused then on the rest of the tale, the dark ribbons that wrapped around and through the hints of Seraphina's real life. Yes, the story had all the typical gothic hallmarks, with a distressed heroine and an atmospheric castle and moody weather and spine-tingling suspense. Yet there was something altogether too real in the descriptions of the dungeon the heroine was kept in, a sense of panic and hopelessness that permeated the pages.

It could be fiction, of course. Seraphina was a talented writer and had the skill of drawing a person in and making them feel all the emotions of a story.

But something deep inside him told him it was not all fiction, that she had experienced these things herself, that she had taken the details from real life and fairly bled them onto the page.

He remembered last night, her wild thrashing, her panicked words, which haunted him even now: *Please, I swear I'm sane. Let me out!* And then her desperate plea for her sisters. Those same words jumped out at him now from the prose before him, almost identical to that moment of terror. His heart had shattered for her, and he'd had the disturbing feeling that the dream had been an echo of a very real event, a passing thought he could not begin to comprehend and had quickly dismissed. But was it possible he'd been right all along? Was this serial of hers, a popular story printed out to titillate the masses, drawn from very real events that tormented her even now?

His heart heavy, he rose from his seat before the fire, taking up his copies of the *Gaia Review and Repository* and carefully replacing them in his bag before firmly closing it up tight. He ached to ask her what had happened to her. But he knew that if she didn't wish to reveal it, there was no amount of begging that would entice her to. Clenching his hands into fists, he went to the fire and stared down into the glowing depths, aware of a latent fury snaking under his skin. If she so much as asked, he would burn down the world for her. And that burning would start with Lord Farrow. Her father had separated them in the cruelest way, causing them unimaginable grief. Worse, if Seraphina's writings held a grain of truth, that man had also tortured his eldest child to such a degree that she had stolen her younger sisters from his care in order to protect them. The image of her terror-filled eyes flashed in his mind, her babbled pleas when that nightmare had held her in thrall ringing in his ears, and he suddenly wished Lord Farrow was within his grasp so he might show the man the full scope of the severity of his mistake in hurting Seraphina.

But it was not his place. Nor would it ever be. He closed his eyes, breathing deep to control the wild sense of loss that stole through him, overshadowing his fury until it was all that he was. Seraphina was right; no matter their nostalgia for the past, no matter that they mourned their old selves and what they had shared, they could not reclaim that time. It was gone for good, swallowed up like an unwary traveler in a peat bog, never to be seen again. He was not the same naïve, rash man he had been. And she was not the same wide-eyed, hopeful girl she used to be.

Though wasn't the woman she had become more amazing than ever before?

He closed his eyes, clenching his back molars tight. God yes. She was incredible, even more fierce and strong and tender than she had been. That girl from his youth had been the other half of his heart. Now the woman she had become felt like the other half of his soul. And in a matter of days, he would have to give her up.

Why? a voice demanded in his head. Why did he have to give her up? Why couldn't they start over again?

Because, he told himself severely, yanking his shirt over his head in sharp, angry movements before beginning to work on the belt that fastened his kilt, even if he wished it, she did not. It was there in the tension of her body if he startled her with his closeness, in every cautious glance she threw his way. It did not matter that she had kissed him and run her hands over his body and straddled him with those strong, smooth thighs of hers. Like she had told him in no uncertain terms, physical desire did not necessarily have anything to do with emotional connection. No matter that those things were becoming inexorably entwined within him where she was concerned.

Naked, he padded on bare feet over the smooth wooden floorboards to the washstand in the corner, taking up a washcloth and dipping it in the basin there, scrubbing it hard over his body in the hopes it might wash away the remembrance of her from his skin. Could he convince her that they might have a chance at something new together? Perhaps if they had enough time. But Edinburgh was but two days away, and then she would be out of his life for good. Two days was not enough time to heal the hurt of nearly a decade and a half.

A slithering idea of a thought crept through the dank halls of his mind like a clinging fog: What if he told her of the dukedom? What if he revealed to her that he was a duke and she was a duchess, that she and her sisters would never have to worry about money again and he could give them all lavish lifestyles safe from any fear of her father?

But even before it finished circulating in his skull he knew that would be the wrong thing to do. For one, Seraphina had never held much store in titles. In his youth, of course, his pride had led him to believe that she did, and she would never be able to overlook the disparity in their stations. It was why he had so readily believed her father's lies.

Now that he was older, however, and hopefully much wiser, he saw with the clarity and pain of hindsight that she had never cared for those things. She had even left the comfort and security of station and wealth in order to protect herself and her sisters and to forge a new life for them. She would not care that she was a duchess and he a duke. In fact, it might turn her from him completely. And besides, he did not want to win her that way, even if she could be won. No, he wanted her to love him for himself, just as she had before.

Love. He let loose a humorless bark of laughter, throwing the washcloth back in the bowl with a splash. He'd thought he was incapable of love, that he'd lanced it from his heart. But it appeared he'd not been as thorough as he'd hoped. The small sliver of emotion remaining in his chest had begun to grow again, filling him up, transforming into something strong. And, he feared, something that would not be so easily gotten rid of this time around, not now that he knew the truth about her part in their past.

Frustrated, heartsick, he doused all the light save for the low fire and headed for the overlarge and lonely bed, climbing between the sheets. A bed that was all the lonelier for how he had held Seraphina the night before and woken with her in his arms. It was something he had never experienced in their tragically short marriage, and it was something he would never experience again.

His self-flagellation was blessedly halted in its tracks by a knock on the door. But his relief was short-lived when he recalled that the only person who would be knocking on that inside door was Seraphina.

He stared at it through the dark shadows of the room for a long moment, frozen, his heart beating heavy in his chest, even as he clutched the covers tighter over his lap, painfully aware that he wore nothing but a sheet. For a mad moment he considered not answering, feigning that he was asleep and did not hear. But she knocked again a minute later, and her husky voice called his name, and he could no more ignore her than he could fly to the moon on wings made of stardust.

"Come in," he called out, his voice harsh and rough in the deep quiet of the room. And then she turned the handle, and opened the door, and he knew that the past and the future did not matter. The only thing that mattered was right now, with Seraphina standing before him in her prim nightgown that nonetheless had him aching for her, with the entire world in her bright blue eyes.

Chapter 20

*T*here had been a moment when Seraphina had padded across the room that separated her bedroom from Iain's when she had faltered. What if he no longer wanted her? And if he did still want her, what if he could not accept her terms, that this was purely physical, that it meant nothing in the grand scheme of things, that it would be a simple night of mutual pleasure and nothing more?

But that moment of uncertainty had not lasted long, the pull of Iain too strong for her to resist. And when she opened his door to find him sitting up in the massive bed, chest bare, skin burnished, and eyes glittering in the faint firelight, looking at her as if he were a parched man and she the sweetest wine, any lingering doubt was extinguished. He wanted her just as desperately as she wanted him.

Even so, she knew in the one small corner of her brain that still possessed clarity that she had to lay all her cards out on the table before they could continue.

"You know why I am here?" she asked quietly, her hand squeezing the door handle with such force she was certain she would see the impression of her fingers in the metal in the morning.

"I have an idea, aye," he replied.

She swallowed hard. "And you also know this is purely physical? That it changes nothing? We shall still head on to Edinburgh to secure the divorce, will still separate when all this is over and done with."

There was the smallest of pauses as what looked to be pain flashed in his eyes. But it must be the shifting light from the fire in the hearth. He did not love her, and so could not feel pain that she did not want emotions involved.

"Aye," he finally replied, quieter now. "I understand."

"Also," she continued, "we shall do everything to prevent a pregnancy."

"Of course," he replied again.

"And you agree to those terms?" she continued, more forceful now, desperate to get this out of the way so she might lose herself in his embrace.

In answer, he threw the covers back, revealing his nakedness in all its glory. Her breath caught in her throat, her gaze roving hungrily over him as he swung his feet over the side of the bed and rose to his full height. Thickly corded muscles, a light dusting of hair across his broad chest, strong legs with feet planted wide. And at the center of it all, his member, standing thick and proud. Her knees went weak at the sight of it.

"Seraphina," he said, his voice gruff, almost a caress on her feverish skin, "I will have you any way I can, for as long as you will allow me, and be thankful for it."

A soft, needy sound escaped from her lips at that, and

before she knew it, she was hurrying across the floor to him. He opened his arms, catching her up against him, his mouth crashing down on hers before she had time to gasp at the feel of him fully aroused against her. Their tongues tangled, breaths mingling, lips in concert, as if this single kiss could help them each reclaim their souls. His skin was unbearably smooth and rough all at once, hard plains silky under coarse hair, and not a bit of cloth to impede her hands from exploring every inch of him. She had explored him some that morning when they had woken in bed together. But it was nothing like this, where she had free rein over unencumbered skin, knowing where these kisses were leading, aching for it.

His hands were not idle either, one large hand splaying across her lower back while the other worked at her night-gown, inching the worn material up, up, until his fingers found her thigh. But he did not stop there, and thank God he did not. No, his hand dipped beneath the cotton, cupping her bare behind, pressing her lower belly into his erection, as if to give proof to his desire for her.

She gasped as the heat between her legs turned molten, ripping her lips from his, her head falling back, the weight too great under the onslaught of his touches. He took it for the invitation it was, his mouth trailing along her neck, tongue and teeth working in concert on her sensitive skin. And then he leveraged his other hand beneath her bottom and lifted her, guiding her legs about his lean hips, his arousal pressing to that most sensitive place.

"Iain," she gasped. "I need you. Now."

He obeyed immediately, walking toward the bed with her wrapped about him, his mouth hungry on the curve where her neck met her shoulder. Each shift of his body had his cock rubbing against her, the thin cotton that separated them only making her wilder to feel him inside her. In the few steps it took to reach the bed, she was writhing against him, silently begging for more.

He lowered her to the coverlet with infinite care. With quick yet achingly gentle movements he removed her spectacles, then lifted her nightgown over her head, baring her to the cool night air. But he did not lower himself over her and slide between her legs, as she yearned for him to do. No, he stretched out beside her, his eyes fairly scorching her skin where they caressed her, his gaze intense and consuming.

"By the saints, Seraphina," he rasped. He reached out a hand then, trailing it over her skin, as light as a feather, leaving a trail of electricity in its wake. "You are beautiful."

And for the first time in forever, she felt beautiful. Not that she had given her looks much thought, or even cared about them, in the past years. Yet now, here with Iain, she wanted to be beautiful to him, to be desirable. She shivered, her back arching as his fingers, incredibly gentle for the strength in them, traced from her collarbone to her breast. Her nipple puckered, begging for his touch. But he seemed intent on dragging this out for all it was worth. The tip of his finger brushed against her nipple, drawing a lazy circle around it, widening the circle before coming back to her nipple again. And she felt every touch straight at the junction between her thighs.

Finally—finally!—he cupped his large palm around her breast and lowered his head, his mouth warm as he closed it around her nipple. A soft cry escaped Seraphina's lips, her hands finding and weaving into the soft curls of his overlong hair, as if she could bind him to her.

That simple, unconscious act seemed to unlock something in him. His movements became quicker, rougher, and she welcomed it. Each nip of his teeth on her skin sent her higher, each hard suck on her nipples making her press her legs together to try and ease the ache there. His hands skimmed down her rib cage to her hips, his grip on her urgent, massaging into her muscles as if he could not get close enough.

"Tell me what you want," he begged, lifting his head to gaze up at her with eyes that reflected the low fire in the hearth.

That desperate plea should not have touched her as it did. Yet knowing he was willing to give up power to her, that he wanted her to take the lead, made not only her body cry out, but her heart as well. Unable to speak, she did the only thing she could think to do: she took hold of his head, and guided it down her body to that place that needed him the most.

The fire in his eyes flared hot with realization before, with a wicked smile, he did as he was bid. Moving down her body, kissing a path down her stomach and over her hip, he eased her legs apart and settled between them. His shoulders were wide, spreading her open, and she felt at once wonderfully exposed and incredibly cherished as he gently dragged his fingertips over the thatch of curls at the juncture of her thighs. He parted the hair there with reverence, as if he were unearthing the greatest treasure, his breath caressing her. The breath caught in her throat as he paused. Then, with a suddenness that sent a sensation akin to a lightning bolt through her body, he lowered his mouth to her.

His tongue caressed her with long, smooth strokes, each

one sending her higher, higher, even as his fingers gripped tight to her hips, as if he feared she might pull away. But she was not about to end this, not while his mouth did such wickedly wonderful things, not while her body sang as it never had before. She reached out blindly, gripping tight to his head, her fingers anchoring in his hair as she pressed him more firmly into the center of her. He growled low, the sound vibrating through her as he dutifully increased the pressure of his mouth. There was no languid lapping of tongue. No, he became almost feral in his loving of her, sucking her into his mouth, his lips and teeth coming into play. And then his finger was there, at the entrance of her, and he eased it inside.

Crying out, Seraphina spread her legs wider, granting him further access, even as she began to rock against his mouth and hand. He groaned in approval, increasing his efforts, and she climbed higher again, shooting through the dark night sky, through the clouds and stars and past the moon before bursting in a shower of sparks and stardust.

In a moment he was beside her, pulling her into his arms, his ragged breathing in concert with her own. "My God, you're incredible," he gasped.

"You're pretty incredible yourself," she managed, even as she clung to him as if he were the only thing holding her to the earth. And perhaps he was.

As her heartbeat began to quiet and a lovely languidness spread through her limbs like warm honey, she relaxed against him, running her hand down his body, reveling in the way his skin, slick with sweat, jumped and trembled beneath her touch. Such strength and power in this man, and the fact that he was so affected by her mere touch was a heady thing.

When her hand brushed against that part of him that was even harder than before, and he very nearly jumped out of his skin, she grinned. She wrapped her fingers around him, and his low, guttural moan as his hips thrust into her hand brought back all the desire she'd felt for him and more.

"You dinnae have to," he gasped, even as he strained up for more of her touch. He threw his head back, the cords of his neck straining and his teeth bared as a hiss of breath escaped his lips. "I want you to enjoy the aftereffects of your pleasure."

"Oh, but this *will* give me pleasure," she purred. Feeling powerful, she pushed him onto his back and, in one smooth movement, straddled his hips.

"Ah, God, Seraphina," he groaned, staring up at her, eyes glittering in the shadows.

She smiled slowly, holding herself above his cock, allowing her wetness to just barely brush against its head. He gasped, and her smile widened.

"Do you wish me to take you inside, Iain?" she whispered.

"Yes." The one word came out on a croak, hot and desperate as his fingers clasped her thighs. "Please."

In answer she took him in hand and lowered herself down onto him. He filled her, inch by glorious inch, almost unbearably hard. She was tempted to throw her head back, to close her eyes, so she might focus on every breathtaking sensation of him stretching her.

Instead she kept her eyes focused on his face. She knew that seeing his reaction would be more potent than anything else. And it was. His face contorted, his mouth opening as short, sharp breaths escaped his lips, his brow knitted in concentration. But it was his eyes that held her captive, his gaze tangling like thread with hers, holding them bound to each other while simultaneously increasing their awareness of one another to an almost painful degree.

Finally he filled her to the hilt, hard and thick and hot. And then his cock twitched inside her, and she gasped.

"Ah, God, Seraphina," he groaned, his fingers clasping her hips, skimming up her rib cage, cupping her breasts. His gaze followed his hands, more potent on her than any touch could be. "Mo chridhe," he rasped.

Mo chridhe. *My heart.* Her own heart squeezed in her chest at the endearment. And then his eyes met hers again, and her entire body shivered with emotion.

Overwhelmed, she lowered her head and took his lips in a kiss, knowing if she continued to gaze into those eyes of his, which seemed to see her so clearly and promised her the world, she would cry. But it did not free her from the spell of him. In fact, it only did the opposite, holding her more firmly in thrall of him as he clasped her to him, hands cradling her face with aching tenderness. Unable to do anything else, she gripped tightly to his shoulders and began to move.

She was slow at first, letting her body adjust, getting used to the sensation after so long, setting the pace. Soon, however, sensation overtook her senses. Pleasure built, the feel of him inside her and beneath her, the low, rough sounds of pleasure that escaped from his chest, even as she continued to plunder his mouth with her tongue driving her wild. Soon she could not keep her mouth on his, her increased pace leaving her gasping, her entire focus shifting to that place where their bodies met. The pleasure wound tighter, more intense, until it coalesced into a shining pinpoint. And then she exploded around him.

Before the waves of pleasure left her, he had his hands

on her hips, flipping her onto her back, his cock still buried inside her. His hips thrust hard and fast, the tip of him hitting a new depth inside her, causing the ripples of pleasure to transform back into crashing waves of ecstasy. She clung to him like a limpet as he rode her, his breath hot on her neck. Just when she thought she felt she was drowning, that she would get lost in the churning surf of pleasure, his hand dipped between their bodies, rubbing against that most sensitive bud, and she broke free of the cloying water and into the golden sunlight.

In a moment he ripped free of her body and, with a strangled groan, spent himself in the sheets. Before she could regain her senses he was there beside her again, pulling her into his arms. She went willingly, curling around him, the tremors of her own release mingling with his. And as, exhausted, she closed her eyes, the last thing she became aware of before she drifted into a blessedly dreamless sleep was the heavy beat of his heart and his ragged breathing in her ear, the most wonderful lullaby.

Chapter 21

*I*ain had stayed awake as long as he was able, certain
Seraphina would be gone when he awoke. He no longer
had any disillusionment that this was anything but temporary and was now only determined to enjoy whatever time
he could claim with her.

What he did not expect when he opened his eyes to the
dawn of a new day, however, was to find Seraphina still
secure in his arms.

He gazed down at her for a moment, allowing himself
to study her as she would never allow him to while awake.
Her features were relaxed, the almost permanent divot
between her brows smoothed out, her mouth slightly parted
in repose. The freckles across the bridge of her nose were
more pronounced in the golden morning light, lending a
vulnerability to her that she would no doubt vehemently
deny were she awake. And her lashes, those impossibly
long lashes, kissed the faint blush that stained her high

cheekbones. Unable to keep from touching her, he traced a finger down her temple, catching a stray auburn curl with his finger and tucking it behind her ear.

Her lashes fluttered then, like a butterfly's wing, rising to reveal the clear sapphire of her eyes. She blinked several times as she gazed up at him, and he braced himself for her reaction. No doubt she would pull away, the barrier between them back in place.

Instead she smiled. And his heart, which had already been on the road to falling back in love with her, completed the journey.

"Good morning," she murmured.

"Good morning," he replied. "Did you sleep well?"

"Mmmm, yes."

The sound she made was erotic enough, especially said in that husky voice of hers that he felt straight to his toes. But she gave a little stretch, arching against him, her leg rubbing between his and fairly melting his bones from the heat that scorched him.

"Lass," he choked out, rubbing his hand over the silky-smooth skin of the arm she had wrapped around his waist, "if you continue to do that, you shall not be leaving this bed anytime soon."

She stilled, and he cursed his loose tongue for ruining the moment. No matter how delicious this was, last night was all there would be between them; he had best get that through his thick skull.

But she shocked him by smiling and dipping her hand beneath the sheets. Her slender fingers wrapped around his quickly hardening cock.

"Perhaps I wouldn't mind that so very much," she replied softly. "Would you?"

"God no," he groaned before his mouth found hers.

This was no slow rediscovery. It was fast, and hard, and not at all graceful. Hands fumbling, kisses clumsy and quick, their bodies were more than ready as he slid between her thighs. He entered her in one swift, smooth motion, their breaths hissing from their lips in mutual satisfaction. He felt as if he was claiming something taboo, a moment that should not have been, a gift that he should have never received. And yet it was all the more precious for it. She wrapped her legs about his waist, tilting her hips, drawing him farther in, and he shuddered at just how deeply and totally he was inside her. Would that he could take his time, that he could focus on remembering every kiss and caress.

But with her hot whispers in his ear, her hungry hands roaming his body and encouraging him to ride her harder, faster, he could do little else but succumb. And when her inner muscles tightened about him as she found her release, only to be replaced by her hands as she pushed him from her sated body and rolled him onto his back to pump him to completion, he gave himself up to it, and gladly.

That soul-shattering ecstasy, however, was not to be held on to. Even as he reached for her to pull her back into his arms, a sudden muffled squawking started up, coming from Seraphina's bedroom. Phineas, awake and looking for attention.

"The damn pigeon," he groaned as Seraphina, having heard the call of her pet, quickly rose from the bed and gathered up her nightgown, further increasing his torment as her delectable body was hidden from view.

But no matter how sated he might be, or how morose he was watching her slip on her spectacles and smooth down her hair as she headed for the damned parrot, none of that mattered when, reaching the door and pulling it open, she turned back to him with a small, intimate smile that had his body stirring to life once more.

"I know we did not intend for things to go beyond what we shared last night," she said, even as her hot gaze roved over him naked in the bed. "But I do think this morning proves there is still a bit more of a particular scratch we need to itch. And as we still have one more night before we reach Edinburgh, would you be open to—"

"Yes," he replied before she could finish what she was going to ask. "God yes."

Her smile widened, filled with promise. "Well then. I'll leave you to dress and pack and shall see you in a bit." And with that she was out the door. And Iain leapt from the bed, more eager for the day than he could remember being in too many long, lonely years.

* * *

"Tell me about your circulating library."

Seraphina glanced up at Iain, who was walking at her side along the pale sand beach near Dunbar, their afternoon stop on the way to Haddington. "The Quayside?"

"Aye." He picked up a small rock, lobbing it out over the waves. "I wish to hear all about it. It is nae small feat, opening such an establishment."

A sudden self-consciousness overcame her. "Nonsense," she replied brusquely. "If I can do it, anyone can. It just took a bit of determination."

"And hard work, and daring, and strength of character," he added, his lips quirking as he gazed down at her.

Seraphina's awkwardness increased at the admiring look, her cheeks warming uncomfortably. "You give me too much credit."

"Nae," he said, his voice soft and gentle. "I daresay you do nae give yourself enough. Now, tell me about this Quayside of yours."

She shrugged. "I needed a stable income to support my sisters, and when we arrived on the Isle of Synne I took a position at the local circulating library. But it was a pathetic thing, with an owner who did not care if it failed or not. When she saw my passion for it, she offered to sell the place to me. I knew I could not pass up such a chance, so I agreed and turned it into the Quayside it is today. It has been mine and my sisters' ever since."

"Such a venture cannae have been easy." Iain's voice took on a different cadence, a sharp interest coating his words, his gaze equally sharp on her profile. "It must have taken quite a healthy bit of capital."

That, finally, made her smile, and not only for the sudden businesslike mien he had adopted. No, the remembrance of just where that capital had come from had her smiling as well.

"I was lucky in that," she replied. "I, of course, did not have nearly enough funds to purchase it, but when Lady Tesh, a permanent resident and the self-proclaimed matriarch of the Isle, heard of the possible change of hands she approached me. She offered to put up the rest of the funds, if I supplied the unmarried women of Synne certain periodicals to...educate them in subjects often lacking in female education."

He blinked. "Subjects of an...intimate nature, I assume?"

She grinned. "You assume correctly. Lady Tesh is of the

opinion that a woman can better protect herself in life if she has the proper tools. As it is an opinion I share, we made a partnership that has become lucrative for both of us."

Iain returned her grin. "She sounds like quite the woman."

"Oh, she certainly is."

"And so you have this Lady Tesh for a patroness. And you are friends with a duchess."

"Two duchesses, actually. And I am acquainted with several others." She chuckled at the absurdity of it, urging Phineas down from her shoulder, stroking a finger over his bright green back. "It is funny, isn't it, that I have not been able to completely escape that world, no matter how hard I tried to?"

He did not speak for some time as they walked on, side by side. Finally, he asked, "Do you ever regret leaving that life behind?"

Without meaning to, a laugh burst free from her lips. "God no. I'm heartily glad I left. I would never wish to return to it. Ever."

"I had thought perhaps your friends would have changed your mind about returning to the aristocracy."

Again a laugh bubbled free. "I assure you, Lady Tesh is a mere outlier. And while I am happy that my friends have found happiness with their dukes, I would not ever want to have those societal strictures on my life again. I'm happy, and independent. What need have I for a title and all the rules that come with it? No, I'm glad I left it all behind."

He was quiet again, an almost heaviness in the silence. When she looked up at him, he was gazing at her with a somberness that stunned her.

"Iain?"

"You are amazing, Seraphina."

Well, that was certainly unexpected. Flustered, she returned Phineas to her shoulder. "Nonsense."

"It is not nonsense. You are amazing." He took her hand and squeezed her fingers. "You have built this incredible life from nothing. You have a successful business, good friends, your sisters are safe. You should be proud of all you have accomplished. I know I am."

She stared at him, struck mute. While her sisters had always been vocal in their gratitude, she had shrugged it aside. She had not done it for their gratitude; she had done it to give them decent lives. And she saw now that it had been in no small part because she had felt she'd owed it to them. Though she did not doubt that what she had done in absconding with them from their father's home had been right, she had felt guilty for taking them from lives where they had not had to worry about money or a roof over their heads or food in their bellies.

The pride shining in Iain's eyes and threading through his words, however, affected her in ways she could not have ever imagined, the emotions overwhelming her. Overcome, needing to change the subject before she lost her composure altogether, she tried ignoring the new glow in her chest, even as she cleared her throat and extracted her fingers from his. "But enough about me," she said firmly. "Why don't we talk about you. You mentioned you had found family?"

The question did what she had wanted, in that it effectively distracted Iain from her. But his response was much stronger than she had intended. He halted in his tracks, his shock palpable. She remembered then his reaction when he had mentioned it before. He had appeared dismayed, and she had not pursued it, telling herself he would tell her when and if he was ready.

Now, however, with the new intimacy between them she found she had the deep and insistent need to know how he had found them, what they were like, where they had been during all his years of loneliness. And, most importantly, that he would not be alone when they parted.

If only they never had to. The rogue thought burst through her mind, rebelling against her certainty that they could never be together. She focused on all the reasons why this closeness must be temporary between them: her business, which she had worked so hard to build; the life she had with her sisters; the horrible, awful secrets she could never share with him. But those reasons were growing dimmer with each moment she spent with him.

Blessedly he spoke then, effectively stopping the traitorous thoughts in their tracks.

"You dinnae wish to know about them," he replied gruffly, reaching down and yanking a long piece of grass from the thick tuft at his feet, tearing it into long strips that he let the wind carry away.

Seraphina, shaken from her moment of weakness, reached up and scratched behind Phineas's neck as he leaned against the side of her head. Of course they would still complete this divorce and go their separate ways. She was not a gambler like him, would not take a chance on a whim. She had a safe, steady life to return to. This trip changed nothing.

"Actually," she finally replied when she realized she had stayed quiet for far too long, "I would very much like to know about your family." When he remained silent, looking out over the white sand beach to the churning sea beyond, thankfully oblivious to the strange moment of uncertainty she'd had, she decided a bit of prodding was in order. "You mentioned a grandmother and a cousin?"

His lips quirked in reluctant amusement as he cast her a sideways glance. "You willnae give up on it, will you?"

She smiled. "What do you think?"

He chuckled, a rough sound, though not nearly as rough and unused as it had been when he had first arrived on Synne. No, now it fit him, like broken-in boots, comfortable and absolutely perfect.

"Verra well," he replied. "But let us get comfortable." With that he removed his jacket, laying it on the ground, and helped her to sit on it.

And Seraphina, who never put any stock in gallantry of any kind, felt cherished by the care he took in getting her settled. To her further shock, she actually enjoyed the attention. Why? She was strong and independent. She didn't care for such things; they invariably came with the caveat that something else was expected, some stroke of the man's ego or simpering on the woman's part. Or worse.

Yet that didn't stop the glow of warmth in her chest as he finished making certain she was comfortable and sat beside her.

"So you wish to know about my grandmother and cousin, do you?" he asked quietly, once more looking out to the waves. Seraphina studied his profile, her gaze tracing the strong-but-crooked line of his nose, proof of a break or two in his youth; at the stubborn jut of his chin with the faintest hint of beard showing; at the lines bracketing his mouth and eyes, lines that had not been there thirteen years ago. And she realized he had never been more handsome or more dear to her.

She cleared her throat, shaken by the realization, and

lowered Phineas to her skirts to distract herself from such thoughts. Thoughts she had no business thinking. She and Iain would part tomorrow, after all.

Tomorrow. It suddenly seemed so very close. Too close.

"Yes," she replied, perhaps louder than was warranted. "Tell me everything. How did you find them after so long? Where were they? Why were you never told of them? Are they from your mother's or your father's side? What are they like?"

He chuckled again, and the sound filled her up. "You have a good many questions for me to answer, lass. Verra well. Where do I start?"

"At the beginning would be a good place," she replied. "Specifically with your parents, and whose side these relations are from."

"Aye." He stretched his legs out and leaned back on his hands. The green-and-blue plaid of his kilt spread over his lap, brilliant against the pale sand and washed-out greens and browns of the tall grasses. "They are my father's kin—his mother, and his brother's child. All that is left of that particular branch of the family."

His lips twisted, but not in humor. No, pain was threaded through it, like the bands of ironstone seams in the brittle shale cliff walls back on Synne. "It seems the MacInnes family has experienced its share of bad luck since my father up and left, cutting off all contact with them. Sickness took two of his brothers before they could marry, infection from a burn took another. There have been all manner of accidents that took the rest. Almost an entire clan wiped out in a matter of just over three decades."

"Oh, your poor grandmother," she murmured.

She expected him to agree. Instead he appeared surprised,

as if he had not considered it. "Yes, I suppose so," he replied, his eyes going distant, a small divot forming between his brows.

In the next instant his frown deepened, as if to banish whatever kind thoughts he'd had for that woman. "Though if she had bothered to look for me or my father, she would have had me to comfort her, wouldn't she?"

Seraphina's heart ached at the anger simmering in him. It was only too obvious that he was incredibly, painfully angry toward the woman he called grandmother. She could not blame him, not truly. From the many secret, heartfelt talks they'd shared when they were young, she knew how much it had pained him to think he was alone in the world.

But while she had never known Iain's father, she had heard something of him. Iain had been shunned in the nearby village because of him, a man who had wreaked enough havoc that it had polluted his son when he'd gone to his Maker. A man who had done nothing for his child but left a stained, lonely legacy. And as anger filled her up for what he had stolen from Iain—a parent's job was to protect their children, protection that had been painfully lacking in her childhood as well—she realized that maybe, just maybe, Iain wasn't truly angry at his grandmother. No, maybe his anger was for his father, but he felt he was betraying the memory of the only family he had known in his youth by admitting as much, even to himself.

She placed a hand on his arm, and he looked at it, startled, as if he had forgotten she was there. "Tell me why your father left his mother's home."

"My father?" He frowned. "To hear my cousin, Cora, explain it, he had a falling-out with his father regarding his excesses. Namely an addiction to laudanum after requiring it for a particularly painful broken bone as a young man."

It was something she had seen often enough in those first years on the run from her father, a malady particularly prevalent in the slums and gutters, the call of the poppy so powerful people destroyed everything else in their lives to get it.

"And do you believe Cora?" she asked quietly.

His frown deepened. "I dinnae ken." His voice had taken on a thicker brogue in his agitation. She shifted closer to him, leaning against his arm, a silent comfort should he need it.

His reaction was instantaneous, his arm stealing about her to bring her even closer. "I suppose it makes sense," he admitted hesitantly, as if her presence alone had given him the courage to face what he had been too fearful to acknowledge before now. "He was always so erratic, in temperament and attention, disappearing for days at a time, leaving me with his landlady when I was younger and, when I was older, leaving me to fend for myself. Then there were the times he lay insensible in his bed, and I could nae rouse him nae matter what I did."

Ah, God, her heart broke for that boy. She leaned her head on his shoulder. Even Phineas, who had until then been quietly sitting in her lap picking at a stray thread in her bodice, waddled over to sit on Iain's leg, as if attempting to offer comfort.

"He did the best he could for me," Iain continued. But his voice lacked conviction, a thread of sound trying to find purchase in the faint breeze coming in off the sea. "I cannae vilify him. He was still my father."

She was quiet a moment, gathering her thoughts. And

then she said, "Yes, he was your father, and he did the best he could under the circumstances. I cannot imagine that raising a child on your own after your spouse dies is easy."

She raised her head and looked him steadily in the eye. "However, speaking as someone whose father failed her horribly, I can say that sometimes the best someone can do for their child is not the best that child deserves. And you did deserve so much more. It is not a betrayal to admit that your father should have made certain you received all that you deserved, whether that was with him or someone else."

He remained silent, and for a moment she thought she had gone too far. But then he rested his head against hers and sighed. "That, to my immense frustration, makes entirely too much sense."

She smiled. "How that must bruise your pride to admit."

"Oh, aye," he agreed readily enough. And to her relief there was a smile in his voice.

"But we digress," he continued, straightening away from her, letting his arm fall, and Seraphina tried not to think how the simple act of him pulling away had her feeling the loss of him. "You wished to ken more of this newly found family of mine. Upon the death of her last son, my grandmother went in search of my father, that son she hadnae seen in nearly four decades. And while she quickly learned he was nae longer living, she also learned he had been married for a short time, and that my mother had died in childbirth, and she went in search of me. And a year ago she found me." He shrugged, as if it was a simple-enough thing, something that happened every day.

She turned to gape at him. "But don't you see how extraordinary this all is, Iain? You thought you were alone all those years. Now you have a family."

Again he paused. Though this time when he glanced her way there was deep emotion in his eyes. "But I was nae alone," he murmured. "Nae when I had you in my life."

"Oh." The breath left her, and she felt as if a thread had been pulled behind her navel, yanking her back into her moment of doubt that she was doing the right thing in staying the course of their trip.

"But enough of this," he continued, even as she attempted to find purchase in the midst of the painfully familiar emotions flowing through her. "We'd best be heading back to the carriage."

With that he encouraged Phineas to return to her lap. Then, rising, he held a hand down for her. She stared at it a moment, remembering the feel of it on her body. Gathering up Phineas, she reached up and allowed Iain to help her to standing.

But even with her feet securely under her in the sand, the next moment she was set completely off-balance.

Iain, his fingers still firmly clasped about her own, cupped her cheek with his free hand. Before she knew what he was about, he bent his head and took her lips in a tender kiss, one light as the breeze that caressed her skin yet powerful enough to steal the very breath from her body. He gazed down at her, his eyes searching her face, and for a moment she thought he wanted to say something more. Something that, to him, was incredibly important.

But then Phineas, who had been silently watching the whole interaction from his perch on her shoulder, chirped loud and spoke up.

"Ye wee Eejit!"

Which effectively distracted Iain from whatever it was he'd wanted to say. Damn it.

He blinked before, giving Phineas a wry smile, he pulled back, letting the cool breeze blowing in off the ocean to chill the space between his body and Seraphina's. Then, retrieving his coat from the ground, he held out his arm. Seraphina took it, and without a word, they began to make their way back up the pale beach.

Chapter 22

The sky had been clear and cloudless when they had retired to their room at the inn in Haddington—they had not even attempted to procure separate rooms this time, both eager for what was to come—the setting sun sending blooms of watercolor hues to splash across the heavens. It had been the perfect accompaniment to the passion that had exploded between them, heralding them into that long night, where they had expressed with touch and kiss what they could not say aloud.

When Iain opened his eyes the next morning, however, the sky outside the large window was heavy and gray, rain dotting the glass pane. As if it sensed what the day was to bring and wept for them.

Seraphina was still curled against his side, as she had been the last two mornings. And as she would never be again. Holding her a bit tighter, he closed his eyes and breathed in deeply, taking the time to memorize the achingly familiar lavender scent of her, the softness of her skin, the way she fit so perfectly against his side it was as if she had been made expressly for him.

He had begun to hope, despite her having insisted that what was between them was merely physical, that she was beginning to change her mind and she might wish to have a future with him at her side. There could be no denying that they had regained some of the closeness they'd had when young. No, he corrected himself, this was no mere echo of what had been. This was something new, with a maturity and understanding of grief that they'd not had before. This was a tempering through fire, coming out stronger on the other side for it. If given a chance, it could be enduring.

But after their conversation yesterday, he knew that any chance for them was so slim as to be nonexistent. She would never wish to rejoin the aristocracy. And his life was forevermore entwined with it, as much as he despised that fact.

But he was spiraling in self-pity, when he should only be focusing on the here and now. There was precious little time left as it was and no sense in worrying about the future. He would survive their separation, just as he had survived it before. At least this time he knew what was coming and could say his goodbyes. Determined to soak in every second he could, he opened his eyes—only to find her looking up at him.

They gazed at one another for a long moment, eyes roving over one another's faces, as if to memorize them. Then, without a word, she slid her hand to the nape of his neck and pulled him to her.

Not a word was spoken, not a sound in that quiet room save for the twin rasp of their breathing and quiet gasps and the faint patter of rain on the glass. He slid over her, between her legs, his hips fitting into the cradle between her thighs, as if he had always belonged there. And as if he always would. Her hands, with her clever, graceful fingers, clasped his head, even as she kissed him as if he were the very air she needed to breathe. When she wrapped her long legs about his hips and urged him within her, he wasted no time, sinking into her ready warmth. They moved together in an age-old dance, their bodies rocking in perfect rhythm, faster, faster, the pleasure building until she came around him. Before the echoes of her soft cries of completion had faded away, he pulled himself from her, spending in the sheets.

He pulled her back into his arms, their labored breathing mingling. Unlike the previous morning, however, when the whole day and next night spread ahead of them with promise, there was no such insulation for them today. He was all too aware of what was to come in mere hours, that separation he had wanted so desperately just days ago but now was the very thing he dreaded most in this world.

She must have sensed that end as well, for there was no languid relaxing against him as their bodies came down from the heavens. No, there was only a vague kind of tension, which grew in intensity with each passing second. He suddenly could not stand the thought of her pulling away from him, watching her go about the day as if they weren't leaving something infinitely precious behind them in this bed. He knew he had a choice to make: to rip his pride to shreds and beg her to stay with him, or to begin the leaving himself.

But as he froze, stuck between the two decisions like a fox caught in a snare, Seraphina was busy making it for him.

"We'd best prepare for our departure," she murmured, pulling away from him. "The sooner we reach Edinburgh the sooner the both of us can get on with our lives."

As she left him alone in the bed, walking away from him without even a glance back, he felt quite literally as if she had taken his heart with her.

* * *

For how silent and tense the last leg to Edinburgh had been, it surprised Seraphina how quickly the time had flown.

Her lips twisted as she peered out the carriage window. Of course, when one dreaded what was to come, the time leading up to it was all the more precious. And all the shorter for it.

They came to a bright-green-fronted inn and turned slowly into the yard. Several people stood back to allow them to pass, including a dark-haired woman with her arm tucked through the arm of a frail, elderly woman. The younger one glanced briefly at the carriage and started violently, then returned her gaze to peer inside. Just as Seraphina caught her eye, Iain, seated across the carriage from her, shifted in his seat and cleared his throat.

"I'll secure a pair of rooms and send a letter on to the Lord President at the Court of Sessions to establish a meeting with him at his earliest convenience," he said, low and tense. "I dinnae see a problem with him being able to see us later this afternoon."

The strange woman already forgotten, Seraphina began busily gathering up her things, the better to distract herself from the volatile emotions churning in her stomach. "I don't require a room," she replied in as even a voice as she was able. "If you would be so kind as to secure a seat for me on the next mail coach, I'll begin the return journey to Synne later today. If I leave in time, I can make it back to Haddington by nightfall. I'm eager to return to my sisters as quickly as possible."

Even in her busyness she felt the weight of Iain's eyes on her. "You would return this verra day?" he asked quietly.

"Yes. Like I've said before. I have a business to return to. The sooner I return the better."

There was a heavy sigh across the carriage as she opened Phineas's cage door. And then Iain spoke, his voice solemn. "Verra well. But I shall hire a private carriage for you." In a tone that tried for lightness but failed miserably, he added, "I dinnae think your pigeon would care for company on your journey."

Throat thick, she nodded. "You have our thanks."

The door to the carriage swung open then, and a groom stood waiting to help her alight. Needing to get away from Iain before she threw herself in his arms and asked him to forget everything she had said and that she wanted to be with him, she hurried to the cobbled courtyard, Phineas perched on her shoulder.

"I'll just take a short walk while you secure your room and write that letter," she said once Iain had descended behind her. "I'll meet you back here, shall I?" Without waiting for a reply, she tucked her reticule against her side and hurried through the busy yard to the bustling street beyond.

But there was no respite from the turmoil inside her. As she walked blindly down the street, a strange, horrible panic rose up in her, making it hard to breathe, hard to think. How could she go through with this? How could she stand before the judge and declare the one piece of information, that she was alive and well, that would separate her from Iain for all eternity? And funny enough—not that there was anything remotely funny about any of this— her fear was no longer that her father might learn that she had resurfaced. No, her sole fear just then was losing Iain.

Though he was already lost, wasn't he? Even if, by some chance, she listened to that voice from yesterday and refused the divorce and claimed a future with Iain, how could she ever be truly honest with him about her past? How could she possibly tell him about her time in the asylum, or what she had done to survive in the years after running off with her sisters? God, she could not handle him looking at her any different, at him pitying her or, worse, looking at her in disgust. No, better that she part from him on her own terms and remain unaltered in his mind.

Even before she completed the thought the rebellious voice returned, louder and more insistent, stomping over all her arguments, attempting to crush them to dust. Hadn't she lived with her sisters for years without revealing the truth? It could be done. Surely she could do the same with Iain as well.

With incredible will she fought back against that line of thinking. She could not live that way for the rest of her life. And neither should Iain. He didn't deserve a wife who would keep secrets from him.

But perhaps she didn't need to. The idea was like a spark in dry brush, cleansing, burning down old ways of thinking. Perhaps she was thinking like her younger self, the one who'd had status and reputation practically beat into her. She was no longer an earl's daughter. She and Iain were both of equal social footing, with no hint of a title hanging over their heads. Perhaps they were meant to have found one another at this point in their lives, to take this trip together, to learn the truth about their separation and heal. They had been given another chance to claim the future that had been stolen from them, but as equals this time.

Against her will, that small hope took hold of her, like the roots of the resilient trees on Synne's craggy cliffs, and it would not let go. Mayhap she had been overthinking it all along. There truly was no great disparity in their stations any longer. They could live a quiet life together, and finally claim some happiness for themselves. And if she did confide the truth of her past to him, who could it possibly affect but the two of them? Surely they could weather it as long as they had each other.

No sooner had the thought washed over her than she spun about on the pavement, determined to return to Iain and see where this new recklessness brought her, brought *them*. Before she had taken a step, however, she came too close to a pedestrian, jarring the package in their arm, sending it to the pavement.

"Oh goodness," she babbled, even as she bent down to retrieve the bundle. "I'm so very sorry."

Whatever else she might have said, however, stalled on her lips as she rose to hand the package back and met the startled eye of the same dark-haired woman she had seen from the carriage window.

But Seraphina's typical raging curiosity, which would have had her attempting to learn why the woman had reacted so strangely to seeing their carriage, was nearly nonexistent now in the face of her determination to return to Iain. Until the woman said, in a breathless voice, "You were with Iain in the carriage."

Seraphina froze. This woman knew Iain? And knew him well if she was using his given name with such familiarity.

"Y-yes, that was me," she replied, tripping over the words in her confusion.

The other woman took her in from the top of her head to the tips of her half boots and everything in between, especially Phineas, whom she eyed with a healthy dose of trepidation.

"And how do you know my cousin?"

"Cousin," Seraphina breathed, her confusion turning to shock. Of all the people in all of Scotland for her to literally run into, for it to be Iain's newly found family was too amazing to comprehend.

"Yes," the woman replied with a delicate, lilting brogue that nonetheless betrayed her disquiet. "But forgive me for not introducing myself. I am Miss Cora MacInnes. My grandmother is in that shop just there, or I would introduce her as well. And you are?"

There was so much more than a request for Seraphina's name in that simple three-word question. She wondered what Iain might have told his family about her, if anything. Out of an abundance of caution for the future she hoped to share with him, she held out her hand and said only, "I am Miss Seraphina Athwart. An old friend of Iain's."

But there was no recognition in the woman's eyes. Not that she thought Iain might have told his cousin about her. From all accounts he had thoroughly despised Seraphina in the thirteen years since they'd parted. And besides, he'd only had his family in his life for the past year; why would he tell them about the woman who'd been out of his life for longer than she'd been in it?

"And this is Phineas," she continued, motioning to the parrot.

The woman nodded, her cautious gaze once more on

Phineas. "A strange companion," she murmured. "I wonder you do not worry about him flying away."

"He's quite tame and well-behaved," Seraphina replied.

Which, of course, was the perfect time for Phineas to look at Iain's cousin and say, loud and clear, "Ye scabby bawbag."

Seraphina closed her eyes and groaned. Of all the times to call a person a scrotum. There was not a noise from Miss MacInnes, and for a moment Seraphina thought she might have perhaps gotten so offended she'd up and left without a word of goodbye. For the life of her, she didn't know which would mortify her more: seeing the woman still standing there, or knowing she'd been so insulted she'd left.

In the end she forced her eyes open—only to see Miss MacInnes appearing for all the world as if she were trying her damnedest not to laugh.

"That is…" Miss MacInnes cleared her throat and tried again, even as her eyes danced with mirth. "That is quite the pet you have there."

"Yes," Seraphina muttered, casting a dark glance to where Phineas sat on her shoulder. That traitor leaned forward and peered at her with one much-too-innocent eye. "He is something else." What that something else was, however, she didn't know.

"But I've never heard a bird speak with a Scottish brogue," Miss MacInnes said. "In fact, I don't believe I've ever heard a bird speak. But while he sounds Scottish, you most assuredly do not. You are English?"

"Yes."

Seraphina saw the questions in the woman's eyes: mainly how her cousin knew an Englishwoman with a parrot that spoke with a Scottish brogue, and why he was traveling with said woman to Edinburgh. She braced herself for a barrage of questions—only God knew what conclusion she had come to. She nearly laughed at that rogue thought, a wild, uncontrolled laugh. Whatever the woman came up with, it could be no more outrageous than the truth.

But at the last minute the woman's eyes clouded, her lips pressing tight, the humor from before gone.

"Well, it was lovely to meet you," Miss MacInnes said, her tone much more subdued than before. "Please do give my cousin our regards." And with that, she turned to head into the small shop she'd indicated her grandmother was in.

It should not have surprised Seraphina that the woman was so cold where Iain was concerned. Iain himself had appeared almost angry when he'd spoken of his family. It was all too obvious that their relationship was one of deep strife.

Yet it was the flash of pain in Miss MacInnes's eyes that made her realize his relatives did not necessarily wish for the estrangement between them. She recalled what Iain had told her, of the pain this family had gone through in the past decades, so much loss and grief. It was all there in Miss MacInnes's eyes, in her voice, in the slope of her shoulders.

Before Seraphina knew what she was about, she called out to the woman.

"Perhaps you might like to accompany me back to the inn to give your regards to him yourself."

The woman stopped in her tracks, causing one older gentleman to stumble and glare at her as he moved past. But Miss MacInnes paid him no heed. Turning and peering at Seraphina, she was silent for a moment before saying, her voice thick, "I don't believe Iain would welcome that, Miss Athwart."

Which was quite possibly true. Even so, she could not allow this opportunity to pass. She was not one for believing in a higher power, of course, or in fate. She believed one had to make what they could of one's life, that there was no one on heaven or earth who could intervene. Her time in the asylum had taught her that. And then after, when it had been her, and her alone, who had done everything she could to save her sisters. No, she did not believe there was anyone looking out for her but herself.

Even so, she could not deny that her meeting Miss MacInnes in the street was too coincidental. Certainly too coincidental for her to pass up this chance to reconcile them. Perhaps this would be just the thing to heal Iain, a gift of sorts, before they began a life together.

Moving closer to the young woman, Seraphina said with all the certainty of her conviction that this was the right thing to do, "I do believe that you accompanying me back to that inn could be a much-needed turning point in your relationship, Miss MacInnes."

The woman considered Seraphina for a solemn moment before giving a reluctant nod. "Perhaps you're right, Miss Athwart. And it would do my grandmother good to repair our relationship with Iain. I'll go fetch her then, shall I?"

Before the woman could so much as move, however, the door to the shop opened and the elderly woman appeared, a footman trailing behind her. The woman's eyes widened when she saw Seraphina, her gaze tripping in agitation to her granddaughter before returning to Seraphina. She truly was a frail-looking thing, her skin translucent, her limbs painfully thin, her shoulders stooped, as if the weight of the grief of the past decades had been too much for her to bear. Seraphina's heart ached for her.

But at the same time an unease had taken up residence in her chest. She had not fully noticed Miss MacInnes's elegant attire before, as distracted as she had been to get back to Iain. But the older woman's appearance made Seraphina realize that these women were of the upper class. It had been a good many years since she had worn such expensive clothing herself, but she had been schooled in proper attire practically since birth, and she would not ever forget it. No, what these women wore was something above the common man or woman, with a quiet luxury that spoke of a striking wealth.

"Gran," Miss MacInnes said, voice gentle as she moved to her grandmother's side and tucked an arm through hers, oblivious to Seraphina's sudden disquiet, "I would like to introduce you to Miss Seraphina Athwart. And her pet, Phineas, of course," she finished with a small smile Seraphina's way.

"And Miss Athwart," she continued as Seraphina looked on with a growing dread, drawing the older woman closer to Seraphina, "it is my honor to introduce you to my and Iain's grandmother, the Duchess of Balgair."

Chapter 23

Seraphina felt as if all the air had been sucked out of her lungs. The Duchess of Balgair? Surely the woman must be jesting. Iain would have never left something of this magnitude out. If this woman, his father's mother, was a duchess, it meant Iain was...

A duke.

"I-I'm sorry?" she asked, certain her ears had been playing a trick on her. Iain had been a poor orphan. There was no way in heaven or on earth he was a duke.

"The Duchess of Balgair," Miss MacInnes repeated, shooting a slightly bewildered look at her grandmother.

Dear God, it had not been her imagination. Seraphina's stomach lurched, and for a horrifying moment she thought she would cast up her accounts. He was a duke. Which meant that every consolation she'd had about their similar low status had been nothing but smoke and mirrors, the mere wishes of a foolish woman. Yes, there was still a title between them. Though this time it was so much worse. It had been one thing for the daughter of an earl to marry an orphan. It was quite another for a former prostitute to marry a *duke*.

But the women were looking at her in expectation. Swallowing down the bile that rose in her throat, she forced a smile and curtsied. "Your Grace, it is a pleasure to make your acquaintance."

Which seemed the right and normal thing to do—truly a miracle for the turmoil Seraphina was in. Miss MacInnes's smile widened as she turned to speak to her grandmother. "Miss Athwart is an old friend of Iain's. She suggested we accompany her back to the inn to visit with him."

Which suddenly seemed like the worst idea in the history of the world. Dear God, she was barely holding herself together as it was. If she had to stand silently by while Iain met with his family, while he came to the realization that she had learned his secret and now knew he was a bloody duke, she would break.

But no, she was made of sterner stuff than that. And besides, no matter that he had omitted the immense fact that he was a duke all this time, the truth of the matter was, even in the shock of the moment she understood why he had done it. He had been determined to secure their divorce and had believed only the worst of her. He had been led to believe she had left him because of his lowly status by her own father. To his mind, proclaiming he was a duke— which meant, dear God, that she was a duchess, but she could not contemplate that right now—could have endangered that.

In his mind at least. She would have never given a bloody damn that he was a duke. In fact, it would have propelled her to agree to his request for a divorce all the quicker. She did not want to be a *duchess*. All she wanted, all she'd ever wanted, was a quiet, safe life with her sisters. Being a duchess would have put that all into peril, pinning her under a magnifying lens, endangering everything she had worked so hard for. It would have brought to light every horrible thing that had happened to her, laying it out for the whole world to see, including those beloved sisters who she had spent nearly a decade and a half shielding from the worst that life had to offer. No, she would never have wanted to be a duchess.

Bile rose in her throat. Which was a bit of horrible, cruel irony, as those were the very things that prevented her from remaining married to him. Her whole reasoning for staying with him had been that they could live a simple, quiet life together. But with Iain being a duke, there was no way that could happen now. The brilliant dreams she'd dared to dream just minutes ago evaporated into the air, not a trace of them left for her to clasp onto.

But the two women were looking at her in expectation. Drawing herself to her full height, taking on a mantle of calm she did not feel, she did as she had always done and kept on the course. No matter that they must see this separation through—now more than ever—she found she still cared for his future happiness.

"If you're amenable," she said, "I can bring you to see him right now."

The duchess's eyes lit with a combination of hope and uncertainty. But in the end she nodded, and Seraphina, falling into step beside the two women, led the way back to Iain and, hopefully, a bit of healing for this family. Though there could be no such healing for her.

* * *

Iain, settled in his room at the inn, the letter to the Lord President written and sent off, paced as he waited with equal parts anticipation and dread for word that Seraphina had returned. While he was anxious to have her by his side again and felt somehow incomplete without her near, he also knew that when she did arrive it would only be to wait for word that they could depart for the Court of Sessions and end things between them. Not only that, but it would finally be time to reveal to her who he was, and what he had kept from her all this time, first out of spite, then out of a need for her to want him for himself and not for his blasted title—a fat lot of good that had done him. She didn't want him at all, at least not in any permanent aspect. And he knew she would hate him for keeping it from her, just as he hated himself.

But where had she gone? She had appeared almost brittle when she'd left, and it had taken everything in him not to take hold of her and beg her to stay with him and ask her to reconsider this whole blasted scheme. His steps increased in speed as he passed back and forth before the hearth, his agitation growing. Was she safe? Should he go looking for her? Just when he thought he would go mad with waiting, there was a sudden knock at the door.

But it wasn't Seraphina who stood there. No, it was a young maid, who looked up at him with wide eyes.

"Miss Seraphina Athwart says she's waiting for ye in the private dining room." And with a quick, clumsy curtsy she was off.

Iain wasted no time, hurrying down the narrow stairs, making his way through the busy dining room to the private room at the back. He threw open the door, certain he would not be able to stop himself from going to Seraphina and pulling her into his arms.

Until, that was, he saw the two women standing beside her.

His boots skidded to a halt on the polished wood floor, the breath sucked from his body. He had not seen his grandmother and his cousin since he'd left Balgair months ago, had not written to them or received word from them.

But after the conversation with Seraphina yesterday, he found he no longer saw these women through a filter of resentment. His anger was still there deep in his gut, of course. But as he stared at the anxious faces of the two women before him, he realized that his anger was no longer directed at them.

As jarring as that was, however, it faded once he realized what their presence here meant. He looked to Seraphina, saw the new knowledge in her eyes, and silently cursed himself. He had been a fool, a damn fool, for holding on to his embarrassment and pride and fear for so long and keeping the truth about himself from her.

"Seraphina—" he began.

But she was already moving toward the door. "I'll leave you three to talk," she said. Then, with a bracing smile Cora and his grandmother's way, she slipped from the room.

He stared after her helplessly, muttering a quick "Excuse me a moment" to the other women, before he followed her. By the saints, she was quick. She was already out on the street by the time he caught up to her. He didn't dare grab her arm to stop her—after her reaction on Synne, as well as all he'd begun to guess about her past, he was not about to cause her further strain. But he did call out to her, sending up a silent prayer that she would stop and hear him out. Not that he deserved it.

"Seraphina, please let me explain."

By some miracle she stopped and turned back to face him. People hurried to and fro on the pavement, weaving between and around them, but he paid them no mind as he stepped up to Seraphina, just barely stopping himself from taking her hand in his.

"There is nothing to explain," she said, hands clasped tight before her. Phineas, on her shoulder, gave a few low, trilling sounds of what appeared to be agitation, but she paid him no heed, the very fact that she was not automatically consoling her pet proof of her own mind's disquiet. And suddenly his reasons for keeping the truth of his title from her seemed pathetic.

"But you deserve an explanation," he rasped. "You deserve to know why I dinnae tell you I am a duke."

She held up a hand, stopping his words in their tracks. "I know why you didn't tell me, Iain," she said, her voice achingly quiet and yet all the more powerful for it. "I used to know you better than anyone; do you think I would not understand your motivation for keeping something so important from me? No, I know you did it because you believed it would endanger your quest to see this marriage dissolved.

"But you do not know me as well as you may think," she continued. "And while much of that can be blamed on the fact that the past years have changed me in ways you can never imagine, I can only blame myself that no one knows my heart. I have kept it bottled up for so long, I even wonder if I know it myself." Here she gave a pained twist of a smile, which caused an answering twist in his chest.

But she was not through driving the stake of truth through his heart. And he deserved every bit of it.

"I don't care that you are a duke, Iain," she rasped, her beautiful eyes dull with pain. "I never would have cared. The only thing that matters to me right now is that you go back there and make things right with those two women, who would very much like to give you what you needed all those years ago: a family."

And with that she turned and walked off.

* * *

Several long, painful minutes later Iain returned to the private dining room, half expecting to find Cora and his grandmother gone—and not knowing if he would prefer to find them gone or still there waiting for him. While Seraphina wanted him to somehow make things right with these women, he did not know if he had the heart for it after watching her walk away.

But no, his cousin and grandmother had remained, looking as brittle as Seraphina had. And suddenly her words from yesterday at the beach came back to him: *But don't you see how extraordinary this all is, Iain? You thought you were alone all those years. Now you have a family.*

Heaving a sigh, he motioned to the seats that circled the table. "Won't you sit?"

They did, sinking into chairs as far from him as they possibly could. It would have grated on his nerves just months ago, proof of their dislike of him, the rough and uncultured brute who had come unwelcome into their lives no matter that they had searched for him. Now he saw it for what it was: uncertainty with him, with where they stood with him, and with their place in this world. He was a stranger to them, as surely as they were to him. But worse, he had control over their lives. They didn't know him or what he was capable of. They only knew he was the son of a man who had caused grief wherever he had gone, a man who had cut ties with his family when his addiction had become too great. And, he was forced to admit, he had not exactly helped matters by his own unwillingness to open up to them. They knew nothing about him, and he knew nothing about them.

Perhaps it was time to repair that.

Leaning forward, he said in as gentle a manner as he was able to—which was so much gentler a tone, now that Seraphina had burrowed back into his heart—"I would verra much like to learn what my pa was like before he left your home. And I would like to tell you about what few years I had with him, and my life after he passed away."

His grandmother gasped, her trembling hand going to her mouth, and tears began to form in her large gray eyes. Eyes the same shade as his own.

Cora, too, looked as if she were about to cry. But, strong lass that she was, she swallowed the tears down and said, a tentative smile on her lips that he had never seen before, "We would like that very much."

Chapter 24

Seraphina didn't know how long she wandered the streets of Edinburgh. All she knew was she needed time to come to terms with the sudden developments that had been thrown at her head in the space of minutes, first with believing she and Iain had a chance at a life together, then meeting his relations, learning he was a duke, and realizing that she could never be with him. She felt as if up was down, right was left, light was dark.

The one thing she was certain of, however, was her feelings for Iain. In fact, she was so certain, she was surprised she had not realized the truth before: she had fallen back in love with her husband.

Her husband, who was now a duke. Iain finally had status and respect. There would be no more people looking down on him for the supposed lowness of his birth, no one treating him like offal beneath their boots. No, he was a duke, a peer of the realm. And she was so happy for him, she wanted to cry—if she were capable of crying.

But his new status also meant she had fallen so far beneath him it was laughable. Which was ironic, really. Hadn't she been the one to proclaim all those years ago that status was not important and she didn't care how unmatched society deemed them to be? Yet here she was, holding on with both hands to the certainty that they could not be together due to his newly elevated status. After all, how could a duke be married to someone with her background, someone who had spent a nightmare of a year at an insane asylum, who had in essence been a fugitive when she had stolen her sisters away, who had gladly taken on the mantle of prostitution in order to survive? Not to mention someone who had essentially been proclaimed dead.

All during her blind meanderings Phineas stayed silent on her shoulder, pressed comfortingly against her neck, as if he sensed she needed time. Finally, however, she realized that if they were to complete what they had set out to do here in Edinburgh she had best return to the inn. And so, with heavy steps, she turned about and made her reluctant way back.

Iain was still in the private dining room, though now he was alone. He looked haggard, wan, with a heavy air about him. When he noticed her, he rose, the chair scraping against the floor. But he did not move toward her. No, he remained where he was, though his eyes burned as he looked her up and down, as if to ascertain she was well.

"Your grandmother and cousin are gone?" she asked. A stupid question, really. She had already noted their obvious absence.

"Aye," he replied, his voice rough as if from overuse. "They left nae long ago."

She nodded, clasping her hands tightly before her to keep

from reaching out for him. "And are things…improved between you?"

"Aye," he said again, quieter now, gentler.

Letting out a trembling, relieved breath, she sagged. Phineas, no doubt feeling his comforting presence was no longer needed to such a degree, alighted from her shoulder and flew to land on the wooden table at the center of the room, where a collection of fruits and green leaves and seeds sat in a bowl. Her throat thickened. It was all too obvious Iain had procured it especially for Phineas.

Iain, watching her closely, motioned to the empty chairs. "There is cold meat and cheese and bread if you've a mind to eat. We have nae eaten since this morning, after all."

Though eating was the very last thing Seraphina felt like doing just then, she nevertheless nodded and took a seat, accepting the plate Iain passed her, picking listlessly at the food as he took his own seat and began to speak again.

"I shall be visiting with my family at their town house tomorrow. It will nae be an easy healing, I'm thinking. But at least it has begun." He gave her a solemn look. "It is thanks to you."

She attempted a smile, but it was a frail thing that could not seem to find purchase. "Nonsense. It would have happened eventually; I just gave it a little push. I am happy for you, Iain. I think you all need each other, much more than any of you know."

But they were getting into painfully intimate territory, weren't they? Clearing her throat, she asked, "And have you heard back from the Lord President regarding a meeting with him?"

His eyes tightened at the corners, and he nodded sharply. "Aye, I have. We can leave as soon as we've finished eating.

If," he continued, his voice wavering slightly, "you still wish to go."

Oh, God, if only she could say no, that she wished to remain with him, to try again.

But she could not. She had her life and her sisters to return to. And he had a fresh start, which would only be polluted by her presence in his life.

She nodded and stood. "We've no need to wait. I'm not hungry anyway. We may as well get this over with. The sooner I get on the road the sooner I may reach Haddington, and I would prefer to reach it by nightfall, if at all possible."

But though he slowly stood, he did not move to leave. "Seraphina—"

His tone told her he was not ready to let her go so easily, either physically or emotionally. Panic flaring to life in her breast, more for the fact that she feared he would be able to convince her to stay, she cut him off.

"No, Iain." Leaning across the table, she attempted to encourage Phineas onto her finger. But the blasted little traitor waddled out of the way and kept on eating, for the first time in his life oblivious of her distress. Or too hungry to care.

Blowing out a frustrated breath, she moved to the other side of the table. But her pet merely waddled in the other direction, giving an annoyed little chirp as he did so around a beak full of apple.

Iain, unfortunately, took this opportunity to try again. "Seraphina—"

"No!" she repeated, louder now, so loud that she startled Phineas, who ruffled his feathers and moved even farther out of reach. Adjusting her spectacles, Seraphina ground her back teeth together and shoved a heavy chair out of the way to try and reach her pet. But yet again she failed.

"You cannae ignore me or what we've shared the last days," Iain persisted, frustration drawing out more of his brogue until it fairly tangled about his tongue.

Giving up on Phineas for the moment, she gave a small growl of agitation and faced Iain. He had moved around the table and was much too close to her for her peace of mind. Stepping back, she glared up at him.

"We have had this conversation already," she bit out. "You agreed that what we shared was temporary, that we could not go back in time and try to reclaim what we had."

"Nae, we cannae do that," he gruffly agreed.

She threw up her hands. "Then what is this about, Iain? You are only making things more difficult than they need to be."

"What is difficult," he growled, "is knowing that in a matter of hours you will climb up inside a carriage and leave forever. What is difficult is knowing that no matter what the hell I do, you willnae give us a second chance."

"Stop it, Iain," she snapped, even as panic and longing and grief writhed inside her.

"The universe brought us together again for a reason," he continued.

A sharp bark of laughter escaped her, colored with pain as she recognized that was one of the very things she had thought when she was convincing herself to give their marriage a try. "As the universe was the one that allowed us to be torn apart in the first place," she replied, the words acid in her mouth, "you will forgive me for not giving any credence to that particular thought."

"Damn it all to bloody hell, Seraphina."

Which, of course, was when Phineas would decide to pipe up. "Damn it all to bloody hell," he chirped with perfect pronunciation.

Seraphina glared at him before turning angry eyes on Iain. "Now look what you have done, you have added more improper speech to his repertoire."

But Iain ignored her. Moving closer, he reached for her hand, taking hold of it before she could think to pull back.

"I love you, Seraphina," he said, his voice thick.

Ah, God, how those words, words she would have given her soul to hear in the hours after her father had torn them apart, or in those first days in the asylum when hope had still simmered in her breast, were now like a finely whetted blade slashing her heart in two. "No, you don't," she managed, pulling her hand from his grip. "You are just emotional from reconciling with your family, and grateful to me for helping you in that reconciliation. You don't know what you're talking about."

"But I do," he insisted, running a hand through his hair in agitation. "You think I dinnae ken my own mind, that I am fooling myself when I say I lo—"

"Don't say it again, Iain," she choked out.

He let out a hot rush of air, his frustration palpable. Then he spoke again, and the combination of his gentle voice—gentler than she could remember hearing from him—and his unexpected words stole the breath from her body.

"I dinnae pretend to ken what you have been through in the past thirteen years. But what I do ken is that, whatever it was, it pains you still. I began to realize something wasnae right when that nightmare took hold of you and wouldnae let go." He paused, as if unsure he should continue. She stood watching him, hardly breathing, fearful of what else he might have to say for all she felt eviscerated in the face of his words and unexpected kindness.

Iain being Iain, however, he was not about to finish there. Reaching into the bag near his chair, he extracted a handful of periodicals: copies of the *Gaia Review and Repository*. She felt the blood leave her face as she spied her pen name on the top sheet.

Watching her closely, he laid them on the table between them. "But then I read through your writing, and realized that your stories, as fantastical as they are, reveal those secrets you would keep unsaid. Somehow, you are able to tell the truth as S. L. Keys as you never could as Lady Seraphina Trew, or Miss Seraphina Athwart, or Mrs. MacInnes"—here his lips twisted, the pain in his expression obvious—"or the Duchess of Balgair."

Ah God, she had feared this would happen. That was why her pen name was such a closely guarded secret. "You read too much into things," she said through numb lips. She dropped her gaze to Phineas, though she did not see him, for the sole purpose that she did not want Iain witnessing the truth in her eyes.

"I dinnae think I do, Seraphina," he said quietly, sadly.

But anger was beginning to rear up like the tide in her chest, brought on by the unfairness of the years and all she could never share with another soul. How could she put this grief on another? How could she possibly share this pain? Her whole life had been focused on protecting others; if she revealed all she had lived through, not only would that have all been for naught, but she would shatter.

And every bit of that anger centered on the man in front of her, who was so willing to give her, someone who could never be worthy of him, his heart. "You have a vivid imagination, Iain," she snapped as she turned on him, with such suddenness that he blinked and took a step back. "You think because I penned some stories with bits of real life in them that the rest is real life as well?"

But her desperate anger did not seem to faze him. "Nae all of it, of course," he replied gently. "But I can see that there is much more of real life in those words than you wish to admit to. And I wish you would confide to me what has happened to you, Seraphina, and allow me to shoulder some of your burden."

"I do not need anyone to shoulder my burdens." Taking up the periodicals, she turned and, with one swift movement, tossed them into the fire. "And you would do well to remember that. All I want to do is to get this blasted divorce over with, return to my sisters and my life on Synne, and forget any of this ever happened."

Iain watched the writhing papers in the hearth for a long, tense moment, the flare of the fire reflecting in his eyes, the muscles working in his jaw as the flames consumed her words. Letting loose a frustrated breath, he paced across the dining room before coming back to face her, his features twisted with turmoil. "So you are fine with me baring my soul to nae only you, but to my family as well. Yet you will nae give up even a bit of the burden of your own."

She swallowed hard at his words, an echo of that day with her sisters, a lifetime ago yet only a week past, when she had told them of her trip to Scotland with Iain. She recalled with stunning clarity the fight they'd had, her sisters begging her to tell them the truth. Elspeth saying, *"You needn't protect us from the truth any longer. Surely you can let go of some of your burdens and confide in us."* And then Millicent's pleading voice, *"Please, let us in."*

Those voices, so very dear to her, clanged about in her head, mingling with the hurt in Iain's voice until they were one and the same. Why could they not leave her alone? Why could they not let her live her life as she had been all this time?

And why couldn't she remain content with keeping things as they had been?

It was that last realization, that not only had she very nearly shared her burden with Iain, but she still wished to, even after knowing how it would affect him negatively, that had panic rearing in her chest. It brought her anger back, that panic, and caused her to lash out, a frightened fox, foot caught in a trap, desperate to chew off its own limb to escape.

"The only thing I want," she said, forcing a coldness into her voice she did not feel, "is to finish with this divorce and to return to my life and to never think of this past week again."

The fire that had lit his eyes, a reflection of his soul, dimmed until, in a heartbreaking moment, it was snuffed out completely. He gazed at her with heavy acceptance, his strong, wide shoulders sagging in defeat. "Verra well, Seraphina," he said. "Let us be off then."

With that, he gathered his things and moved toward the door, holding it wide for her. Seraphina knew she should feel victorious and relieved that he was finally accepting her words as truth. But all she felt was a peculiar lethargy in her limbs and a strange prickling behind her eyes.

Nevertheless, she retrieved Phineas and, without a second look at Iain, walked from the room.

Chapter 25

*F*our days later—four days of mind-numbing travel in which Seraphina had only her torturous memories of Iain to keep her company—her carriage rolled into Durham.

Well, not her carriage. And not even a rented carriage. No, Iain had insisted she use his own carriage, with the men he trusted, the same men who had driven them north. They turned down a street, and a familiar inn came into view, the very same inn she had spent that horrible night with Iain, when they had learned the truth of their separation and had gotten so drunk they had wound up in bed together. What would have happened, she wondered listlessly as she started gathering her things, if they had never had that fight? Would they have continued hating each other all through their long journey? Would the break with him have been so much easier, a relief instead of the misery it was?

But there was no sense in *what ifs*. What had happened

had happened, and there was no changing it. No amount of cursing her father would bring them back to that time.

Her father. Fury sizzled under her skin for all the heartache that man had caused. The bastard was most likely sitting comfortably and unconcerned at Farrow Hall this very moment. She glared in the direction that place would be, just six or seven miles away, a mere hour's journey. Would that she could face him, to tell him exactly what she thought of him.

Iain's voice suddenly drifted through her mind, a memory she had forgotten, spoken during that frantic, inebriated night of a week ago: *If it got out that you were alive, and he lied, he would be ruined.* She stilled, her focus suddenly to a pinpoint. She had not paid Iain any heed when he had first said it, as concerned as she had been with keeping him from going to her father. But she realized now that it was true. Her father had proclaimed to all and sundry that she and her sisters had perished. He had essentially buried them, no doubt taking advantage of the attention it brought. All this time she had used her supposed death as a kind of shield. Surely no one would come searching for her now.

She had never once considered that there was an even more powerful armor protecting them from her father searching them out.

An idea took shape then, absolutely mad, and yet shining with possibility. Was it a gamble to try out this new plan of hers? Absolutely. Inwardly her body rebelled, her heart speeding up and her hands beginning to shake. But hadn't Iain made her see that she was stronger than she had even realized? Hadn't he shown her with his own triumphs that taking chances could be worth the risk? And after all, she was so damn tired of hiding, so tired of knowing her father

was out there living his life without a care while she and
her sisters had been struggling to survive. She was tired
of living in fear, and she was tired of her sisters living in
fear. She recalled the day after Iain had arrived on Synne,
and the terror in her sisters' faces when they had seen him
and believed they were found and would have to leave their
home. It was time to put an end to it once and for all. She
did not want her sisters to feel that fear ever again.

The carriage pulled into the yard of the inn, slowing to a
stop, the men descending to see to the horses. As the groom
made to open the door, however, she put a hand on the latch
to stop it and leaned out the window. "I would very much
like to visit a house nearby before we stop for the night,"
she said. "Is that possible?"

The man looked confused but touched a finger to the
brim of his hat and nodded. "Of course, miss. And where
would you like to stop off?"

Seraphina took a deep, steadying breath. And then, before
she could rethink her decision, she said, "Farrow Hall."

* * *

Farrow Hall looked the same as it ever had, the gray stone
structure sprawling and elegant, spreading across the flat
land as if determined to take possession of everything in its
purview. *Just like its owner*, Seraphina thought with trepidation as she descended to the gravel drive and stared up at
an edifice that was at once achingly and terrifyingly familiar. She'd spent happy days here, of course, though they had
been few and far between. Most of her early memories had
to do with this place and her mother, ever sweet and loving
if constantly sickly. And then after, when her sisters had

been born and her mother was no longer with them. She had tried to take what would have been her mother's place in their lives, to give them some of what they would have had if Lady Farrow had survived that last birth.

But by then most of her memories—her happy memories anyway—centered around the outdoors and the adventures she had with her sisters. Those that centered around the house itself, those that her father had been part of, were only darkness. He had never been a kind man when her mother had been alive. But at least then he had made himself scarce. After her mother had died, he had become a stifling presence, like a great dark vulture looming over them. As she had gotten older, his unkindness had turned to cruelty, his unceasing need for perfection and obedience making life nigh unbearable.

And when she had dared to love someone he had not approved of, to plan a life with that man, he had treated her no better than an animal, locking her up in a place designed to break her spirit.

She had been back to Farrow Hall once after that, when her father had taken her from the asylum with the belief that she would finally be the meek daughter he had always wanted her to be. But the house had been as much a prison as the asylum had been—until, that was, she had gathered her sisters up and left, stealing them away in the dead of night.

She shivered as that old fear coursed through her, the unforgiving gray stone walls of the house before her looking more like a jail. And here she was, ready to climb those front steps and enter that place of her own free will. A manic laugh escaped her lips. Perhaps she was as mad as he had tried to make her believe all those years ago; why else would she willingly re-enter the house of the man who had tried for years to track her down like a dog to do God knew what after she had found the will to leave him?

But this man had taken enough from her; she was determined to finally take back, to break free of his hold on them once and for all.

Adjusting her spectacles, she turned to the groom, who had stood silently by while she dithered. "Will you please watch Phineas for me?" she asked, her voice shaking. At least her pet would be safe should anything happen to her while she was inside.

"Aye, miss," the man said, concern knitting his brow.

Nodding her thanks, she straightened her shoulders and climbed the front steps, pausing only slightly before ringing the bell.

The sound of it echoed through the house like a death knell. Before it had faded away there were heavy footsteps from within. And then the door was thrown wide, and the butler stood there, ancient and wiry and frighteningly familiar.

"Hello, Barnes," she said, keeping her voice as steady as possible. "Is my father in?"

Though now that she thought of it, arriving unannounced like this may not have been the wisest thing to do. While Mrs. Campbell had somehow been aware that she was alive, Seraphina had not considered who else might have known or guessed at that fact. Obviously, it was not the butler, that was certain. The man gaped at her, turning white as a sheet before stumbling back and clenching a hand over his heart.

"Ah, God," he croaked. "Lady Seraphina, come back from the grave."

Seraphina winced. Damn and blast, that was all she needed, for the man to keel over dead on the spot from shock at seeing her.

"I'm not a ghost, Barnes, but alive and well," she tried to say. But the moment she stepped toward him, hand extended to offer him assistance, he gave a gurgling shout, throwing his hands before his face. And then he was off, loping through the house as if she were a spirit come to steal his soul.

"Dear God," she groaned. And then, because she didn't know what else to do, she stepped into the house and closed the door behind her.

At once she felt as if she were being buried alive, her chest tightening almost unbearably as the walls of the building seemed to close her in. But she had come this far; she would certainly not turn tail and flee now. Straightening herself to her full height, she stalked through the house, ignoring the wan faces of the servants who peered out of corners as she passed, no doubt given ample warning by the terrified butler, whose wails of ghosts and demons she could still faintly hear echoing through the bowels of the house.

But she hardly heard him or the anxious whispering of the servants over the rush of blood in her ears. It was like she had stepped back in time, as if her sisters would come tearing around the corner as they searched for her, as if her father's angry face would appear from the shadows to terrorize them into behaving. She half expected the latter to happen at any moment. Surely that man must be aware that something was amiss by now. Was he searching for her as she was searching for him? The very idea had her heart pounding hard and anxious in her chest, had her rubbing at her wrists, as if she expected the manacles to already be there.

But no, he never appeared. Nor was he in his study when she finally reached that place. It had been his favorite room, the one where she had been certain she would find him. He had never been far from it, his need for control in every aspect of his life having him poring over correspondence and ledgers at all hours of the day and night. Unperturbed, she made her way to the library. Surely if he was not in his study, he would be there. But no, he was not there either. In fact, the room was decidedly cold and dark and smelled oddly musty, as if it had not been used in some time.

Biting her lip, she turned back to the hallway. Where else could he be? She could try asking someone, of course. But with the way the servants squeaked and scurried into the shadows when she looked their way, she rather thought that would not necessarily be as easy as it sounded. It was up to her to search her sire out. Mayhap he was in his rooms. And so, on shaking legs Seraphina went back to the front hall and climbed the stairs. The floor that housed the family quarters was just as dark and musty as the library. Not wanting to look too closely at her surroundings, she attempted to keep her head down and hurry on to the primary suite of rooms at the far end.

But the moment she passed one very familiar door she slowed and stopped quite against her will. Before she could think better of it, she put her hand on the latch and pushed it open.

Her room was the same as it had been, with the massive four-poster bed that dominated the space, the white desk in the corner, the blue-and-silver wallpaper. It had been a haven from her father when he had forced her from the nursery, then later a prison when he had brought her back from the asylum. She saw now it had been kept exactly as she had left it, down to the small book on her bedside table and the gray shawl draped over the chair before the hearth. It shocked her, that this place had not changed even a bit. On a whim she went to the corner of the room, dropping to her hands and knees, yanking back the rug with shaking hands—and let out a breath when she saw the loose floorboard beneath. Clawing at the board with suddenly desperate fingers, she pulled it up to reveal a small box hidden in the space underneath.

The breath left her body as she gazed down at it before lifting it out and opening it almost reverently. Every one of the keepsakes she had saved from her friendship with Iain, every flower he had given and that she had pressed and preserved, every bit of ribbon she had kept, was all still there. Her eyes did that strange prickling that they had taken to doing occasionally since Scotland. But she did not have time to understand it; she was here for a reason, and she would get it over with. When she was done here— God willing she was able to leave this place—and back in Durham at the inn, she could take the time to look these items over to her heart's content. Or maybe she should wait until she was back on Synne. Or maybe someday down the road when everything was not quite so raw and painful.

Closing the box back up, she held it tight to her chest as she left the room and made her way to her father's suite. She swung the door wide without bothering to knock, only to find...

...Nothing. Not that the room was empty, of course. Her father's taste in interior design, after all, was to gather as many expensive pieces as he could fit into a single space.

But beside the massive, intricately carved furniture and the costly fabrics, the room was empty.

Letting out a frustrated breath, Seraphina felt as if every bit of her confidence went with it. Mayhap he was out. Which was incredibly inconvenient, as she did not think she would ever have another chance like this again. As she turned to leave the room, however, and find someone, anyone, who could tell her where her father was, she heard the rhythmic clomp of horses' hooves, the rumble of a carriage in the drive, and a driver calling out. She wasted no time, hurrying across the room to the window to peer down at the scene below.

Her father's carriage, Farrow crest emblazoned on the side, pulled to a stop before the front door alongside the carriage she had come in. As she watched, frozen, a gray head popped out of the window, an all-too-familiar stern face peering out: her father.

Bile rose in her throat, filling her mouth, and it was only with utmost will that Seraphina kept herself from casting up her accounts then and there. Fear snaked through her body, urging her to run, to hide. She ignored it as best she could, forcing herself to exit the room and descend to the ground floor. No, she would not run and hide. She was through being frightened, through with her sisters living in fear, and would have things out with this man once and for all.

Just as she made it to the front hall on shaky legs, her father threw open the door. "Barnes," he barked in that harsh voice that Seraphina recalled all too well, "where the hell—"

The rest of his question was cut off as he spied her at the bottom of the stairs. His eyes widened in shock, his nostrils flaring as he took her in, and Seraphina felt as if she had stepped into a dark tunnel, with only a pinprick of light and her father's cruel face on the far side. She gripped tight to the banister, forcing air into her starved lungs, praying she could keep herself from keeling over on the spot.

He looked the same as he had all those years ago, though perhaps a bit grayer, a bit more wrinkled. But still, he stood straight and tall, with the same vitality he'd always had. As she watched, he shook his head, as if trying to clear cobwebs from it before narrowing his eyes on her.

"Seraphina?" he demanded, incredulous.

She swallowed and then spoke, praying her voice was even and without inflection. "Hello, Father."

He took her in from the top of her head to the tips of her toes, his expression going from disbelief to outrage in the space of a minute. When he looked again at her face, his eyes blazed with fury.

"What the fuck are you doing here?"

She flinched at the venom in his voice. And yet it had the welcome effect of jarring her back into herself. Was she still frightened? More than she could ever say. She rubbed at her wrist, as if to comfort herself with the fact that she was free.

But she also knew who she was, and who she had become. She was strong, so much stronger than that frightened girl who had fled in the dead of night more than a decade ago. She had walked through the fires of hell and come out the other side. She would not let this man cow her.

Pushing away from the banister, needing to stand on her own two feet, she stepped across the gleaming tiles of the front hall, right toward her father. "I am here to make certain the ties are cut between us for good."

A sharp, cruel laugh escaped his thin lips. "Cut ties with me? Girl, the ties shall be cut when I say they are." Suddenly he narrowed his eyes, looking behind her. "But where are your sisters?"

Ice seeped into her bones. There was entirely too much interest in those cold eyes of his. She had the sudden, panicked urge to run from this house and to not stop until she was on Synne and had her sisters safe in her arms.

Instead she drew herself up to her full height and looked down her nose at him. "Where they are is no concern of yours. But perhaps we had better take this conversation to a more private place." She motioned to the shadows, where more than one pair of eyes was peering out at them.

The change in her father was instantaneous, the fury in his face replaced with wary frustration as he looked about. He had no doubt built up the story of his daughters' deaths for all it was worth, and would not appreciate the mirage being dispelled, even among his staff. It was all the verification that she needed that the gamble she was taking in coming here could very well pay off.

"To my study," he snapped, low and fierce. "Now."

Which might have rankled Seraphina. But she was ready for this final confrontation to be over and done with, and was not about to squabble about his tone.

What she had not counted on in her determination to face him and put this part of her life behind her, however, was how much his fury and hatred could grow in thirteen years' time.

The moment she stepped into his study, he slammed the door behind him and turned the key in the lock, dropping it in his waistcoat pocket as he did so, effectively trapping her in.

"I could send you off to that asylum again, girl," he hissed as he approached her. "No one would blame me for it. I could have you committed, and this time you would never see the light of day again. You would rot in there."

Once more she struggled to draw breath. As he came closer, she felt the walls close around her, shrinking down to the size of that dank cell. The cold seeped into her bones, and against her will, she began to shiver.

But as her arms unconsciously curled around herself as if to stave off a cold that wasn't there, she felt the bulk of the box in her arm. *Iain.* Ah, God, Iain, whom she should have had a happy life with, a life that had been stolen from her by the man before her. At once the cold dissipated, strength returning to her limbs, the heat of cleansing anger burning away her fear.

"No," she said, drawing herself up, "you won't do that. And do you want to know why, my lord?"

He stopped in his tracks, looking vaguely surprised. But the haughty disdain did not leave his icy eyes. "Oh, I'm certain you'll tell me, girl."

Knowing it would infuriate him, she leaned insolently against his massive desk, and was rewarded with a furious flush creeping up his throat.

"Besides the fact that my sisters and I have reached our majority and you have no power over any of us any longer," she drawled. "I could tell by your readiness to get us away from prying eyes that you would not like the truth that we are in fact alive to get out. I remember your need for a spotless reputation, you see. Which, no doubt, was why you fabricated the information to separate Iain and me all those years ago."

For the first time in their exchange he appeared vaguely

uncertain. It did not last long, however, the cruel mocking back in place. "You are still as much a fool as you ever were. That boy was nothing but an opportunist. He was using you, girl, but you were too blinded by him to see it."

But she refused to listen to another word he had to say. "You are wrong there, my lord. I have recently returned from a very informative trip with that very man, where the truth came out in spades."

Pushing away from the desk, she stalked across the room toward him, the anger of all he had stolen from her and Iain and her sisters eating away at the last remnants of fear. "You lied to separate us. And then you put me in that hell on earth to further break my spirit."

"He was a commoner," he hissed, apparently through with any pretense of lying in the face of her fury. "You are Lady Seraphina Trew, daughter of an earl. You could not marry a penniless orphan whose only claim to lineage was an addict of a father who was looked down upon and ridiculed by even the lowest of men."

"I am not Lady Seraphina Trew," she said, acid filling her mouth at the name she had willingly given up. "I ceased being Lady Seraphina the moment I married that boy you despised so much."

He rolled his eyes heavenward. "Are you simple, girl? Do you truly believe that pathetic excuse for a marriage, without banns read, without a priest, was legal?"

"Now who is the fool?" she spat. "We were in Scotland. I assure you, our marriage was legal. No, that day I ceased being your daughter, and became Mrs. Iain MacInnes, all quite legal and binding."

She smiled, a slow thing, more a baring of teeth. To her immense pleasure, he appeared faintly alarmed.

"And when Iain learned he was the Duke of Balgair, I became a duchess."

She wasn't certain what his reaction would be to that piece of news. God knew it had taken her more than her fair share of time to come to terms with it—not that she had truly come to terms with it, even after all these long days of travel, when it had been all she'd thought about.

Yet after an initial incomprehensible staring, when he started laughing, long and loud and gratingly mocking, she felt a certain satisfaction for what was to come. If anything good could come out of this heartbreak with Iain, it was knowing that her father would soon learn he had let a dukedom slip through his fingers.

His laughter finally fading away, he gave her a mocking glance. "A duke, eh? You truly are as stupid as I always thought you were. How could that boy become a duke? Do you think dukedoms form on trees like fruit, ready to be picked by any man who wishes it?"

"I assure you, he is indeed the Duke of Balgair," she replied quietly. "His father, while an addict, was also the youngest son of the previous duke. And when all of the males in the line tragically died, they went searching for Iain." She smiled coldly. "You may look into it if you like. Though you'll find all I've told you is true."

The scorn on his face transformed to confusion as he peered at her. "That cannot be possible," he rasped. "I'd heard of the tragedy surrounding that title, of course. And that they'd found an heir. But it cannot possibly be that boy who used to shovel shit in my stables."

"I assure you, that is precisely who it is."

He blinked as understanding finally took hold. "And you are a duchess."

Pain lanced in her breast. "I am. Or, rather," she continued, raising her chin, "for the time being. The reason I was with Iain, you see, was to secure a divorce."

"A divorce," he hissed.

"Yes. A divorce."

"You fool," he snarled. "You have such a prize dropped right into your lap, and you would turn your nose up at it?"

"But that was never a prize I wanted." *No, all I ever wanted was Iain's love, even when he was just a poor orphan with only dreams to live off of.*

His eyes blazed, and she rather thought he would have gladly struck her down. She had never seen such hate in his eyes, not even when he'd sent her to the asylum. Instead of shrinking back, however, she stepped closer. It was only then she realized they now stood eye to eye. She no longer had to look up at him. That fact gave her a small thrill.

He seemed to see it as well, for his eyes flared wide in shock as he took her in. "You are unnatural," he spat.

"I shall take that moniker, and gladly, if it means I am nothing like you."

He stared at her in outraged confusion, and she smiled. "But telling you about all you lost in driving us away—not only the comfort and care of three daughters who would have been loving companions into your old age, but the status you so desired as father of a duchess—was not why I came here today. No, I came to tell you that my sisters and I now hold much more power than you do over us. And we shall use that power should the need arise."

He scoffed. "You have no power over me, girl. No, even if I should allow you to leave here today, you can be certain I shall find you again. And then you shall rue the day you crossed me. As shall your sisters."

Seraphina saw red. Stepping up to him so they were nose to nose, she said, low and cold, "And *you* can be certain that if you ever seek us out you shall regret it. I am aware how you must have leveraged your daughters' supposed deaths to further your connections and your career in Parliament. I am also aware how dearly you hold your reputation. If word ever got out that my sisters and I are alive and well and you lied to hide the truth, you would be ruined." She stretched her lips into a smile that was more a baring of teeth than anything else. "And we will gladly tell all and sundry the truth should anything happen to any of us."

Her father's face paled before turning florid in his rage. "You bitch," he hissed, his body shaking. As she watched, he raised a hand as if to strike her.

"Oh, I wouldn't do that if I were you, Lord Farrow," she drawled. "I have not been idle these past years. I have friends in high places now, ones who would be more than happy to assist me in seeing you suffer, and greatly. Now," she continued as she held out her hand, "the key."

His eyes fairly popped from his skull, so furious was he. For a moment she wondered what she would do if he dropped dead at her feet from apoplexy. She rather thought she would gladly retrieve the key from his pocket and step over his still-warm body.

In the end he reached into the pocket himself, handing the key over with impotent disgust.

Taking it, she brushed past him and headed for the door. As she opened it and was about to leave, however, she paused and said over her shoulder, "As this is the last time you or I will ever see one another again, I shall bid you adieu. I hope you get exactly what you deserve, Lord Farrow."

With that she sailed out the door, through the house, to Iain's carriage in the drive. And as she settled inside next to Phineas, and in the growing twilight the carriage began the trek back toward Durham to the inn, leaving Farrow Hall and her father and all the memories wrapped up with him behind, she felt that, for the first time in thirteen long years, she could finally breathe.

Chapter 26

Candles were glowing in the windows of the rooms above the Quayside Circulating Library when the carriage pulled up. Seraphina looked with a full heart at that place she had worked so hard to build for her sisters, knowing that if she was going to finally stop living in fear, as she had determined to do back at her father's home, she had to trust them with the truth and tell them everything. Which in and of itself frightened her nearly beyond bearing.

Dragging in a shaky breath, she allowed the driver to help her down to the pavement. The air, she noted absently, was already beginning to cool, the end of the summer season having come and gone while she was away, a stiff autumn wind coming in off the sea. It wrapped around her like a caress as she and Phineas waited for Iain's men to retrieve her bag, and she closed her eyes as the comforting feel of home filled her up. Or, at least, home as she had believed it to be, before she had gone off with Iain on that ill-conceived trip to dissolve their marriage—a trip that had changed everything for her, ripping apart at the seams what she had believed to be true, patching it up again into something new and brilliant and frightening.

"Miss Athwart," the groom said, and she opened her eyes to find the man holding her bag out for her.

"Thank you," she murmured, taking the bag. She cleared her throat and adjusted her spectacles. "And thank you both, for everything."

"It was our pleasure, miss," the driver said, touching a finger to his brim. "Would you like us to help you inside?"

"Oh, no. That won't be necessary." She pointed down the street toward the Promenade. "The Master-at-Arms Inn is just that way. They will take fine care of you for the night."

They nodded, climbing back up on the carriage. As the driver was about to urge the horses on, however, Seraphina, feeling as if she was about to lose Iain all over again, panicked and stepped forward. "When you get back to Scotland, please tell His Grace—"

But what message could she send to him? That she loved him; that she was sorry she never told him that; that she missed him and wished she were with him and wanted to take back everything she had ever said about how they could never be together? No. Because though all of that was true—so much so it broke her battered heart—she still had no doubt that she had made the right choice. She had burned all her bridges to a life as a respectable member of the aristocracy. And while she could never regret the decisions she had made to save her sisters, she could still mourn the fact that a chasm had opened between her and

Iain when he had taken on the dukedom, a chasm that could never be crossed.

But the men were watching her with mounting concern. "Please give His Grace my thanks for the use of his carriage," she finished lamely.

Nodding, they waved and were on their way, the last link to Iain rumbling down the street. Resolutely she turned back to the building, looking up at the golden stones of the facade to the windows above. As she watched, a shadow passed across a window: one of her sisters. Battered heart swelling, she retrieved Phineas's cage from the ground and, squaring her shoulders, marched around the side of the building to the small door and narrow stairs that led to the upper floor.

A comforting warmth enveloped her as she stepped into their apartment, the sound of her sisters' chattering, like busy magpies, making her eyes prickle. They sat close together on the small, worn sofa, their backs to her and bright red heads bent together, a beloved sight she had not known how dearly she had missed until now. Quietly pushing the door closed behind her, she placed Phineas's cage down and opened the small door. At once he scrambled from the contraption, eagerly flying to her sisters, alighting on Millicent's shoulder with a happy little chirp.

"Oh!" Millicent exclaimed. "Phineas!" And then both girls turned and saw Seraphina, and the excitement and love in their eyes was like a balm to her soul.

"Seraphina!" Elspeth cried, jumping up and running to her, arms outstretched. "We have missed you!"

Seraphina embraced her, holding her close, pressing her cheek to the soft crown of her sister's hair, even as she closed her eyes tight against the sudden burn in them. Soon

Millicent joined them as well, and Seraphina thought her chest would burst from happiness.

But that happiness was tempered by the knowledge that there were things that needed to be said before she lost her nerve entirely. Things that could not wait a moment longer, not if she wished to finally move on from the past and stop living in fear.

Pulling back, she looked down into their sweet faces, that same blind trust in their eyes that had always been there. She had counted on that blind trust for far too long, a one-sided thing she had not reciprocated as she should have. No, she needed to also put her trust in them.

Drawing in a deep breath, she said, not even attempting a smile, "Let us sit. There is much I have to tell you."

At once their joy dimmed, uncertainty taking its place. But they did as she bid, making their way to the comfortable circle of well-loved seats, huddling together as if they knew they would need one another after Seraphina was done.

And they would. As much as she might wish otherwise, the coming conversation would be painful. Yet she also knew it could not be put off a moment longer. If she did not do this now, when the confrontation with her father was still fresh in her mind, when Iain's admiration was still bolstering her spirit, she would never be able to do it. And her sisters deserved better than her continued secrecy. Drawing in a steadying breath, Seraphina began, her voice warbling.

"I have not been fair, to either of you. I have kept things from you, all in the name of protecting you. Just as I have tried to protect you for these past thirteen years. But in doing so, I have disrespected you both. You deserve to know the whole of our history, *my* history. And it is past time I told you."

"Seraphina," Elspeth said, even as her knuckles turned white where she gripped tight to her sister's hand, "you needn't tell us if it pains you."

Which would have been an easy out. But Seraphina was through with keeping these two women—for they were women now, though she had tried to keep them children for so very long—in the dark.

"No, you need to know. You have begged me for years now, asking me to let you in to my most secret heart. And I, fool that I was, locked you out at every turn." She closed her eyes for a moment, gathering her strength before, opening them again, she looked her sisters in the eye. "I'll begin with why I went to Scotland with Iain. I told the truth when I said that Mrs. Campbell's death brought up something that needed to be taken care of, and that is why he came to Synne for me. But what I did not tell you is that he learned I was not dead all this time as our father let everyone believe, and he wanted to secure a divorce from me. Because we were married."

Both girls blinked myopically at her. "Married," Elspeth repeated, as if the word did not make any sense.

"Yes. Which, naturally, leads me to the rest." She took a fortifying breath and launched on, telling her sisters in as gentle a way as she could manage the whole of it: how she had loved Iain and married him with the intent of heading to Montreal to start a new life; how she had returned to the house to say goodbye to them but that her father had caught her; how he had made her believe that Iain had betrayed her, then sent her off to an asylum, where she had stayed for a year until, finally, he brought her back home in preparation for finding husbands for the younger girls. They gazed at her with horror and grief and disbelief as she spoke, not interrupting, simply listening.

When she fell silent, however, Millicent, whose face had gone as pale as the sea foam made by the churning waves at the shore, spoke.

"Oh, Seraphina," Millicent whispered, her eyes welling with tears. "An asylum? He sent you to one of those awful places?"

"No wonder you were so altered when you returned," Elspeth said thickly. "How you must have suffered."

"That was why I agreed to take you away from Father," Seraphina explained, "so you would not have to suffer as I had. You were ready to rebel against his plans for you to marry those awful men, and I had no doubt, none at all, that he would have done the same to you once he even guessed at your intentions to leave."

The girls paled, no doubt the reality of how close they had come to that fate beginning to sink in.

"That is the reason for your nightmares, isn't it?" Millicent asked mournfully. "You still suffer from your time there."

Seraphina felt the blood leave her face. "You know about those?"

"Of course we do," Elspeth answered before giving her a sad smile. "Our walls are quite thin, you know."

"We ached to go to you when they took hold of you," Millicent added. "But we knew you would not wish it."

"We did not imagine, however, that they were brought about by your time in an asylum," Elspeth rasped, her eyes wide and full of a pain that Seraphina had never wished to put there.

Then she said something that further tore Seraphina's heart in two.

"We believed you had nightmares from having to sell yourself in order to keep a roof over our head and food in our bellies those first years."

Seraphina blinked back the hotness in her eyes. "You know about that as well?"

"Of course we do," Millicent replied. Though tears poured freely down her face now, she continued, her voice thick. "And we can never apologize enough for the horrors you had to shoulder to keep us safe."

"No, you will never apologize for that, do you hear me?" Seraphina demanded. Her throat burned, and she swallowed hard to relieve it, but it only grew worse as she gazed into the grieving eyes of her sisters. Reaching out, she took their hands in hers. "I would do it all again if I had to, a hundred times over."

They squeezed her hands tight, their eyes full. Though there was grief freshly etched into their beloved faces, and though she suspected there was some guilt in their hearts as well, she could not detect a bit of anger or disgust. No, their love for her was still as clear as it had ever been.

She shook her head slowly. "But... aren't you angry at me? Aren't you sickened by what I've revealed to you?"

The smiles on their faces, as watery as they were, only grew. "You silly thing," Elspeth said gently. "We could never be sickened by what you have done, especially as you did it for us, and out of love. We'll love you forever, Seraphina."

Unable to speak for probably the first time in her two and thirty years, everything suddenly appeared out of focus. It was only when she blinked and her gaze momentarily cleared, however, a strange warmth tracking down her cheeks, that she realized why. And when her sisters, seeing her reaction, exclaimed and enveloped her in their arms, she finally gave herself up to it, letting the sobs rip freely from her chest, feeling the burden of nearly a decade and a half wash away in cleansing tears.

Chapter 27

One Month Later

Seraphina, perhaps you should take the afternoon off and go for a walk on the beach," Elspeth said.

Seraphina, who had been arranging and rearranging fans and perfumes on a small table in an attempt to keep busy, started and glanced up at her sister. No matter that she had been trying to distract herself, her mind had been elsewhere—namely back in Scotland, with a certain duke whom she had not been able to put from her mind for even an hour since her return no matter how she had tried.

Though after the letter she had received that morning, succinctly informing her that her marriage to Iain had been successfully dissolved, she did not wonder at her distraction. Her deep and aching sadness, however, was another matter entirely.

Her sisters knew of the finalization of the divorce. Seraphina's new openness with them had not stopped at that emotional evening when she had returned to Synne. It had taken practice over the past month, of course, years of holding her cards close to her chest having made it difficult to confide her troubles to others. Which really was putting it mildly.

But she had told them of the divorce—and had been rewarded with their vigilant eyes on her all day. Like now, as they both watched her with concern.

She flushed, frowning. "Nonsense," she replied. "I cannot leave. It's the middle of the day."

But Elspeth merely pursed her lips and raised a brow, eyeing her from her position behind the gleaming counter. "And we do not have a single patron right now. Truly, it's silly for all of us to be here. Take the afternoon off."

"Yes, do," Millicent piped up from her place at the window, where she was dusting an already spotless display of their latest arrivals. "There's nothing to do here anyway. And besides, you've yet to figure out how to end S. L. Keys's latest story. I'm so excited to see what will happen to Josephine."

Both girls nodded at that, their eyes glowing, and despite the heartache from the letter this morning, Seraphina's chest warmed. She had told them about her secret writing, and had told the Oddments as well, and for the rest of her life she would never forget just how thrilled each and every one of those women had been that she had made a success of herself with her writing.

Unfortunately, Millicent was also too correct, in that Seraphina had been unable to write these last weeks. She might be tempted to blame it on her decided lack of nightmares, or on finally sharing the burden of her past.

But she knew only too well what it was: She missed Iain, so much her chest hurt with it. Even now, as she thought of him, she found herself unconsciously rubbing at her chest, right over her heart.

Phineas, of course, would sense her disquiet. He had kept close to her as he usually did these past weeks. Yet his attentions had seemed somehow more than they had been, his mood almost morose. Like now, as he flew from his perch to land on her shoulder and rubbed his cheek against hers. Right against a patch of wetness. It was then she realized she had begun to cry.

Reaching under her spectacles, she dashed the tear away, scowling down at the swipe of moisture on her fingers. She had spent nearly a decade and a half remaining dry-eyed, in complete control of her emotions. But ever since her return to Synne she had found herself crying at the drop of a hat. The cover of one of her favorite novels came back damaged? Tears. A small plant grew out of a crack in the pavement and bloomed with a brilliant flower? Tears. No matter if the occasion was even remotely happy or sad or even something that should be seen as absolutely mundane, she found herself blubbering like a baby.

Really it was most annoying.

"Seraphina?" Elspeth said, concern lacing her voice.

Seraphina threw her hands up in the air. "Fine. You wish me to take a walk? I shall take a walk." She scowled at them. "But I want you both to know I am not happy about it."

Her sisters merely smiled serenely. "Of course you're not," Millicent said placatingly. Retrieving Seraphina's pelisse from the back room, she took Phineas while Seraphina shrugged into it before placing the parrot back on her shoulder. "Now, Phineas," her sister said to the bird, who looked at her with bright eyes, "you take good care of your mistress. And don't let her return for an hour at least."

With that, she herded Seraphina and Phineas out the door of the Quayside, closing it firmly behind her.

* * *

But at the end of that hour, Seraphina found she was no better than she had been. In fact, her mind was even more tangled in grief and memories. Truly, what was wrong with her? She knew there could be nothing between her and Iain, and had made the decision to leave Scotland with that knowledge. And she had spent the last month trying to forget him. Like she had told him that last day, they could not go back to what they'd had, no matter how differently they might wish it.

Yet with one letter informing her that their divorce was now complete, she found that emotionally she was in an even worse place than before.

Sighing, she kicked a small rock. It bounced across the pale sand before being swallowed up by the surf. Her heart was heavy in her chest, and even Phineas was quiet on her shoulder, as if he was mired in his own sad thoughts. Reaching up, she scratched him behind his neck.

"Let's go back then, shall we?" she murmured to her pet. "Being out here with only our thoughts for company is doing neither of us any good."

Phineas gave a subdued little chirp, which Seraphina decided to take as agreement. Turning about, she began the long trudge back down the beach. The wind whipped up, biting through her clothing, and she cupped a hand about Phineas to protect him from the cold. "We'll warm up in the office, and have a nice hot drink," she said as they left the beach behind and made it onto the Promenade, which had only a few stragglers walking on its wide path that ran parallel to the beach. "By then I'm certain there will be plenty to keep us busy, certainly enough to get our minds off of Iain."

But even as she thought it, she knew it was merely wishful thinking. No amount of hard work would keep her from remembering what it had felt like to be held in his arms. Nor would it erase her wish to find herself back in his arms, this time for good. She was so mired in these morose thoughts, she did not immediately notice the decided crowd of bodies in the Quayside when she returned.

"There," she grumbled as, Phineas having alighted from her shoulder, she worked at removing her pelisse. "I have taken a walk. I do hope you're happy—"

But the words stalled in her throat as she spied the group of familiar and much-beloved faces gathered in a circle of seats that had been placed in the middle of the space.

She blinked as she took them all in. Besides her sisters and, for some reason, Lady Tesh, there were also the Oddments: Adelaide, Honoria, Bronwyn, with her husband, Ash, and…

"Katrina?" she breathed.

Miss Katrina Denby—or, rather, the Duchess of Ramsleigh since her marriage earlier that year—rushed forward, tears in her eyes. At once Seraphina was enveloped in her friend's arms.

"Oh, I have missed you, dearest," Katrina said.

"I have missed you as well," Seraphina managed, just before her throat closed up from tears. Damn and blast, these emotions were highly inconvenient.

Blessedly Katrina's overlarge and exuberant dog, incongruously named Mouse, decided he was due for his own welcome. He pushed his muzzle between them, demanding attention, long tail whipping back and forth in a dangerous manner.

"Oh, very well, you brute," Seraphina managed as she knelt and buried her face in the animal's neck. A perfect subterfuge, for it allowed her to compose herself.

Her tears successfully wiped dry on Mouse's black-and-white-spotted coat, she gave a sniff for good measure and rose. "But what are you both doing here?" she asked her friend, even as she accepted a hug from Katrina's husband, Sebastian.

To her surprise, however, Katrina—and everyone else present—looked exceedingly sheepish. Before she could make sense of it, Lady Tesh spoke up, her brusque voice carrying and firm.

"You've a great many people who care about your well-being, Miss Athwart," she said, her heavily beringed, gnarled fingers combing through the frizzy mop of white fur atop her pet Freya's head. "So when your sisters sent out the call for help, we did not hesitate to answer. Even my former companion here," she grumbled as Katrina, with Sebastian sticking close to her side, resumed her seat beside her. "Though she would not come when it was merely *I* asking her."

"Oh, Lady Tesh," Katrina said with a smile, none of her former nervousness around the woman present now. Leaning toward the dowager viscountess, she gave her an affectionate kiss on her paper-thin cheek. "You know we love you dearly and would have been back soon. But we have been gone only a few months."

"Hmmph," Lady Tesh said, though her sharp brown eyes sparkled with pleasure. She leaned forward to glare at

Sebastian on Katrina's other side. "Just see you do not keep Katrina from me, Your Grace," she scolded. "You know I am a frail old woman, and I do not have much time left."

"I would never dream of keeping Katrina from anyone she loves as much as she loves you," Sebastian said with impressive solemnity, before he ruined it spectacularly by grinning. "Though we both know it's me you wish to see."

"Scamp," Lady Tesh said affectionately.

But Seraphina had heard enough. Or, rather, she had not heard anything beyond Lady Tesh's unexpected confession. "What do you mean, my sisters put out a call for help?" she demanded.

At once the lighthearted mood changed. Elspeth stepped forward, taking Seraphina's arm and guiding her to the circle of chairs—of which she now saw there was an empty space.

"Now, I know you have done your best to stay positive this past month," her sister said, encouraging her to sit. "But it has been clear to all of us that you aren't happy."

"I am not happy because I have been ambushed by people I thought I could trust," she grumbled. Glaring about the circle, she demanded, "Does this have anything to do with a certain letter I received this morning?"

"Oh, no, that was pure happenstance," Honoria piped up. "They sent out letters to all of us a week ago."

"A week," Seraphina breathed, looking at her sisters with hurt eyes.

But neither of them looked the least abashed. "You have been so very sad since you returned from Scotland," Millicent explained.

"We could not do nothing," Elspeth added.

But that did not assuage Seraphina's hurt and sense of

betrayal. "And so instead of talking to me yourselves in private, you invited everyone here to, what? To attack me for not being happy?"

Yet again they did not look ashamed of their actions. "Of course it is not an attack," Elspeth replied. "It just seemed the best course of action. We have been trying to make you see that separating from Iain was not the best thing for you. But you have not listened."

Which was all too true, she realized begrudgingly. But she had not taken their urgings to write to Iain and try to work things out seriously. Her decision had been the right one. After all, who in their right mind could possibly believe that she, with the history she had, could possibly have anything respectable with a duke? If she were to take on the mantle of duchess, a position that brought with it such close scrutiny, eventually the truth of her time in the asylum and her work as a prostitute would find its way into the clear light of day. And she could not bring Iain down with her.

Millicent motioned across the circle. "And when we talked to Bronwyn, she suggested that drastic measures had to be taken to convince you to finally listen to us."

"Bronwyn?" Seraphina demanded, looking at her friend.

But Bronwyn did not look even faintly guilty. Adjusting her spectacles, she speared Seraphina with a stern look. "We all know how stubborn you can be," she said in her clipped matter-of-fact tone. "And that it would take an incredible amount of effort and intent to get you to listen to us."

But anger was beginning to replace Seraphina's hurt. Blowing out a sharp breath, she stood and paced within the circle of friends and family, feeling much like a caged lion.

"And so you banded together, all so the pathetic divorcée would see what a monumental mistake she made in leaving her husband?"

Adelaide rushed toward her, enveloping her in arms that held the comforting scent of baked goods.

"You are not, and never have been, pathetic," she said in a thick voice. "What you are is incredibly unhappy, and you are sabotaging any chance to change that. And if we, the people who love you best in this world, can help you to see that you are as deserving of happiness as any person, then we shall."

"Adelaide is right," Katrina added, wide blue eyes shining with tears as she wrapped her own slight arms about the both of them. "You have made certain we all live our best and happiest lives. Why can we not do the same for you?"

"And while you are incredibly stubborn," Bronwyn added, joining in the group hug, "you are no match for the combined stubbornness of the rest of us."

"Well, hell," Honoria grumbled as she stood and added her embrace to the rest, "if you think I'm going to be left out of this, you've got another think coming."

Seraphina, standing in the middle of her friends' embrace, held on to her outrage with pure will. As if she could be swayed by such nonsense. As if she would suddenly change her belief that she and Iain had no business being together.

But as the warmth from their collective bodies began to seep into her, forcing her to come to terms with the fact that these people would not go to all this trouble for nothing and must truly believe what they had to say, she felt her stubbornness begin to waver. If every single person present believed, after knowing what they did about her past, that she could find happiness with Iain, and that a life with him was not doomed for failure and heartbreak, how could she possibly continue to retain her certainty that she could not?

Desperate, uncertain, she looked to the one person whom she knew would tell her the truth. Lady Tesh motioned to Sebastian that he should take her pet, then grabbed her cane and leveraged herself to her feet, making her way with her hobbling gait to Seraphina. A few swift swipes with said cane, and she soon had Seraphina's friends dispersed and entered the fray, standing before Seraphina and looking up at her with a tenderness not often seen on her heavily lined face.

"Lady Tesh?" she begged, not knowing how to voice what she needed.

The woman, however, was quite the shrewdest person Seraphina knew. Immediate understanding filled her face, and she nodded and drew in a deep breath. Seraphina, not knowing what she wanted to hear from this woman, tensed.

"You are a strong, independent woman, Miss Athwart," she began. "You have been through much in life, and have succeeded where so many have not. You have protected your sisters, and started a thriving business, and you have even made something of yourself with your stories."

She frowned, white brows dropping over stern eyes. "And yet you refuse to follow where your heart leads you. Come along, my girl. You're made of sterner stuff than that."

Seraphina, blinking back those damnable tears, shook her head. "But how can I make a life with him, my lady?" she demanded.

"How?" Lady Tesh demanded right back. "Because he is a duke and you have a past? Do you think your friends here should have given up happiness with their dukes simply because they had a bit of baggage?" Here she motioned to Katrina and Bronwyn, who stood with their husbands' arms wrapped about them. "Would you tell your other friends to forgo happiness with dukes of their own should they happen to find ones to love?" Here she motioned to Adelaide and Honoria before saying in an aside, "And don't think I'm not actively looking for some dukes to match you with, ladies."

"Oh, I'm not certain dukes are for us," Honoria said slyly before taking Adelaide's hand in her own. Adelaide, for her part, blushed crimson but held tight to Honoria's.

"Oh!" Lady Tesh said, straightening, even as Seraphina stared at her two friends, seeing them in a new light, pieces clicking together that had not fit before.

"Well, good on you," the dowager viscountess said with an approving nod. "Men can be such a headache at times. Current company excluded, of course." She nodded to both Ash and Sebastian, who gave her wide grins, before turning to Seraphina. "And excluding your own duke, of course."

She took Seraphina's hand in hers then, giving it a squeeze. "Believe you me," she said in a full voice, "if I could have my own dear husband back for even a day, I would and gladly. Don't turn your back on happiness if you have a chance at it, my girl."

Seraphina shook her head helplessly, looking over Lady Tesh's head to her sisters. "And what if he doesn't want me any longer?" she demanded. "What then? Am I to lay my heart at his feet and wait for him to trample on it?"

Which was when Phineas decided it was time to join in on the conversation. He landed on her shoulder and rubbed his cheek against hers, bringing her attention once more to the tears that had unknowingly been tracking down her cheeks. But this time Seraphina didn't care that her emotions were on display for everyone to see. And then her pet spoke.

"Keep the heid!" he squawked, nodding his head up and down before adding, "Damn it all to bloody hell."

A sputter of a half sob, half laugh escaped her lips at the echo of Iain in that blasted phrase. And then her sisters were before her, their own eyes welling as they gazed up at her.

"If I remember anything about Iain," Millicent said softly, gently, cupping Seraphina's cheek and wiping away the tears that would insist on falling, "it is that he was kind, and just as stubborn as you. If he has fallen back in love with you, as you say he has, then there is nothing on heaven or earth that will change it this time around."

"Claim some happiness for yourself for once in your life," Elspeth said through her tears.

And as Seraphina stood there, surrounded by these people she loved, and who loved her in return despite everything she had revealed to them, she felt that maybe she could claim that happiness. She thought of Iain that last day in Scotland, when he had declared his love to her, how he had all but begged her to reconsider. She had thought she was doing right by him in refusing.

Now she wondered if she hadn't made the biggest mistake of her life.

"I can't leave you," she said to her sisters now, one last attempt to hold on.

But her sisters only smiled, as if sensing victory was at hand.

"We're grown now, Seraphina," Millicent said gently.

"You've been mama bird to us for so long, keeping the nest safe."

"But it's time for us to fly," Elspeth added.

With that, a permission she hadn't known she needed, she felt the last of her doubts fall away. Drawing in a deep, fortifying breath, she let it out in a sharp exhale, her mind already spinning with what was to come. Was she afraid of the journey she was about to take? More than she'd ever been in her life.

But if Iain was at the end of that journey, she knew that any fear she might feel would be well worth it.

Smiling truly for what felt like the first time in too long, she said, "You've all wished to know how the story of Josephine is to end?" Her smile spread into a grin, one she found she could not contain even if she had wanted to. "Well, it looks as though you're about to find out."

Chapter 28

*I*ain, the *Gaia Review and Repository* is here."

Iain, who had been deeply immersed in the accounting books before him, looked up to see his cousin in the doorway of his study holding up the periodical. She smiled, with no hint of the distrust and wariness that used to fill her gaze. It was a wonderful sight, proof that the more than two months of work they had all done in repairing their broken relationship had succeeded, giving hope for the future.

Or, rather, it would have been a wonderful sight, if Iain hadn't been completely and totally focused on the paper in her hand. He stared at it, his heart pounding in his chest, fighting the urge to race across the room and snatch it from her. He had been religiously asking both his cousin and his grandmother—and the butler, and basically any servant who would listen—to inform him when the magazine arrived. As it was only published monthly, and had to travel all the way to the wilds of Scotland before it arrived on the doorstep of Balgair Castle, he'd had no idea when it would finally appear.

But he had not expected it to arrive so close after the last issue, which they had received a mere two weeks ago. He would certainly not complain, however, for here it was, a bit of connection to Seraphina.

But Cora was waiting for him to speak. Managing a smile, he put the accounting book aside and stood. "Shall we go see Gran then?"

Together they made their way through Balgair to their grandmother's sitting room. The duchess was dozing in a stray sunbeam, a bit of embroidery in her lap. As they watched, a light snore escaped from her lips.

Cora, chuckling fondly, made her way to the woman's side and gently shook her shoulder. "Gran, the *Gaia Review and Repository* is here."

"What was that?" the duchess asked blearily, peering about. When she spied Cora she smiled. "Oh, I'm sorry, dear. I must have fallen asleep. But what have you got there?"

"As if you don't know," Cora teased with a grin, even as she removed the embroidery from the duchess's lap and packed it away.

The dowager caught sight of the periodical as Cora and Iain settled near her—that same paper that Iain was eyeing so hungrily. She frowned in confusion. "So strange. Didn't we just receive an issue a fortnight ago?"

Which was just what Iain had been wondering. Cora, however, merely smiled. "We did. But this is apparently a special issue. S. L. Keys, it is rumored, is finishing off her series."

At once a sharp ringing started up in Iain's ears. He lurched forward in his seat. "What do you mean, finishing her series?" he demanded.

His reaction should have shocked Cora. But she only smiled wider, holding the periodical up as if it were the greatest treasure.

"Yes," she murmured. "It seems Josephine's story is about to come to a close and they printed off a special edition to say farewell." Then, with a raised brow, she held the paper out to him. "Would you like to do the honors, Iain?"

He did not need to be asked twice, taking the paper, gazing down at it hungrily. There it was, on the front page, Seraphina's pen name, and the notice that her serial would be coming to an end. He scanned the short notice a bit desperately, certain it must tell the reason, or if not that, at least tell if she would write something new. But no, there was nothing but a quick, simple announcement. Panic flared in his gut that he would lose this last connection to her.

But Cora and his grandmother were waiting for him to begin reading. Clearing the thickness from his throat, he began.

He ached to hurry through the prose, desperate to read every word she had penned. But knowing he might never read another from her hand, he soaked in each and every line, seeing her in the strength of her heroine, hearing her voice in his head when Josephine spoke. So invested was he in it, he did not even know if he continued to read aloud, the picture in his head as brilliant as any live play before him.

And then he came to the twist, that ever-necessary plot device of the gothic tale, and his breath left him entirely.

There, on the page, Josephine had learned that her long-lost lover, Drummond, was not the villain she had believed him to be. And she had gone off in search of him, to claim her happily-ever-after. He turned the page, desperate to learn if she had been reunited with him.

And found only a blank page.

Staring in disbelief, he worked at the page with his fingers, trying to see if they had been stuck together. But there was nothing, just a gaping emptiness.

"What happened to Josephine and Drummond?" he cried, glancing up, only to find Cora and Gran gone—and Seraphina standing there before him.

He blinked, certain his eyes must be playing tricks on him. But no, she remained solid and wonderful.

"I rather think," she said thickly, "that how the story ends is entirely up to you."

"Seraphina," he breathed, lurching to his feet.

She smiled, but it was a nervous thing, more nervous than anything he had ever seen from her. "Hello, Iain. Phineas is having a nice visit with your cousin and grandmother. Do you mind if we talk?"

He shook his head, still not able to comprehend that she was here. "Am I dreaming?" he muttered to himself.

She stepped forward until she was right in front of him. And then she cupped his cheek with her palm. "Not dreaming," she said, the words broken, tears pooling in her clear eyes and making the blue so much bluer.

But wait. Tears? His Seraphina did not cry. As if to make a liar of him, a single tear broke free, tracking down her cheek. Unable to stop himself, he raised a hand, dragging his thumb across its path.

She gave a small, embarrassed laugh. "I listened to what

you told me that last day in Edinburgh," she whispered, "and gave up a bit of my burden to my sisters. And now it seems I am a watering pot."

Her expression altered, the small bit of lightheartedness replaced by a solemn nervousness. "And I would share it with you if you'll let me. And we may see how you feel about me after it is done."

* * *

She waited for what felt an eternity for him to respond. Yet he stared at her as if she were a ghost.

But then, finally, he motioned her to the sofa.

She settled herself, smoothing out her skirts. Her hands were trembling violently, which he seemed to notice at the same moment. The warmth of his long fingers as he took her hands in his seeped into her bones, soothing her as nothing else could.

"Seraphina," he said, his voice deep and oh so dear. "You dinnae have to tell me anything if you dinnae wish to."

"I know," she replied quietly. "But that's just the thing, you see. I *do* want to tell you. I want to share all of my secrets and burdens with you. You used to know me better than anyone. But I—we—are different people now. And I would have you know who I have become."

He sat silent, waiting. But the silence wasn't awkward. No, she found she felt a strength in his quiet presence. Drawing in a steadying breath, she began. She told him everything, of the asylum and the horrors she faced, of how she endured being chained, of the beatings and the cold and the fear. She explained how when her father finally brought her back to him, she stole her sisters away. And then she told him of selling her body to survive, and fighting tooth and nail to put food in her sisters' bellies, but that she would endure it all over again to make certain the ones she loved were protected.

He did not say a word through the whole ordeal. His face, however, darkened with each word, until by the end he looked as if he was ready and willing to rain hellfire down on the entire world. It was only when she fell silent, exhausted beyond belief, that he finally spoke. And his words were like a cleansing balm to her heart.

"I cannae begin to know how you got through that, Seraphina," he said thickly, and it was only then she saw the glimmer of tears in his eyes. "I am so sorry, mo ghraidh."

My love. Her heart, which had already been full, nearly burst at the endearment. "You are not disgusted by what I've told you?" she asked quietly, needing to hear it in plain words from his lips.

"Disgusted?" He looked at her as if she had grown a second head. "Of course I am nae disgusted. How can I be?"

"But society will destroy you if it's ever found out. You will be shunned."

He let loose a derisive bark of laughter. "As if I care about all that. Society can hang for all I care. The only thing that matters to me is you."

He pulled her into his arms, drawing her against him. And Seraphina felt as if she had truly come home. "You are the bravest, the most amazing woman I have ever known, Seraphina."

Tears, those blasted tears, would insist on blurring her vision just then. She blinked them away, not caring if they tracked down her cheeks, only needing to see his beloved face.

"I certainly hope so," she said thickly, "because there is something infinitely braver I am about to do, that is much more difficult than telling you the truth about my past."

She cupped his face in her hands. "I love you, Iain MacInnes. I have always loved you."

"Ah, God, lass," he choked, lowering his head to hers.

This kiss was unlike anything they had shared before. Even when they had loved each other all those years ago, the love of two young people with open hearts who had dared to defy the world, it was nothing like this. No, this was the coming together of two souls who had walked through the fires of hell itself and come out the other side, who had been burned and damaged but were stronger for it, who had found a healing in each other.

She opened her mouth under his eagerly, running her hands up his broad shoulders, marveling in the strength under her hands, in the tenderness in his touch as he cradled her like the most precious treasure. They drank of each other, a new beginning in the act, and she did not think her heart could be more full.

Until he pulled back and gazed down at her with a love stronger than any she had ever seen. And then he lifted the chain around his neck to reveal that simple silver ring he had slipped on her finger all those years ago.

His own hands shook as he removed the chain from the ring, but his voice was sure and strong when he spoke.

"I know our marriage has been dissolved," he said gruffly. "But you have always been the wife of my heart. And I have nae stopped loving you for even a moment. I love you, mo ghraidh. Will you marry me again, and make my heart whole?"

"Yes," she whispered. Then, stronger, "Yes, Iain, I will marry you."

And as he slipped the ring on her finger and pulled her close for another kiss, this one filled with all the promise of their tomorrows, she knew no one would ever separate them again.

Epilogue

*H*aud yer wheesht."

"Haud yer wheesht!"

"Nae, you feathered menace. Dinnae be copying me."

"Dinnae. Dinnae. Haud yer wheesht."

"Damn it all to hell. Nae! Dinnae you dare repeat that, you blasted pigeon. Seraphina!"

Seraphina, who had been diligently writing out the latest chapter of the newest S. L. Keys serial in her spacious sitting room, looked up from the stack of papers before her, trying her damnedest not to laugh as Iain came storming in, Phineas bobbing happily along on his shoulder. Her pet had taken quite a fancy to her husband once he saw how happy the man made her, and when he wasn't with her, he was with Iain.

Probably because the man had the horrible propensity of teaching the parrot a whole slew of new—and completely inappropriate—things to say.

Phineas, seeing her, took off from Iain's shoulder and landed on her desk, where he proceeded to pick at her quill with his sharp beak.

"That bird," Iain said in a highly offended tone as Seraphina worked at removing the quill from her pet's grasp, "is the devil incarnate."

"Oh, nonsense," she said, giving the parrot a good scratch behind his head. He tilted his head to one side, in obvious ecstasy. "He is an angel."

When Iain merely stared at her in disbelief, she laughed. "Very well, not an angel. But you have to admit he's a sight better now than he was when you first met him."

"Well, aye," Iain admitted grudgingly, his hand going to his ear, an old habit he hung on to out of pure wicked glee. "At least he is nae about to give me a piercing any longer."

"And perhaps," she added fondly as he pulled a chair up to sit beside her, "if you did not keep all those treats in your sporran for him, he would not be quite so keen on you."

The look he gave her was of mock outrage. Then, with exaggerated movements, he dug into said sporran and produced a handful of nuts.

"You cannae expect the creature to starve, can you?" He dropped the whole lot on the desk. "And besides," he added with a wicked smile as Phineas made fast for the bounty of treats and dug in with fervor, "it provides me with the perfect distraction when I wish to kiss my wife."

With that he wrapped his arms about her and pulled her close for a kiss, to which Seraphina gladly and willingly gave herself up.

Some time later, both pleasantly flushed and mussed from their endeavors, he pulled back to gaze tenderly down at her. "Ye see?" he murmured. "Perfectly distracted."

"Mmm, yes, I do see." Smiling, she pushed a stray lock of hair back from his forehead. "And is that kiss the only reason you came here? Or is it you're hoping to see what might be happening to my newest heroine and her brooding count?"

He grinned. "Never say there are nae perks to being married to the popular S. L. Keys. But that is nae the reason. At least, nae completely." He reached back into his sporran and retrieved a handful of letters. "It seems the women of Synne have been quite busy writing as well."

"Oh!" she exclaimed, grabbing the letters, shuffling through them, her heart glowing brighter with each familiar bit of handwriting that jumped up at her.

"Nae only that," he murmured, a smile in his voice as she tore into the one from Millicent, "but it seems your Lady Tesh has continued with her correspondence to my gran, and is now even inviting her for a stay on Synne."

Seraphina, who had been ravenously reading Millicent's missive—the distance from her sisters had been the hardest thing to adjust to upon marrying Iain—gasped and looked to her husband with eyes that welled with tears.

"Then we may take your gran to Synne ourselves, and Cora, too, if she's a mind to come. It seems Mr. Tunley has finally proposed to Millicent and they are to marry just before the start of the summer season, in two months' time."

She passed him the letter, watching him as he read it, chest warming at the smile that lifted his lips when he reached the part where Millicent sent him her love. In her mind she could not help but recall that lonely boy he had been, wanting nothing but a family.

Now here he was, surrounded by family. And they were

adding on new members by the day. She smiled to herself. Though there was one particular member that would be making an appearance soon, one he was completely unaware of.

"The timing is perfect, really," she reflected slyly, pursing her lips to keep herself from smiling as he gently extracted a piece of paper from Phineas's beak. "We can travel to Synne, stay for perhaps a month or so, and be back well before I should refrain from travel."

"Refrain from travel?" He frowned, glancing up at her, hand frozen in the air. Phineas gave an aggrieved chirp at being ignored before he waddled off to do God knew what to her writing supplies.

"Yes," she replied.

"But why must you refrain from travel?" he demanded, the worry in his eyes increasing. "Are ye well?"

In answer—for, truly, she was beyond words at that point—she took his hand and placed it over her still-flat stomach.

The realization on his face, followed swiftly and completely by a joy so rapturous she felt it in her very soul, brought tears to her eyes.

"A babe?" he whispered. When she happily nodded, he pulled her close.

"A babe," he repeated, the words hot on her neck, followed quickly by the warmth of his own tears. "I love you, mo bhean, so much. You've given me a life I never dreamed."

And as he took her lips in a tender kiss, she knew their reality was so much better than any dream could ever be.

About the Author

Christina Britton developed a passion for writing romance novels shortly after buying her first at the impressionable age of thirteen. Though for several years she put brush instead of pen to paper, she has returned to her first love and is now writing full-time. She spends her days dreaming of corsets and cravats and noblemen with tortured souls.

She lives with her husband and two children in the San Francisco Bay Area.

You can learn more at:
  Website: ChristinaBritton.com
  Facebook.com/ChristinaBrittonAuthor
  Instagram @ChristinaBrittonAuthor

*Get swept off your feet by charming dukes and
sharp-witted ladies in Forever's historical romances!*

A SPINSTER'S GUIDE TO DANGER AND DUKES
by Manda Collins

Miss Poppy Delamare left her family to escape an odious betrothal, but when her sister is accused of murder, she cannot stay away. Even if she must travel with the arrogant Duke of Langham. To her surprise, he offers a mutually beneficial arrangement: a fake betrothal will both protect Poppy and her sister and deter Society misses from Langham. But as real feelings begin to grow, can they find truth and turn their engagement into reality—before Poppy becomes the next victim?

ALWAYS BE MY DUCHESS
by Amalie Howard

Because ballerina Geneviève Valery refused a patron's advances, she is hopelessly out of work. But then Lord Lysander Blackstone, the heartless Duke of Montcroix, makes Nève an offer she would be a fool to refuse. Montcroix's ruthlessness has jeopardized a new business deal, so if Nève acts as his fake fiancée and salvages his reputation, he'll give her fortune enough to start over. Only neither is prepared when very *real* feelings begin to grow between them…

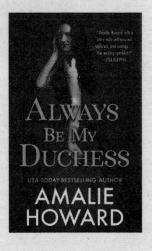

Connect with us at Facebook.com/ReadForeverPub

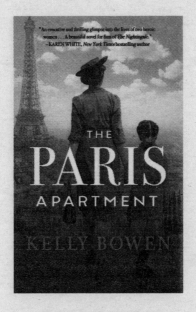

THE PARIS APARTMENT
by Kelly Bowen

2017, London: When Aurelia Leclaire inherits an opulent Paris apartment, she is shocked to discover her grandmother's secrets—including a treasure trove of famous art and couture gowns.

Paris, 1942: Glamorous Estelle Allard flourishes in a world separate from the hardships of war. But when the Nazis come for her friends, Estelle doesn't hesitate to help those she holds dear, no matter the cost.

Both Estelle and Lia must summon hidden courage as they alter history—and the future of their families—forever.

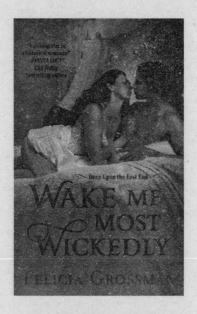

WAKE ME MOST WICKEDLY
by Felicia Grossman

To repay his half-brother, Solomon Weiss gladly pursues money and influence—until outcast Hannah Moses saves his life. He's irresistibly drawn to her beauty and wit, but Hannah tells him she's no savior. To care for her sister, she heartlessly hunts criminals for London's underbelly. Which makes Sol far too respectable for her. Only neither can resist their desires—until Hannah discovers a betrayal that will break Sol's heart. Can she convince Sol to trust her? Or will fear and doubt poison their love?